DOVER MYSTERY CLASSICS

E. C. R. Lorac
Murder by Matchlight

DOVER PUBLICATIONS, INC.
Mineola, New York

Bibliographical Note

This Dover edition, first published in 1988 and reissued in 2015, is an unabridged, unaltered republication of the work as published by Collins ("for the Crime Club"), London, in 1945.

Library of Congress Cataloging-in-Publication Data

Lorac, E. C. R., 1894–1958.
  Murder by matchlight.
  I. Title.
  ISBN-13: 978-0-486-25577-4
  ISBN-10: 0-486-25577-8
PR6023.O66M8   1988   823'.914   87-27605

Manufactured in the United States by LSC Communications
25577804   2018
www.doverpublications.com

CHAPTER ONE

i

" WELL, the war's done one thing at any rate. It's got rid of those damned awful railings."

Bruce Mallaig lighted another cigarette and stood still to get his bearings in the dark. The railings to which he had referred were those which had once divided Regents Park from the roadway of the Outer Circle. Bruce, who was now thirty years old, had known Regents Park all his life, and had often regretted the fact that at sunset, when the wide stretches of the Park seemed so desirable in the misty twilight, the public were sternly driven out into the streets. Standing in the darkness of war-time London on a moonless night, Bruce Mallaig conjured up the shout of the park-keepers in peace-time: " All out! All out!" Ghostly echoes of their call seemed to come to him now from the blackness beyond the lake. It was a very dark night. " If I didn't know exactly where I was, damn it, I might be anywhere," he said to himself.

Fortunately, he knew very well where he was. He had turned into the Outer Circle at Clarence Gate, and crossed the road, and he now stood at the approach to the iron bridge which spans the lake. Mallaig was a sentimentalist, though he would not have admitted it. He stood in the searching damp chill of a black November evening just because it gave him pleasure to be reminiscent. As a schoolboy he had learnt to scull and to punt on Regents Park lake, and he had learnt to skate there as well. On summer afternoons in the holidays he and Peter and Pat had taken picnic teas to eat in their skiffs under the shady trees of the islands. Now Peter was in the R.A.F. and Pat was in⁄the Waafs. She should have been on leave this evening, and she and Bruce had made a date to dine together at Canuto's. When Bruce had reached the restaurant he was given a telegram saying that her leave was deferred for twenty-four hours. Too disappointed to eat his dinner in solitude he had had a drink, and had then come out to wander in Regents Park.

" Some bloke wrote a book called ' Outer Circle '," he said to himself. " I'll write one one day and call it ' Inner Circle.' Jolly good title."

He set out over the bridge, reflecting that he and Peter used to have sculling races from the boat house at the end of the

5

lake up to the bridge where Pat had waited in a Canadian canoe to judge the result. Once he had taken a header into the water, and had started to swim to the bank, only discovering later that the water was but waist deep. He crossed the bridge and turned to the right along the path by the lake side. To his left were the grounds of Bedford College—their railings still *in situ*, else he would have walked across to the Botany garden and the tennis courts. The college was evacuated elsewhere now, and strangers roamed the once trim lawns. Pat had been a student at Bedford, and Bruce knew the grounds well.

He walked on briskly towards the small gate at the eastern end of the path; this led into York Gate and the Inner Circle and he determined in a warm glow of sentiment to walk right round the Circle and return to Marylebone Road by York Gate. As he walked he continued to think of Pat. She had said that she would marry him after the war, and Bruce kept on discussing with himself where would be the ideal place to live. A tiny flat in London and a nice cottage in Bucks or Berks—or a not so tiny flat in London and a houseboat on the river somewhere, or even a caravan for week-ends. So immersed was he in this pleasant cogitation that he decided to sit down for awhile and think the thing out. There was a seat beside the path— his torchlight showed it when he switched it on—and he sat down in the darkness feeling that the whole world belonged to him.

He was just beginning to weigh up the advantages of a fair-sized flat in Dolphin Square as against a single-roomed one in Trinity Court when he heard footsteps a few yards away from him. Just before the gateway which led into the York Gate there was a little wooden bridge: beneath this bridge a path in the College gardens led to the lake side. The newcomer had paused on the bridge, and stood there for a few seconds. Then, rather cautiously, he flashed a dim torch light around. A moment later, much to Bruce's interest, there came sounds indicating that the newcomer was climbing the wooden railings of the bridge, and this surmise was clinched by the sound of something solid alighting on the ground—some six feet below the bridge.

" Well I'm dashed!" said Bruce Mallaig to himself, wondering what the devil the chap was up to. A spy? a thief? . . . but why on earth should he choose that means of entry to the erstwhile College grounds? There was a gate a little farther along. An assignation? Bruce chuckled, not unsympathetically. The chap who had climbed over the little bridge was keeping tryst, perhaps. Bruce sat still and listened. The man down below had certainly not moved from the spot where he had landed: he must be waiting down there in the darkness. "Ought I to do anything about it?" Bruce asked himself, and sat and listened.

A few minutes later came the sound of further footsteps approaching, this time from the roadway beyond. Another person turned in at the gate and presently stood on the bridge.

"Anyone about?"

The unexpected inquiry nearly made Bruce Mallaig reply "Yes, I'm here. . . ." The voice had been so conversational, so calmly chatty, as though it were the most natural thing in the world for a man to ask such a question in the apparent solitude of a black dripping November evening in Regents Park.

Bruce had a lively imagination and the situation intrigued him. Sitting very still, he began to work things out. Number two was obviously expecting a friend. Perhaps he made a habit of meeting here—and number one (now under the bridge) had discovered the trysting place and was going to listen in.

"Dirty dog!" said Bruce to himself. He felt kindly disposed to all lovers to-night. "I'll stay here until the girl-friend turns up and then put them wise," he determined.

Meantime number two was humming a little air to himself, quite unconcernedly. Next he struck a match and lighted a cigarette. Bruce had a momentary glimpse of a thin pale face, rather whimsical, under the shadow of a trilby hat. "That chap's an Irishman," said Bruce to himself, remembering the voice he had heard—even those two words gave the brogue away. Number one, down on the path below the bridge, was silent and still. The Irishman finished his cigarette and flung the end away, so that the lighted tip made a tiny glowing arc before it fell into the damp grass beyond. A moment later he lighted another match, and Bruce rubbed his eyes, wondering if he were dazed by the bright splutter of light in the intense darkness. It seemed to him that beyond the small bright circle of matchlight there was another face in the darkness—no body, just a sullen dark face. The Irishman had bent his head, his cupped hands were shielding the match flame, and then he shook it to and fro and the light went out. Bruce Mallaig heard a dull thud, and then another sound, as of a heavy body lurching, thumping, falling . . . and then silence again.

7

Mallaig said later that he was so surprised that he must have sat stock still for a few seconds, not believing what his ears had told him. Then he snatched his torch from his pocket and jumped up. Of course he dropped the torch and wasted further seconds fumbling for it. By the time he reached the bridge, a full minute must have elapsed since he heard the dull thud.

The light from his torch showed him two things; first, a man's body lying on the bridge, and second, another man just astride the rail of the bridge. As Bruce Mallaig sprang forward, the second man tried to get back over the bridge with the obvious intention of reaching the ground below.

" No you don't!" cried Bruce, and seized the other, dragging him forward with all his might. It was a ' catch as catch can ' performance, in which Mallaig clawed and tugged, and the other struggled to get free, hitting out and wriggling and heaving in his efforts to get away. Mallaig, who was by no means a powerful fellow, was uncertain of his ability to hold his opponent, and he shouted " Police! police! " while he persisted in the struggle. It was both a grim and a ludicrous performance, because the probability of the police hearing the calls seemed pretty remote. Bruce Mallaig, by sheer determination, succeeded at length in dragging the other fellow over the handrail, and then they both collapsed heavily on the bridge, Mallaig uppermost, kneeling on his panting captive.

It was at this juncture that there came the sound of running footsteps—heavy plodding footsteps of one unaccustomed to making speed, and Mallaig gave another breathless howl of " Police " which sounded as much like a squawk of distress as anything else, and at last a hoarse, breathless, unmistakably constabular voice demanded, " What's all this?"

Mallaig gave up his efforts to hold his captive and rolled over breathlessly, gasping out, " Cop him! Don't let him go . . . He bashed that other chap. . . ." In the light of his torch, Constable Bull of D. division, proved himself quite equal to an emergency. He collected Mallaig's captive by tripping him up just as he had regained his feet and was making a dive for freedom, and he stood over him with regulation boots, reinforced by fourteen stone of constabular pressure, holding the overcoat firmly down on the planks of the bridge. He then blew a whistle vigorously, and promptly gripped Mallaig with his free hand.

" All right. I'm not going to beat it," protested Mallaig. " It was I who yelled for you."

" We'll see about that," said Constable Bull.

It was at this moment that the gleam of another torchlight helped to light up the scene, and a voice said " Can I help, officer? I'm a doctor—if anybody happens to be hurt."

The voice was the kind of voice which commanded respect, and Bull, glad enough of the arrival of a responsible-sounding party, replied:

" If you'll just glance at that man on the ground, sir, I'll deal with these others till my mate arrives."

Mallaig stood still, panting from his recent efforts, bemusedly reflecting that this was the craziest scene ever staged in Regents Park. The big constable still pinned down the man who Mallaig had in very truth " arrested," and the down cast light of the bull's-eye lamp on the constable's belt fell on the Irishman's crumpled body, and the bending figure of the newly arrived doctor. The latter, torch in hand, was examining the original victim, and Mallaig could see enough of the latter's face to feel suddenly sick. Blood had trickled down the pale face, and the dark eyes stared dreadfully as the doctor pulled the crumpled hat away.

The doctor did not spend very long on his examination.

" Nothing I can do here, officer. The man's dead—his skull is smashed into his brains."

Constable Bull immediately sounded his whistle again, and as though in strange reply a dog raised his voice close by and howled in piercing notes of melancholy.

iii

Half an hour later Bruce Mallaig was asked to make a statement concerning the events of the evening to Inspector Wright at the Regents Park Police Station. Wright was a big powerful fellow, but apart from his inches he was quite unlike Mallaig's notion of what a policeman looked like without his helmet. Wright had a meditative, almost a philosophic air, and his voice was kindly and encouraging. (Mallaig learnt later that this gentle aspect concealed a sceptical mind—Wright was a man who never took any statement at its face value).

" Bruce Charles Mallaig, age 30, British subject. Address 31 Marlborough Terrace, N.W.8. Occupation, Analytical chemist to the Ministry of Supplies."

Wright wrote down this information, returned to Mallaig's identity card and then said: " And now if you would care to make a statement, sir?"

Bruce Mallaig gave a clear, terse description of his evening's experiences, beginning with the telegram he had received at Canuto's and ending with his tussle with an unknown man on the little bridge in Regents Park. Wright listened and wrote industriously, putting an occasional question, such as, " You just thought you'd like a walk, sir? You had no particular reason for going by that route? It was just as the fancy took you, so to speak?"

" You sat down for a rest, as it were. . . .? You weren't expecting to meet anyone?"

Finally, Bruce arrived at the moment when the Irishman struck his second match, and he paused a moment, realising that it was necessary to be very careful. " The match light dazzled my eyes a bit, but I had a very strong impression that I saw another face just beyond the first chap's shoulder . . . I could only see his face, no collar or tie or coat."

" Did he wear a hat?"

" I don't know . . . I just don't remember," replied Mallaig. " All I can remember is the face—and I should recognise that if I saw it again."

" Did you hear the footsteps of this third man arriving, sir? You say you had heard the footsteps of the man who climbed over the bridge, and you heard the footsteps of deceased when he arrived."

" Yes—I heard both of them, but I didn't hear a single sound of the third chap : that was why I was so surprised when I saw his face. I didn't hear him walk away, either. I just heard a thud, and then the sound of a body falling. I tried to get my torch out quickly—but I dropped it through being in too much hurry. When I got it switched on, the first chap was astride the bridge—and I went for him so that he shouldn't do a bolt."

" You say the first chap, sir—meaning the man who had originally climbed the bridge, I take it—but you hadn't seen his face until you lighted your own torch after the thud of the falling body?"

" No, that's quite true," replied Mallaig. " I saw the dead man's face by the light of the match he struck, and I saw that other face—a dark flushed heavy-jowled chap—but I didn't see number one—the bridge man I call him—until I got my own torch on."

" So you can't be certain it was the same man who climbed the bridge?"

Bruce took a deep breath. " No, I suppose I can't—but it's absurd to suppose that *another* one joined the party. Dash it all, I should have heard him. . . ."

He broke off, realising that he had already described one face —minus the appendages of a face—and denied hearing the arrival of the feet which presumably belonged to the disembodied face. He began to realise more clearly than ever what his story must sound like to a sceptical hearer.

" Look here, officer," he broke out. " I realise that you're probably thinking I'm telling you a tall story. It must sound the most utter drivel, but I'm telling you exactly what happened, and I'm not adding one single thing. I heard the first chap come and I heard him get over the bridge. I didn't see his face, because although he lighted a torch to examine the bridge, the light—a very feeble one—was thrown downwards. I heard the second chap arrive, and I saw his face in the matchlight and heard him ask ' Anybody about?' I did not hear the third chap arrive, but I saw his face, I'll swear to that. When I heard the thud and realised there was dirty work afoot, I tried to cop the chap on the bridge in the interests of justice, and I yelled for the police to help me. If you think I'm trying to lead you up the garden—well, you're wrong."

" That's all right, sir. Don't you get worked up," replied Wright cheerfully. " We've got to look into this very carefully, you'll understand that. Now I shall have to trouble you to step round to the Mortuary with me, just to see if you can recognise deceased."

" All right, I'll come—but I don't know him from Adam," replied Mallaig.

A few minutes later Bruce Mallaig stood and looked down at the shrouded figure of the Irishman, as he described the dead man to himself. When the sheet was turned back, the stare of the dark eyes in the dead man's face was horrific at first, but otherwise the face looked very peaceful. The wide thin lips were set in a half smile and the dark brows were whimsical, tilted at the corners. The Irishman might have been any age from thirty-five to fifty: he was lean, black-haired and pale skinned, certainly not a " tough." Rather the sort of chap one might have opened up to in a theatre buffet or bar, thought Mallaig, a nice looking bloke, humorous and promising. Wright inquired formally:

" Can you identify deceased, sir?"

Mallaig turned to him with a worried look. " No. I can't tell you who he is, and it's quite probable I've never seen him before—but something about him is familiar. I might have seen him in a bus, or in the tube, or in a pub for that matter. I can't place him, but I believe I've seen his face before somewhere. What's his name—or don't you know that yet?"

" According to his Identity Card and some letters we found on him, his name's John Ward, and he lives in Notting Hill."

" John Ward." Mallaig meditated. " It's a commonplace sort of name—nearly as common as John Smith. . . . Anyway it doesn't convey anything to me. I've known several men named Ward—but he's not one of them. I should have expected him to have an Irish name—O'Connell or O'Brien or something like that."

Wright replaced the sheet, and as they left the building he said: " I'll get you to sign that statement, sir, and then I needn't trouble you any further to-night. We shall need you at the Inquest, I expect—and you'll probably be asked further questions when the Yard take over. You won't be moving away from your present address, I take it?"

" Lord, no! You can find me whenever you want me," said Mallaig, and to his own ears the words had an ominous sound.

CHAPTER TWO

i

WHEN the crime in Regents Park was referred to the Commissioner's Office, the case was immediately handed over to Chief Inspector Macdonald for investigation. Macdonald, when he heard the brief salient facts, said: " Well—that's an unusual story: murder isn't uncommon, but murder in the presence of witnesses is quite uncommon. In the circumstances I'll finish off this report and get it done with. Tell the Regents Park fellows I'll be with them shortly. Meantime, they can carry on."

So it came about that Inspector Wright, much to his own private satisfaction, was able to continue the job by interrogating the second witness of the crime—he whom Bruce Mallaig had described as the " bridge man."

" Stanley Claydon, aged twenty-eight, address 115A Euston Passage. Discharged as unfit from the Army (Middlesex Regiment, Nth Battalion). Discharged as unfit from the Arsenal Small Arms Factory. At present of no occupation."

Inspector Wright absorbed this information and studied the man to whom the information referred. A tall weedy fellow, pale and unhealthy looking, was this Stanley Claydon, but he looked fairly muscular—by no means feeble.

" What's the matter with your health?" asked Wright.

" Asthma," was the answer. " Never know when it's going to lay me out. It just comes on—and then I'm kippered."

" Yes. Nasty thing, asthma," agreed Wright amiably. " Now what was it took *you* for a walk in Regents Park this evening?"

' Well, it's a rum story," said Claydon miserably. " I know before I start you won't believe me."

" I haven't the chance of believing you until I've heard your story," replied Wright. " It's up to you to choose if you want to make a statement—or if you want a solicitor present before you do so."

" Solicitor? Likely, isn't it? A solicitor couldn't tell you what he doesn't know, could he? It's just my luck. I always said I was born unlucky."

Wright enjoyed listening to Claydon's story—it was interesting and unusual—" ingenious " Wright called it when he was talking to Macdonald later—frankly the Inspector did not believe a word of it.

" I woke up feeling fed to the teeth this morning," began Claydon. " I'd been fired from the works because the doctors said I wasn't fit. Told me to get an out-of-doors job, but I was to have a holiday first to get fit. Well, I thought I'd ring up my married sister—she's got a house in the country, near Bedford. I went into St. Pancras Station to telephone—one of those call-boxes in the booking hall. It's dark in there—you know it?"

" Yes. I know it." (" Why did you choose a call-box there, I wonder?" Wright asked himself.)

" Well, I had to wait a longish while before I got on, and while I was waiting I heard a bloke talking in the next call-box. I could hear every word. I wasn't listening in particular, but I just couldn't help hearing. He asked for a doctor somebody—I didn't catch the name—and then he said ' Just say it's Tim—Timothy you know.' He'd got a rum voice, not quite English somehow. Next thing he said was ' That you, Joe? This is Tim speaking. Tim. T. I. M..' He went on for quite a bit, saying it was Tim, and he was quite O.K. and in the pink. Then he changed his tone a bit and said ' You and me had better get together and have a talk, Joe.' Something in his voice made me think he was threatening, and he went on, quite sharp, ' now don't argue. I'll be waiting for you at 8.30 this evening on the little wooden bridge close by the gate of Regents Park in York Gate. You know the place—near that island at the end of the lake. Oh yes, you know it all right. You've got to be there. Got that? Don't try any funny stuff because this is Tim and we've got to have that talk.' I think he rang off then, but anyway my own call came through and I didn't hear any more."

At this juncture Stanley Claydon glanced round nervously: another man had come into the Inspector's office and stood listening. Wright got up, but the newcomer said:

" Carry on. Finish the statement," and Wright sat down again and turned to Claydon.

" Yes—you said your own call came through."

" Yes, I was ringing up my sister, Dora. Mrs. Steven her name is. She's got a house near Bedford and a small business—cigarettes and confectionery, leastways, she had. The woman who answered the 'phone said Dora had joined the ATS and parked the kids out somewhere and the business was sold. I was fed-up, I tell you. What can a chap like me do when he's told to take a holiday? Dora's the only relation I got. I came out of that call-box more fed-up than ever. I've got nothing to do and no one to do it with. The woman at my digs won't give me any dinner and won't make me a fire in my room. I just mooched about and went into cafés and had cups of tea—and all day long I thought about that Tim and his doctor bloke, and the more I thought, the rummer it seemed. You see, I know that bridge in Regents Park. It's a lonely place after dark. Of course the park used to be shut at nights, but now the railings've been taken away, so it's always open. Well, I tried going to the flicks, only the stuffiness of them places always makes me cough, and then later on I went to the Corner House and had a real blow-out and felt better. I didn't want to go back to my room and think—so I jolly well made up my mind to go to Regents Park and see if these chaps turned up. I thought it might be funny. Just my luck. . . ."

Stanley Claydon was a big fellow, but his loose underlip quivered as though he were on the verge of crying. " What can a chap do when he can't keep a job?" he asked querulously. " In the Army they set me to work peeling potatoes—millions of them—only that gave me asthma, too. The place we peeled 'em in was that damp."

" Never mind about that," said Wright. " You get on with Regents Park."

" I wish I'd never bloody well gone near Regents Park," said Claydon, plucking at his loose underlip.

" It's a bit late to think about that now," said Wright, " so get on with your story."

" Well, I got on to the bridge about twenty-five past eight—I looked at the time in Baker Street Station. It was black dark, and I didn't quite like the idea of waiting on the bridge till the chaps came there—this Tim and Joe. I didn't know which way they'd come for one thing, so I thought I'd just jump over the bridge down on to the path below—it's only a few feet. Then I thought I could hear 'em talk. Anything for a bit of fun. I can see now it was a silly thing to do—but I was bored stiff and wanted to get my mind off myself. I turned my torch on— just to see there was no one about—and then I climbed over and got underneath the bridge. I hadn't been there very long when I heard someone walking along York Gate and then they turned on to the bridge, and a voice asked ' Anyone about?' I recognised the voice—it was the bloke Tim who'd been in the telephone box. No one answered, and presently he struck a match and lighted a cigarette. I could see the light gleaming between the planks of the bridge, and I could smell the cigarette. I don't smoke myself, it gives me asthma. It was perishing cold there, and I couldn't move about in case Tim heard me, and I began to wish I hadn't come. He threw his cigarette away—the end fell in the grass nearby where I was and it give me an awful turn—it shone so bright as it fell. Then he lit another match: leastways, I suppose it was Tim, though I couldn't see him, and then there was a sort of schemozzle and an awful bump on the bridge . . . and something warm dripped on my face as I looked up into the dark.'' Claydon shivered, and his breathing grew laboured as he spoke. '' I was frightened stiff,'' he said. '' I hadn't expected anything like that. I'd have run for it—but I didn't know if the gates of them college grounds was locked, and it wouldn't have looked too good if I'd got copped there—so I thought I'd climb up on the bridge again and beat it down York Gate. I pulled myself up on to the bridge somehow, and then someone went for me—nearly throttled me. I couldn't get away, and I couldn't even yell out because I'd lost my breath . . . I just knew he was going to do me in, too. I tell you I was scared stiff. . . .''

ii

There was no mistaking two things: first, that Stanley Claydon had been '' scared stiff,'' and second, that he was an asthmatical subject. His narrative had worked on his own nerves until he was as breathless as a man in the throes of bronchitis. Macdonald, who had been standing listening to Claydon's story, came forward at this juncture saying:
'' You needn't be frightened of that any longer. In any

15

case, if another man's going to kill you, he doesn't generally shout for the police while he's doing it."

"He wanted to put it on to me, that's what he wanted," said Claydon. "I knew it when I tried to beat it. 'Oh, no, you don't he says '—and I understood."

"Now don't you worry your head about that," said Macdonald. "I want you to answer this question. You say that you heard the second match struck—and then the thud and the body falling: had you heard a second person walk on to the bridge?"

"No, sir. There wasn't a sound." Claydon turned eagerly to the plain-clothes officer, sensing the humanity in the quiet voice. "There was just this chap Tim. I knew where he was standing, just above my head, because I heard him shift his feet once or twice, but I never heard a sound of no one else coming—the other one, he must fair have crept up like a mouse. I didn't hear nothing."

"Think back to the time when you climbed up on to the bridge again," went on Macdonald. "How did you get up?"

"I caught hold of the bars and pulled myself up—you know, like a monkey," said Claydon. "I got my foot on to the edge and hauled myself on to the rail—and I'd just got there when this other chap turned his torch on me and came at me."

"The chap with the torch *was* on the bridge then?"

"No, sir. Not then he wasn't. He'd gone away a bit—further from the gate. He was about three yards along the path. If I'd known there was anyone there, I shouldn't have climbed up like I did. I thought Tim must have thrown a fit, or been poisoned and fallen dead. You see I never heard no one else—and that's rum, you know, because when you're underneath that bridge there's no mistaking when anyone sets foot on it. It sort of echoes."

"Rum it is," agreed Macdonald, and Claydon put in eagerly:

"Could it've been a bit of bomb or shrapnel or something like that hit 'im, sir? Something dropped out of a plane, say? A bit of stone'd do no end of damage if it was dropped from a height."

"Maybe it would, but it wasn't any bit of stone or bomb which killed this man," said Wright. "It was something like a small coal hammer."

Claydon, whose face was as pallid as a potato, turned a shade greener when supplied with this information, and after a moment's pause Wright said to Macdonald:

"Shall I ask him to see if he can identify the body, sir?"

Macdonald nodded. " Yes, Inspector. I'll look through your notes in the meantime, and read this other statement. I'll be here when you come back."

iii

Macdonald read through the statement which Bruce Mallaig had signed, and then studied Wright's brief but admirably legible notes giving the gist of Claydon's statement: this latter document he handed to an attendant constable to be typed. Just then a sergeant came in to report. He had been sent to the address on the dead man's Identity Card, and had returned with what information he had been able to collect. John Ward had lived at 5A Belfort Grove, Notting Hill Gate. This house was divided up into six self-contained single-room flatlets, of which John Ward had rented the topmost—and cheapest. On the same floor lived the resident caretaker, a talkative and ancient charlady whose erstwhile occupation had been that of lavatory attendant. This body, who gave her name as Mrs. Maloney and her age as sixty-five (the sergeant guessed that eighty was nearer the mark) said that she was employed as " house-keeper," her duties including answering the front door, cleaning the stairs and landings and the bathrooms shared by the tenants, as well as rendering such " service " as her other duties permitted to those tenants who wished to employ her. She had identified the dead man as Mr. John Ward of 5A Belfort Grove. He had lived at this address for six months, occupying the room of a Mr. Claude d'Alvarley, an actor, now in His Majesty's Forces. Mr. d'Alvarley still paid the rent of the flat, and Mr. Ward occupied it on a basis of friendly agreement.

Concerning Mr. Ward himself, Mrs. Maloney could—or would —give no information. " 'E was a gentleman—which is more'n I'd say of some," she volunteered, " and 'e kep' 'isself to 'isself and caused no bother."

" Relations?"

How was she to know? Mr. Ward wasn't one of those who made confidences not asked for, and she'd got too much to do to gossip. " I did out 'is room once a week by arrangement— Tuesday's my day for 'im, and 'e always obliged by going out so's to leave me free to get on with it. And I've never 'ad no dealings with the police, nor don't want to, and I say so straight. I've me character for twenty-five years since me 'usband was took, and never been in no trouble at all."

17

When this ancient lady had retired, Sergeant Phillips grinned at Macdonald.

" I went and found her in the local—the Duke of Clarence—and she was properly annoyed. No lady likes to be inquired for by the police, she told me, accident or no accident. The landlord says she's highly respectable and to be trusted. Drinks like a fish but she's never any the worse for it, and all the tenants say she's as honest as the day—so the pub people say. The tenants are mostly in the profession—variety folk. There wasn't a soul in the house this evening."

When Wright came back he said, " Claydon couldn't identify him—but I didn't expect him to."

Macdonald nodded, and then said: " These two statements —Mallaig's and Claydon's—tally remarkably well over the events at the bridge. Remembering their relative positions, there isn't a single discrepancy. Mallaig said he saw another man's face in the matchlight—but both men agree that they heard no other footsteps after deceased came on the bridge. That's a bit remarkable. Claydon did *not* say that he heard Mallaig approach the bridge, and Mallaig states that Claydon, to the best of his belief, was *below* the bridge when deceased was struck. Since it doesn't seem probable on the face of it that there's any collusion between those two witnesses, we're faced with the probability that another man arrived on the bridge unheard by the man immediately beneath it."

" You accept these two statements without doubt, sir?"

" No. I never accept any statement until I can prove it, but the fact that these two independently narrated identical facts makes me believe that both statements are true so far as they go. They both told exactly what they saw and heard—though that's not to say that they told all that they saw and heard, or that they are truthful and innocent people."

" How do you suppose that the man Mallaig says he saw got on to the bridge—since Claydon, immediately underneath, didn't hear him?"

" Mallaig didn't hear him either. He says that he saw a face. It might have been an optical delusion—matchlight is very confusing. However, we have the one objective fact we can't get away from: deceased had his skull smashed in by a whacking great blow which was probably struck by that coal hammer your man picked up from the lower path which goes under the bridge."

Wright pondered. " If both Mallaig and Claydon are speaking the truth, it beats me how anyone else got on to the bridge without either of the other two hearing footsteps. Do you think there could be any other possibility: could the hammer have been thrown, for instance?"

Macdonald replied: "I always hesitate to say that a thing's impossible, and I'm quite willing to experiment, but I feel very doubtful. If you throw a hammer it tends to revolve in the air owing to the fact that the two ends are unequal in weight, and it would be very difficult to throw it in such a manner that the weighted end would hit its objective with the necessary force. I was playing about with a similar idea in my own mind. I thought of a catapult, but again I doubt if any projectile from a catapult could have struck with the force that was used in this case, not merely cracking but smashing the skull. In addition to this, there is the evidence from Mallaig that he saw another face in the matchlight—a face which he says he could recognise again. Of course I haven't seen Mallaig myself—what was your own opinion of him and of his evidence?"

"He was a good witness, and he seemed a sound, trustworthy sort of fellow," said Wright, "but I don't feel disposed to take either of these witnesses at their face value. Both of them told stories which it would be difficult to disprove—but both stories could have been made up in advance, just to account for the witnesses' presence at the spot."

"That's perfectly true," agreed Macdonald, "but it's worth bearing in mind that Mallaig could have got away without attracting any attention at all, and that he chose to give the alarm quite deliberately. Had he been concerned in the murder, I doubt if he would have shouted for the police."

"Maybe not," said Wright, "though it's an old trick to pretend to discover a body when you've just committed the murder yourself."

Macdonald nodded. "Admittedly—and I don't want you to think I'm accepting either statement without reserve. Both men's careers will have to be looked into very carefully. However, I should like to spend a little time considering that bridge where the murder took place. Have you got a man posted there?"

"Yes, sir. I thought there might be some other evidence to be found in daylight. The ground is soft between the park gates and the bridge, and it's just possible we may get some footprints which might help. We've got a fair idea of the prints Mallaig and Claydon made this evening. Bond had a look at their shoes as they came in. Mallaig had crepe rubber soles—size nine. Claydon wears size eight, and there's a hole in the sole of his right shoe."

" Good man ! " said Macdonald. " You're one of the fellows I like to work with."

Wright grinned happily. " Thank you, Chief. A word like that from you makes the day seem a good one—but I'm afraid my efforts with the shoe soles won't be worth much to you. The ground's been trampled over a lot. Still, I've had a cordon put round, just in case."

" Again—good for you. Co-operation in the early stages is often worth a lot more than brain-waves later," said Macdonald. " I'll have a look at deceased, and see what he had in his pockets, and then I'll go and glance around in Regents Park."

iv

Macdonald stood and studied the dead face of the man whom Mallaig had called " the Irishman "—and the Chief Inspector admitted that he himself would have attributed the same nationality to the owner of that smiling whimsical face. He studied the long thin hands and the condition of the dead man's skin and hair. A healthy, well-kept skin and carefully tended hands denoted a man of the professional class rather than an artisan. A writer or an actor perhaps, thought Macdonald, for there was something that suggested an imaginative faculty, or artistry, in that pale smiling mask of death.

Macdonald next turned his attention to John Ward's clothes. His suit had been a very good one once, though it was old now. The tailor's name had been cut away, but the workmanship of the suit denoted a good tailor. The linen was less good in quality, but was clean and fresh. The only markings on it were those stitched in by a laundry. The contents of the pockets told very little : there was a wallet holding Identity Card and Ration Book, some printed cards giving John Ward's name but no address, and three letters. Each of these was written by a different woman : each was a love letter of sorts, and each had had the address torn off. Elspeth, Meriel and Jane all expressed their affection for " Johnnie " in the current idiom of young women of to-day. Apart from the wallet and its contents the pockets contained four shillings and sixpence, a packet of Players, a box of matches, a fine linen handkerchief, a fountain pen, a pencil and two latch keys. The preliminary surgeon's report told Macdonald that deceased appeared to have been in good health, but that he had been slightly lame, due to a badly set fracture in the left femur. " That probably kept him out of the Services, but it didn't save his life," pondered

20

Macdonald. Something about John Ward interested the Chief Inspector. Even in death the Irishman had an invincible charm.

CHAPTER THREE

i

WHEN he left the Mortuary, Macdonald made his way to the Marylebone Road and turned up York Gate. The night was intensely dark and the streets were deserted; the buses were no longer running and not a single car was in sight as the Chief Inspector crossed the wide roadway opposite Marylebone Parish Church. London was silent, with a silence which had no quality of peacefulness: in its shroud of darkness the place seemed tense, uneasy, as though waiting for the first banshee howl of sirens which seemed a fitting accompaniment to the listening darkness. Had Macdonald not known his way very well he would never have found the entrance to the little bridge. He had not turned his torch on because he liked finding his way in the dark, steering by reason since the sky was so overcast that the keenest vision could not perceive the outline of roofs or trees against the clouds. Macdonald, using his memory, noted every kerb as he negotiated it, the roughness of asphalt and gravel, the smoothness of tarmac in the roadway of the Outer Circle, the slight rise in the ground as he crossed the road-bridge over the lake. When he did turn his torch on, he found himself exactly at the point he had calculated, and as he flashed the torchlight on the ground he was challenged by the constable on duty.

For the next fifteen minutes he examined the ground on, around and below the bridge. The latter told the plainest tale. Claydon's footmarks showed clearly on the damp path, and it was evident that he had stood still for some considerable time, for the pressure of his shoes had made distinct imprints. He tended to dig his heels in, and the evidence was plain to see. Next Macdonald made his way to the seat where Mallaig had observed the earlier part of the evening's proceedings, and here again his footmarks showed clearly, the imprint of the crepe rubber soles clearly discernible, as were their tracks when he had run to the bridge. On the bridge itself it was less easy to read the traces. There was a patch of mud at one point, at the place where John Ward had stood, and Macdonald guessed that he had walked across the muddy path recently trodden by

21

pedestrians on the grass bordering the Outer Circle. Bending low, Macdonald brought the ray of his torch close to the surface of the bridge, while the constable stood by watching. At last Macdonald said: "There's the print of bicycle tyres here —only as far as the point where deceased stood: perhaps that explains the most puzzling part of the story—how a third party approached the bridge without being heard by the man below it."

Following up the prints, Macdonald found evidence that a bicycle had recently been ridden—or wheeled—along the side-walk of York Gate and had turned in by the gate giving access to the bridge. The wheel tracks were fairly plain on the side-walk, but only just discernible on the bridge where they were partly obliterated by footsteps. Macdonald stood and considered. It seemed possible to him that a man could have free-wheeled a bicycle down the slight incline of the side-walk, swerved in at the gate and come level with the man on the bridge without being heard. If the evidence of Mallaig and Claydon was to be trusted, the blow which killed Ward had been struck while his head was bent over his cupped hands as he lighted a cigarette. The matchlight had made him a clear target for a few seconds. While he stood considering this possibility, Macdonald saw a light approaching in the road and realised that a bicyclist was close at hand.

"Hi there, cyclist! Police speaking. Stop just a minute."

"Lord, what's up now?" demanded a resigned voice. Macdonald's torchlight revealed the figure of a man in Civil Defence uniform, and the C.I.D. man replied:

"Nothing for you to worry about. Can you spare your bike for a couple of minutes while I try an experiment?"

"O.K. What's the idea?"

"Would you like to co-operate?" asked Macdonald, and the other replied:

"You bet—provided it won't take too long. I've got ten minutes."

"That'll do. Let me have your bike. I want you to climb over the bridge and wait underneath it—and tell me what you hear afterwards."

"Right oh. That sounds easy."

"Good. Get over the railing here—we're trying to get some evidence from footprints further along . . . That's right. Just wait there—and when you hear me whistle, listen for all you're worth."

Macdonald then gave a few words of instruction to the attendant constable, who was bidden to stand at the same spot that

John Ward had stood and to strike a match and light a cigarette after he had counted twenty. Macdonald himself then wheeled the bike a dozen yards up the side-walk of York Gate and whistled shrilly. He stood with the bike on his left, and then with his left foot on the pedal shoved off and free-wheeled to the gate. Just as he came level with the gate the match spluttered and the constable's face and hands showed up clearly in the flickering light. Macdonald swerved on to the bridge close behind the constable, brought himself to a standstill with one foot on the ground and made a swipe with his right hand at the constable's helmet. Still with his left foot on the pedal the Chief Inspector shoved off again and the bike moved forward into the darkness of the park. The constable, following previous instructions, had collapsed noisily on to the bridge. Macdonald returned to the bridge and called to the Civil Defence man below:

" Experiment's over. Can I give you a hand up?"

" That's all right." The chance collaborator was an active fellow and he hauled himself up with ease. Macdonald asked:

" Exactly what did you hear after I whistled?"

The other replied: " I heard the sound of a match being struck and saw the gleam of light—surprisingly bright in the dark. I think my attention was completely taken up by the light, because I didn't really notice any sound before there was a good healthy biff and then a commotion and thud which made me think the bridge was breaking down. Thinking back, I can remember hearing a sort of faint click-click. It was the bike of course, free-wheeling—but then I knew you'd borrowed my bike. If I hadn't known, I shouldn't have tumbled to it that a bike went over the bridge."

" Thanks very much. You've done your bit admirably and I'm much obliged," said Macdonald.

" Glad to be of use. What's the racket?"

" I expect you'll see something about it in the paper to-morrow. Someone got biffed over the head, and it's a bit difficult to understand how the assailant came up unheard."

" I follow. Hence the bike idea. All the same, it wouldn't be easy to biff anyone efficiently from a bike—not unless you're a bit of a trick rider."

" I think I agree with you—though I landed quite a fair one on that chap's helmet," replied Macdonald.

The Civil Defence man chuckled and then said, " You know it's not in human nature to have no curiosity at all. It makes me hopping mad to have heard just this bit of the story and then have to clear off and not know another word about it."

" Yes, I quite see that," replied Macdonald. " Incidentally, what's your job?"

" I'm one of the Post-wardens in that block up by the corner there: there's quite a party of us near the searchlight."

" Have you just come off duty?"

" More or less. My mate's there, and I've taken the opportunity of coming to get some cigarettes: it's O.K. provided one warden's at the post."

" I see. You might be useful to me if I want to learn more about the nocturnal habits of Regents Park. Can I see your Identity Card?"

Again the other laughed. " Here it is. Don't go thinking I biffed anyone over the head—because I haven't."

Macdonald examined the Warden's card in the gleam of his torchlight, saying, " One of the disadvantages of being a policeman is that every innocent citizen imagines one's suspecting him. Well, Mr. Tracey, I'll probably look you up at your Post. If you could manage to keep this experiment under your hat for the time being it might be advisable. It's not essential —but less said's soonest mended."

" O.K. ' Careless speech ' and all that. I'll remember. I'd better be beating it. What's your own name, if I'm allowed to ask?"

" Macdonald. I'm a C.I.D. man."

" Lawks! I've heard of you . . . in that Rescue Squad do down Lambeth way. May 10th '41. Shan't forget that in a hurry, by gum."

" Neither shall I," replied Macdonald feelingly. " You Civil Defence blokes earned George Crosses, every man jack of you, that night."

" What about yourself?—Well, so long. Come and see us at the Post sometime. Cheer oh!"

When Mr. Tracey had mounted his cycle, the constable came to Macdonald. " D'you reckon that's how it was done, sir? You caught me a good wallop as you passed."

" I don't know: it's just an idea," said Macdonald. " Incidentally, did you hear the bike as it approached you?"

" Yes, sir, but I was expecting to hear it, and also it was a very old bike. Real bone shaker."

" That's true," replied Macdonald. " I'll try the same experiment again with a good machine and see that it's well oiled. There's one point which puzzled me a bit though: those bicycle tracks only show as far as the middle of the bridge: there wasn't a sign of them on the side of the bridge away from the gate, and the bridge isn't wide enough to turn round on—so I

24

shouldn't like to offer the idea to Counsel for the Defence to make merry over—even if we had any other evidence of the bicyclist's existence, which we haven't."

" All the same, it's a good idea of yours, sir," said the constable. " It does explain that puzzling bit about the chap below the bridge not hearing a footstep—and you hit me harder than I'd have thought possible in the circumstances."

" Devil take it!" said Macdonald unexpectedly. " It's beginning to rain, Drew. Even if it had kept fine those prints would have faded out by morning, but two minutes of rain will ruin the lot—and you can't put a tarpaulin over half Regents Park. Oh well, I suppose it's better not to have too much luck to begin with."

" It's a good thing you saw those prints when you did, sir. Gave you an idea, so to speak."

" Quite true—though ideas are dangerous commodities," replied Macdonald. " Child's guide to detection—evidence without ideas is more valuable than ideas without evidence."

The constable chuckled: " I've heard that evidence interpreted by ideas is the ticket, sir."

" Losh, don't be too intellectual, Drew—on a foul November night in the blackout in Regents Park. What was that low ditty—' Can your mother ride a bike . . . in the park after dark . . .' I'm afraid you're going to have a poor night of it, Drew. Keep listening for cyclists—and remember the old adage."

ii

Macdonald glanced at the luminous dial of his watch when he had turned his coat collar up. Eleven o'clock—only two and a half hours since John Ward had walked on to the bridge. Remembering the sergeant's statement that the tenants of the flats at 5A Belfort Grove were mostly ' in the profession '—on the stage in other words—Macdonald guessed that late to bed and late to rise was more likely to be their motto than the one generally approved by moralists. He decided to go to Belfort Grove and see if any of the household could be helpful. He walked back down York Gate, crossed the now unrailed space of the church-yard opposite and recovered his car where he had parked it in Marylebone High Street and was soon driving westwards along the empty darkness of Marylebone Road—a darkness slashed by the incredible brightness of the traffic lights shining out at the road junctions ahead. Belfort Grove had the same quality as every other London street in the blackout:

it seemed completely blank and dead, as though it were impossible that cheerful normal human beings could live and move behind the dead façade of blackened houses. Macdonald parked his car at the entrance to the " Grove," and turned his torchlight discreetly on to the nearest doorway to ascertain its numbering. After several such attempts he concluded that the numbering of the houses must be continuous—up one side and down the other. As he descended the steps o : No. 27—having previously examined numbers 2 and 16, he heard footsteps approaching him and a cheerful voice enquired:

" Are you looking for any particular number—or are you just looking?"

" I'm looking for number 5A," he replied.

" Well, well, I thought you might be. You see I live there. Just popped out to the post so's to catch it in the morning. Number five's back that way. If you'll wait till I've posted my letter I'll show you. You just wait here."

The voice was a woman's voice, good-tempered and full of confidence. Macdonald heard the click of her heels as she walked briskly along the pavement. He waited as she had bidden him, amusing himself by visualising the owner of the cheerful Cockney voice. A woman as old or older than himself, he judged (Macdonald was looking fifty in the face) a Londoner undoubtedly, one of the undaunted millions who take blackout and bombs in their stride, and prefer the hazards of those " twin b's " to the " 'orrible 'ush " of the safe countryside. He heard her footsteps returning and heard her humming a tune which took him back twenty years.

" Let the great round world keep turning . . ." Macdonald whistled the tune under his breath and was greeted with " Fancy you knowing that! I always says the last war had the tunes. Not a tune worth singing this war. I suppose you've come about poor Johnnie Ward."

" That's it," replied Macdonald, falling in step beside her.

" I guessed that'd be it," she went on. " Funny, isn't it? I can't see you but I bet I know just what you look like. You police are a good class these days—not like some of 'em when I was a gal. The minute I heard your voice I said to meself, ' Not one of us and not a newspaper man either. Must be police,' I said. I fell down in Piccadilly the other night—after the sirens had gone too, and a young Bobby helped me up— you should just've heard his voice. Eton. Not half! ' Madam ' he called me. This is number 5. Now what've I done with me latch key. Hope I didn't pop it in the pillar post . . . no, here we are . . . come right in."

The entrance hall in number 5 was partially illuminated by a melancholy blue bulb which shed sickly beams on worn linoleum and colourless walls.

" Who d'you want to see?" inquired Macdonald's guide, and he replied:

" Well, say if I start with you. You've been very helpful so far."

" Righty oh. Always glad to do me best. There's a lot of stairs though. Heaven's not in it. You follow me. Remember the old song? ' So *up* the stairs he went again, the shopman said ' How do?' . . . It's been a lovely day to-day, what can I do for you?' . . . Law! my poor feet. . . .''

Macdonald followed the lady up three flights of stairs and then she halted on a dimly-lit landing, produced another latch key and opened a door from which a flood of light poured out on the landing.

" Pop in!" she adjured him. " Landing blackout's N.B.G. I *do* like a bit of light. This dark business is enough to give a girl the creeps. Come right in. That's better, isn't it?''

" Much better," replied Macdonald cheerfully, blinking a little in the strong light. His first impression was of a prevailing pinkness: pink walls, pink curtains, pink cushions: artificial pink roses stood in ornate vases, artificial cherry blossoms trailed over mirrors and peeped coyly round elaborately framed photographs. Macdonald disliked pink as a colour, and this room seemed to him to resemble pink blanc-mange. He turned in some relief to study the owner of all this roseate effect—a neat little black-coated figure, she stood and returned his stare sedately.

" I'm Rosie Willing," she said cheerfully. " Not that I'm expecting you to know me name. I've been in variety since the year dot, but mostly in the provinces. Now all the youngsters are in the services I've got a contract with Stolling Ltd. I know me stuff, you see, and if I'm not the world's chicken I can still get a laugh when there's a laugh to be got. Sit down, won't you?''

" Thanks very much." Macdonald lowered himself into an ancient chair, whose springs were almost defunct under its blanc-mange coloured cover. Rosie Willing was very much as he had visualised her—over sixty years old he guessed, but gallantly and obstinately youthful of aspect. Her fair hair should have been grey, and her cheeks pippin coloured rather than ashes of roses, but her blue eyes were as serene as a child's. Her figure was still trim and slim, and it was probable that she looked a well-preserved forty behind the footlights. Somehow

Macdonald liked her, despite her partiality for very pink pink.

"Poor Johnny Ward!" she said. "So he's got his number, has he? It was only yesterday he said to me 'Reckon I'm on to a good thing this time, Rosie. You and me, we'll have supper at Oddy's next week, you see if we don't.' Always the optimist, Johnny was."

"You knew him well, then?" asked Macdonald, and she shrugged her shoulders.

"In a way, yes, in a way, no. These days you get to know your neighbours, don't you? What with the raids and shelters and all that, and no one able to get any help. I nursed Johnnie when he had flu' last month—you know the way one does, these days. He was a nice fellow and full of jokes—but as to knowing him—who he was or where he came from, well, I just don't."

"Say if you tell me just what you *do* know," said Mac-Donald, and she nodded in her bird-like way.

"Righty-oh—but it's not a lot, so don't be too hopeful."

iii

John Ward had first been seen in Belfort Grove about nine months ago, in February: he was introduced to Rosie Willing by Claude d'Alvarley, the actor who was tenant of the room which Ward had been living in. "Claude used to be on the Halls, he did a very good dance turn—tango and all that," said Miss Willing. "Then he did some work for the flicks and got a contract at Denham. It wasn't much use to him, because he got called up soon after. He told me he'd let Johnny Ward have his room, and that was that. Johnny just moved in—in May it'd've been, and here he's been ever since. He was a nice fellow, you couldn't help liking him; he'd got that Irish way with him, so you could have forgiven him anything. We soon got matey, and he popped in and out most days. I shall miss him."

"What did he do?—was he on the stage?"

"Bless you, no. Fellows like Johnnie never do any work. He couldn't have held a job down for five minutes. The only thing about him you could rely on was that he was unreliable."

"Then he had enough money to live on?"

She laughed at that. "Money? Not he. He made a bit here and there, and when he'd got a note in his pocket he blewed it at once." She studied Macdonald quizzically. "Now look here. Don't you think you're going to put me in a witness-box to give evidence. Nothing doing in that line. If I'm asked to swear what I know about Johnnie Ward, I don't know anything. See?"

"Yes, I see," replied Macdonald—"but you've done a bit of guessing, haven't you?"

"I won't say I haven't, but that's not evidence," she replied. "I don't mind talking to you, but you've got to remember it's only ' say so.' I don't *know* anything."

"Right you are," replied Macdonald. "Now according to ' say so ' how did Johnnie Ward scrounge a living?"

"Scrounge?" she echoed meditatively. "That's about the right word. He picked up what he could where he could. You know what it is these days: coupons and ration cards and short of this and can't get that. Johnnie got a bit of this and a bit of that and he sold it again to the highest bidder. Mind you, I'm only guessing—but I guess it was silk stockings here and a bottle of gin there, and clothing coupons somehow."

"Black market, then?" inquired Macdonald.

"I didn't say so—and I don't *know*," she replied, "but when governments go making all these rules and regulations, why then the Johnnie Wards of this world say ' Where do I come in?'—same's they did with prohibition in America. Always happens."

She broke off again, studying Macdonald with her shrewd blue eyes. "I've been in vaudeville since I was a little kid," she went on, "and I tell you you learn a bit about human nature. I've seen Johnnie Wards by the hundred—except that our Johnnie had got more of a way with him than any of them. He was educated, too. What I call a college boy." She chuckled a little. "If he hadn't a bean to pay for a meal, he'd just gate-crash into somebody's party. Always got away with it, too. There wasn't a woman in the world could be angry with Johnnie when he got wheedling." Her head cocked on one side, she concluded "I've sure said a mouthful, as the dough-boys say—and not a fact nowhere—because I don't know any. Take it or leave it. That was our Johnnie—scrounging his way along. Never quite in trouble but always asking for it, though he said he'd die any day to save himself trouble."

"You've given me as good a picture of him as I could want," said Macdonald, "but can't you help me a bit further? He must have had some relations somewhere."

"If he did, I never saw them or heard about them," she said. "He said he was alone in the world. Oh, he told me lots of stories, but one always contradicted the other. His father was an Irish Peer one day, and a Viceroy of India the next: he was born in New York and in Dublin and in Park Lane. Oh, he made me laugh, he did. He knew I never believed him. I think one thing was true—he was lame, you know—and he said he got wounded when he was a boy of twenty in the Black and Tan rows in Ireland. 1919 wasn't it? He was lame all right, and had a bit of shrapnel or something in his lung. He went for his medical when he registered— he wanted to join up. Loved a scrap—but they wouldn't look at him."

She yawned, a good wide honest yawn, and then said: " Sorry—but I've been on the go since I queued up for the fish this morning—and never got a sprat for me trouble. Now just tell me this—what happened to Johnnie? Traffic accident was it?"

" No. Someone knocked him over the head. Do you know what he was doing to-day, or who he was doing it with?"

" No. Not the foggiest. He never told me what he was going to do—thank goodness. I might have had to tell him not to, and what was the use? Might as well've saved me breath." Yawning again, she added " And you might as well save yours if you're thinking of asking me if I can guess who knocked him on the head. I can't. I just don't know."

Macdonald got to his feet. " All right, Miss Willing," he replied. " I'm ashamed to keep you up answering questions because you're tired and it's very late. Just answer two more questions. Where is Claude d'Alvarley now?"

" Search me! In the Forces out east somewhere—India or Burma, that's all I know."

" Will you tell me the names of the other tenants in this house and the number of their flats."

" That's easy. First floor, Mr. and Mrs. Rameses, conjurors and illusionists—they've a contract with Flodeum Ltd. at the Surrey Met. Second floor, Mr. Carringford, scenario writer or something like that, and Odette Grey—separate flats they've got of course. She's in the chorus at the Frivolity. Third floor, Mirette Duncan. She's on tour with Ensa in Egypt. Fourth floor, Johnny Ward and me, and old Ma Maloney in the corner attic. That's the lot." She yawned again and Macdonald said:

" Right. Thanks so much for answering all my questions. Good-night. I'll find my own way out."

" Rightey oh. I'm tired and that's flat," she replied. Macdonald was tired, too, but he stuck to his job. While the facts were fresh in his mind, he made a summary of the timetable of the case so far—a precaution which had stood him in good stead on other occasions. The murder had occurred at 8.30.

The body had been taken to the Mortuary in an ambulance at 8.55. As soon as the body had been examined and the Identity Card found a sergeant had been sent to 5A Belfort Grove, arriving there at 9.30. The sergeant could get no reply to bell or knocker at 5A, but inquiry next door had directed him to the public house where Mrs. Maloney was known to spend her evenings. The sergeant had returned to the station at 10 o'clock, just after Claydon had finished his statement. Macdonald left for the Mortuary at 10.5 and reached Regents Park at 10.15. He was at Belfort Grove from shortly after 11.0 and left there just before midnight.

CHAPTER FOUR

i

JOHN WARD'S Identity Card—a much worn document—showed two addresses, the first one being in South London, in a street which Macdonald remembered vaguely as being somewhere near Camberwell Green. Before he went to bed Macdonald decided that first thing next morning he would go to Dulverton Place—the first address on the Identity Card—and see if he could get any information about John Ward in that quarter.

When Macdonald had left Miss Rosie Willing he had gone into John Ward's room and examined his effects. He had gained no information from his careful scrutiny. The room held but the minimum of furniture: there was a divan bed, with a long drawer beneath it, a small table, an easy chair and an old bedroom chair and a dressing chest. In one corner of the room was a built-in cupboard. A door gave access to a tiny slip of a room under the sloping roof; here was a very small bath and wash basin, with an electric hot plate and miniature oven on a shelf at one end. There were a couple of tumblers, some cups, two plates and a few knives, forks and spoons. On the bedroom walls hung a number of photographs, mostly unframed and pinned up in haphazard fashion. These photographs were inscribed " to good old Claude," " to Claude d'Alvarley from Pip," "——Ever, Leonie," and so forth. They were obviously theatrical photographs belonging to the original tenant of the room. A very small hanging bookcase contained a few obscure thrillers and some " Wild West " novelettes, paper covered and dilapidated. For the rest, the contents of drawers and cupboard contained one dress suit—

old, but of good cut and material, four shirts, two pairs of pyjamas and a very small stock of underwear, collars, ties, socks, and handkerchiefs. There was a worn pair of pumps and a pair of walking shoes whose soles and heels needed repair. Macdonald registered a guess that the dress suit had been bought second-hand and the shirts likewise—they varied in material and size. From the contents of the room one or two things could be assumed: their owner had very little money, and he had used the room to sleep in, but for no other purpose. His meals must have been eaten elsewhere; his friends—if he entertained any—entertained elsewhere. The room, from a detective's point of view, was like a negative—but it was a negative from which the imagination could develop a positive.

When Macdonald reached Dulverton Place the next morning, he was quite prepared for what he found: it seemed a logical continuity with the negative room. The short street still existed as a thoroughfare, but it ran through a level open space where small hummocks of rubble alone had been left by the demolition of bombed premises. There were acres of such open spaces between the Elephant and Castle and Camberwell Green. After one prolonged stare Macdonald made his way back to the main road and stopped the first Civil Defence worker he met. The C.I.D. man stated his identity and then, pointing to Dulverton place he inquired " When did that happen?"

" Last February," was the answer. " Funny thing—that street survived all through the '40-'41 blitz—never touched. Then on the night of February 10th a load of incendiaries came down on it. We got everybody out and put them in the big surface shelter at the end there—and then a big H.E. hit the shelter. Shocking business. Sheer bad luck."

Macdonald nodded. " All that," he said. " Some of them survive?"

" Oh yes. A surprising number. My God! I shan't forget going in with the Rescue Squad . . . Some things you can't forget."

" I know," said Macdonald, and for a few seconds they both stood in silence. Then the C.I.D. man said:

" Well, I've got to trace one of the inhabitants in that terrace. D'you live around here?"

" I'm at No. 10 post there, but I don't know this district well. I lived in Westminster—Horseferry Place: the big block that copped it in May '41. Since then I haven't what you'd call a home. All went west—my missis, too."

" Rough luck," said Macdonald and the other shrugged his shoulders.

32

" I'm not the only one, and I shan't be the last," he said. " Look here—if you want to talk about Dulverton Place, stop that postman over there. He knows all these streets round here."

" Thanks, I will," said Macdonald, and the Civil Defence man moved on, a dogged sturdy figure in his blue uniform. " All went west. . . ." Macdonald knew that phrase. Many Londoners did.

The Postman turned out to be a helpful person: he was a tough stringy little fellow of sixty or thereabouts and he had been sorting and delivering letters in the same district ever since 1918. Macdonald's first inquiry was " What sort of houses were those in Dulverton Place?"

" Two storey dwelling houses like many of those here-abouts," replied the postman. " Small garden front and back. Let out in rooms many of them. Any special house in mind, sir?"

" Number 15."

" 15? ar . . . lodging house that was. Belonged to an Irish body named Casey. She was killed that night. She was a decent woman, always ready for a joke and a bit of back-chat and did her best to keep the house decent-like. She let rooms to single gents—always coming and going."

" You wouldn't remember any of their names?" inquired Macdonald.

The other shook his head. " Can't say I do—but there's a chap named Mason who lived at the far corner, newsagent he was, delivered papers and always out to spot the winner. Did a bit of book-making between you and me. He was badly hurt that night—lost both feet. He's living along there on Camberwell Green—Albert House, number 95. He could tell you more about the folks in Dulverton Place than anyone else. They've all scattered, them as survived. You know what it is."

Macdonald nodded. He knew. Again with the brief word of thanks which had an unusual note of sincerity in it Macdonald went on to Camberwell Green.

Alf Mason was a fat cheery fellow, despite his crippled con-dition. Reposing his enormous weight in a wheeled chair, Alf winked at Macdonald and extended a vast flabby pink hand.

" Glad to see you, sir. Always glad of a bit o' company. Lives like a lord, I do: fair treat to sit in a chair and watch others do the work. D'you know, a few years ago I was as lean as you are yourself, sir, worked to skin and grief. See me now—never believe it, would yer?"

33

Alf was full of reminiscences, and Macdonald slowly and good-naturedly led him to the matter in hand, namely, the inhabitants of Dulverton Place. Inevitably the story of the bombing had to come first, the tragic record of fire and destruction, horror and misery—a story no less tragic because it had been so often experienced in south London. Gently but persistently Macdonald led Alf Mason back to the days when Dulverton Place still stood, its shabby little brick houses a dingy grey under the London sun.

" Number 15," repeated Macdonald, " Mrs. Casey's house, wasn't it?"

" That's right—and a fine woman she was—bigger'n I am now," said Alf. " Dearie me, many's the laugh I've had with Ma. All called 'er Ma down our street. Let lodgings, she did, and often as not they diddled 'er and never paid a bean. ' Single gentlemen ' she called 'em. Well, depends on what *you* call a gent."

" Gentle is as gentle does," said Macdonald. " Now I wonder if you remember any of the lodgers by name? I believe there was a man named John Ward used to live there."

" Mr. Ward? Quite right, so there was. He'd been at Ma's for a long time—a couple o' years it'd 've been. I often wondered about Mr. Ward. Never saw 'im again after that night. 'Is name wasn't down among those killed, I do know that, but 'e never came round to see me, same as many of the others."

" Can you tell me anything about him? How old would he have been, and what was he like?"

" Well, I reckon he was getting on for sixty—same's me. He was a little bit of a chap, bald, with ginger hair what there was of it and a fine big moustache. Put me in mind of a butcher I knew once, down Dulwich way."

" Do you know what his job was?"

" Nothing very much. Something down by the river side— fish porter or that. 'E wasn't in no union, I do know that. ' I'm what they call casual labour ' 'e used to say, but 'e made what 'e could while 'e could, if you follow."

Macdonald nodded. This description of Mr. John Ward of Dulverton Place did not surprise him in the least. He had been expecting something of the kind.

" Do you remember any of the other lodgers at Mrs. Casey's?" he inquired. " Were there any who you'd have called superior—educated men, so to speak?"

" Bless you, there was all sorts. Some of 'em might 've been toffs once, come down in the world. Ma often said to me that it was always the 'igh and mighty ones went off without paying their rent—— Life's like that. ' Gimme an honest working man, ma,' I told 'er. ' These down-at-'eels used-to-be's— they're no one's money.''

'' Do you remember any Irishmen staying there?'' asked Macdonald.

Mr. Mason would have been only too glad to talk to his visitor for hours, but Macdonald soon found that there was no further useful information to be obtained from him. Mr. Mason's reminiscences of Irishmen in Mrs. Casey's lodging house had no bearing on the inscrutable unknown in the Mortuary, who, for reasons of his own, had carried the Identity Card of John Ward of Dulverton Place, a one-time casual labourer of Thames side.

ii

After he left the stout and talkative Mr. Mason, Macdonald called in at the local police station before he returned north of the river. Here he obtained further information about the destruction of Dulverton Place and the shelter to which many of the inhabitants had been directed as the fire made their own homes untenable. He also inspected a list of the names of those killed and those missing, believed to be killed. Amongst the latter, the name Timothy O'Farrel occurred. Enquiry about the bombing of the shelter elicited just those facts which Macdonald had assumed for himself from grim experience in Rescue Squads. The shelter was divided into compartments: the section struck by high explosive was at the north end of the structure, and here the destruction had been complete. Identification of remains rested on assumption. In the middle section of the shelter a few persons had survived: at the south end the majority had been brought out alive. All that could be learnt about Timothy O'Farrel was that a silver identity disc bearing his name had been found among the debris as well as a cigarette case containing a card bearing the same name but no address. Both these relics had been found in that part of the shelter where the victims had been damaged beyond hope of recognition. One of the constables in the station during Macdonald's visit had been on duty on the night when the shelter was destroyed, and he talked with Macdonald about it. The latter put forward the theory he had deduced from his morning's inquiry.

'' It looks as though a man whom we will call O'Farrel was in the shelter when it was hit. O'Farrel seized the chance of losing his own identity and taking that of another man. In other words he managed to get hold of John Ward's Identity Card and left his own disc and cigarette case behind. I take it you had several casualties who couldn't be identified?"

" Yes. There were several bodies in the Mortuary which nobody recognised—and for the rest, there was an unknown number who couldn't have been recognised. Nobody knows—you know what it's like when such ' incidents ' happen, sir."

" Yes," replied Macdonald laconically. " I know."

iii

Macdonald drove back over Westminster Bridge pondering on such facts as he had collected. There seemed little room for doubt that John Ward's Identity Card had been acquired by the Irishman in some such manner as Macdonald had guessed. The man known to Alf Mason as John Ward of Dulverton Place had never been seen again after the bombing: neither had a man of that name asked for a new Identity Card at the office which issued these documents after the bombing. The man who had lived at Belfort Grove carried the Identity Card once issued to John Ward of Dulverton Place, and the man of Belfort Grove had been an Irishman in the opinion of those who had heard him speak. In addition was the fact that Stanley Claydon, in describing the telephone conversation which had caused him to go to Regents Park, had said that the man who telephoned had called himself Tim.

There was no proof at all that ' Tim ' who had been murdered in Regents Park was identical with Timothy O'Farrel whose identity disc had been found in a bombed shelter in South London—but there was a possibility that the two were identical. In any case, it seemed obvious that " Tim " had taken an opportunity of changing his identity by using another man's Registration Card, and no man goes to the trouble of changing his name and concealing his original identity without a very good reason for doing so.

It was getting on for mid-day when Macdonald arrived back at Belfort Grove. He had guessed—rightly—that the inhabitants of that house would not be early risers, and his mid-day visit was judiciously timed to catch those he wished to interview before they went out to lunch and the business of the day. To theatrical folk the morning hours are spent in resting and in a leisurely toilet before the real business of the day. Macdonald made his first call on Mr. and Mrs. Rameses—the pair who had been described by Miss Willing as conjurers and illusionists. They lived in the flat on the first floor and the door was opened by a plump highly coloured lady dressed in a puce-coloured, wadded silk dressing-gown and jade green mules garnished with dispirited ostrich tips. Macdonald had much ado to keep his eyes from studying the intricacies of her hair curling arrangements, for the coils and adjustments and spring-like contrivances reminded him of a dismembered wireless set.

" Be blowed! I thought you were the milkman," she explained. " Didn't see his van in the street, did you? Half a pint between two, and lucky if you get that. Awful, isn't it? Sorry. Come in, do. Was it the gas meter?"

Macdonald explained that it wasn't the gas meter, raising his voice in competition with the strains of a gramophone issuing from an open door just behind him.

" Scotland Yard! My! how wizard. You come in and talk to Birdie: he's just finishing his daily dozen. Has to practice every morning to keep up to the mark: just let him finish the record. You watch—he's a wonder Birdie is."

She gave Macdonald a friendly push and he stepped inside the door of the gramophone room and stood watching. A tall stout man clad in trousers and a shirt with rolled up sleeves stood on the hearthrug, executing a swaying movement in rhythm to the blare of the gramophone record: around and above his head a surprising number of objects were being kept in the air: two plates, a tumbler, a teddy bear, a beer bottle and a ping-pong ball were thrown up in rhythmic succession as though supported by jets of water from a fountain: Birdie's enormous pink hands weaved a dexterous pattern as he panted out the rhythm like a Yorke-Trotter baby. " Taffy—tiffa—teffy," he grunted, " taffy—tiffa—teffy . . ." It was not until the gramophone shrieked its final bar that Birdie fielded his miscellaneous selection and laid them down on the table beside him, executing an elaborate bow on the final beat.

" Snappy, isn't it?" demanded the lady at Macdonald's elbow and the latter replied politely " Very snappy indeed," as Birdie turned and studied the visitor with melancholy dark eyes.

" Not what I call first-class work. Common, not to say undignified," said Birdie mournfully. " All they ask these days. Something to make them titter. What can I do for you, sir?"

The man's voice astonished Macdonald. It was a beautiful voice, very deep and quiet, and might have done credit to a don. For the next moment or two there was an elaboration of introductions, during which Mrs. Rameses introduced herself to Macdonald, and Macdonald to her husband, while both apologised for the state of the room. It was inded as chaotic as any room Macdonald had ever seen: it contained all Mr. Rameses' stock in trade as well as all Mrs. Rameses' costumes, and in addition was a carpenter's bench where the raw material of further " illusions " was being shaped. After a moment or two of vociferous explanation from Mrs. Rameses, Birdie seized her firmly by the shoulders and put her outside the door. " You leave this to me, lady bird," he said in his profound bass and closed the door. " Now then, what about it?" he asked Macdonald. " There's a chair to sit on by the window. I'm not bats by the way. I'm a hard working bloke with my living to earn."

" So am I," replied Macdonald equably. " I am in charge of the investigation into the death of a Mr. John Ward who lived upstairs."

" Rather you than me. Seems a waste of a good man's time," said Mr. Rameses. " No use pretending we can help you. We can't. Johnnie Ward sometimes tried to cadge a drink off me and once cadged a fiver from my missis. Once. Not twice. Told him it wouldn't wash. He understood." He stood with his back to the mantelpiece and studied Macdonald with his melancholy dark eyes. " Lots of his type about. Some of 'em in the Black Market. Some in gaol.· Some being kept by silly women. No use to anyone. Why fuss?"

" The man was murdered. That's why," replied Macdonald. " It's the man who murdered him we want. Can you tell me anything at all that would help?"

The other went through a complicated series of manœuvres with a ping-pong ball which seemed to run round and round his bare arm like a mechanical toy.

" No. Nothing," he repeated. " Who was he? Do you know? Certainly I don't know. He was an Irishman, probably of good family and certainly of good education. He understood good clothes—even though his own were threadbare: knew how to behave; knew how to speak. Funny for me to be telling you this—but I know what I'm talking about."

" I realise that," replied Macdonald. " D'you mind telling me what your own name is?"

Again that slow scrutiny of the frowning dark eyes. " My own name is Richard Nightingale. I ran away from school and got in with a circus. Then I did conjuring. Travelled all round the world. Not a bad life. I've seen things—and I'm not boasting when I say I've worked for my living. " *This*"—

and he indicated the ping-pong ball which now appeared from inside his open shirt collar—" isn't as easy as it looks. It may be piffling, but it means work—honest sweat. Johnnie Ward didn't believe in work. He believed in living easy and letting other folks foot the bill."

" How do you know?"

" Know? Didn't I tell you I'd earned my living in a circus? I soon learnt to recognise the chap who left you to pay for the drinks. I once took Johnny Ward by the ear and put him outside this door when he was trying to sell my missis a pair of silk stockings. ' That's where you belong ' I told him. ' Outside. Got that?' He went. He'd got a grain of sense somewhere."

" I should say you have several grains of sense, Mr. Rameses —so will you tell me what you were doing between eight and nine o'clock last night?"

" I don't need to—but I will, to save you bother. You go and ask the manager of the Surrey Met. He doesn't pay me good money for not doing the show I contracted for."

From the empty air Mr. Rameses collected three billiard balls and a stuffed canary in rapid succession. " Sorry to bore you with this tripe," he said, " but it's my practice time. The only way to keep in training is to respect your practice time. If I'd wanted to kill Johnnie Ward—which I didn't—I shouldn't have done it in a way that would have brought Scotland Yard to my door next morning. Oh, no. If I'd done it, no one would have been any the wiser. I may be a clown, but I'm an efficient clown. I'm afraid you'll have to try somewhere else."

" I've no doubt I shall have to try a variety of places," rejoined Macdonald. " When did you see him last?"

" Yesterday morning . . . on the pavement there . . . about ten o'clock. He went out early for once in a way."

" When did you speak to him last?"

" Sunday night. At the front door. He began ' Could you by any chance . . .' and I cut in ' No. I couldn't. Not by any chance. Ever.' " For a moment Mr. Rameses stood still and faced Macdonald squarely. " It's just waste of time, Inspector—your time and mine. I haven't said ten words to Ward in ten weeks, and my missis hasn't either. I told her not to. No use for him. I don't know how he lived and I don't know how he died, and I don't want to know."

" But I've got to find out," said Macdonald. " I don't want to waste your time, any more than my own, but I've got to find out every single thing I can about John Ward. You lived in

39

the same house with him. You may know more about him than you realise."

Mr. Rameses leaned on the mantelshelf and spoke deliberately: "I'll tell you everything I know—and it won't take long. I first saw Ward last May. He cadged acquaintance in the front hall. I didn't like him. Can't stand Irishmen anyway. Don't trust 'em. He's been in this flat three times: first time he tried to sell me a bottle of whisky. I'm a teetotaller. Next time he got a fiver out of my missis. I told her not to do it again. Third time he wanted to sell stockings. I told him to git. I don't know any of his friends, any of his business or anything else about him. That's the lot."

" I shall have to ask your wife the same questions."

" Right oh. Go outside and yell. She'll come. I'm not interfering."

Mr. Rameses went up to Macdonald and picked a grotesque furry spider off his coat—it measured an inch across and ticked like a clock. " Pardon me," said the conjurer mournfully. " It's like this," he added earnestly. " I'm not unwilling to help. I like you. You're a decent chap and you look sensible, but I just don't know the first thing about that blighter except that he was a parasite—lived on other people's stupidity. I knew that because I've seen so many of his sort. Whoever killed him did quite a useful job. That's all."

Macdonald laughed. He couldn't help it. The deep solemn voice coupled to the man's grotesque appearance and preposterously skilful hands made a combination which was irresistibly comic.

" Right you are," replied the C.I.D. man. " I'll leave you to your labours."

" You just give her a shout," replied Mr. Rameses. " She'll be in the kitchen. I warn you, she likes talking. She'll talk from now to doomsday. Non-stop. Wonderful gift."

Macdonald did as the conjurer suggested: he walked into the passage and called, " Mrs. Rameses."

" Here in the kitchen: come right in, I'm just beating a batter and it'll go flat if I stop and then it'll be a pancake and Birdie can't abide pancakes. Dried eggs and synthetic milk and imaginary lemons. Awful isn't it?—but what I say is . . ."

Macdonald at length checked the torrent, or at least guided it in the desired direction. Mrs. Rameses was perfectly willing to talk about Johnnie Ward, but the sum total of her evidence was identical with that of her husband, so far as their acqaintance with Ward was concerned. The facts she produced were so precisely the same as her husband's that Macdonald suspected she had listened to the conjurer's statement in the adjoining room. The only divergence was that Mrs. Rameses, like Miss Willing, had been impressed by the Irishman's charm.

" Boy, he was a peach—the loveliest eyes he'd got, and the manners of a king, but there, he was just one of those slackers —*you* know, not a worker like me and my Birdie."

All the time she talked she went on beating the batter in a pudding basin held on her knees, and Macdonald wondered if she and her husband were ever still : he also wondered uneasily if a snake or a frog would suddenly pop out of the batter and make faces at him.

iv

It was a relief to Macdonald when he at last got out of the Rameses' flat and stood in the little lobby contemplating his next call.

The first floor flats were inhabited by Mr. James Carringford and Miss Odette Grey, and just as he reached the door of B flat it was opened by a tall, thin elderly man who looked at Macdonald with enquiring eyes.

" Are you wanting anybody? " he inquired.

" Mr. Carringford? I am an Inspector from Scotland Yard."

" Right. Come in. Case of Johnnie Ward? Poor old chap . . . an amusing fellow, what I call a natural wit . . . come along in, not that I can help you I'm afraid."

The room into which Macdonald was ushered was a pleasant, tidy room with long windows facing the street. It was well furnished and had a sober comfortable aspect. There were large easy chairs, a number of bookcases and some good etchings on the walls. It presented such a contrast to the flat downstairs that Macdonald felt he had stepped into another world. Carringford was a man about sixty Macdonald guessed, with very white hair and deep set eyes—a lawyerly looking fellow in his neat dark suit—a very sober looking tenant in comparison with those other inhabitants of this melancholy house. He asked Macdonald to be seated and then said:

" What can I do for you, Inspector?"

"I am inquiring into the death of a man about whom I can find out nothing at all," said Macdonald. " It's possible that relatives or friends may appear later to enlighten us, but at the moment we can find nothing to indicate who deceased was or anything about him. My only course at present is to interrogate his neighbours."

41

" And I'm afraid his neighbours won't be very helpful—at least this one won't," replied Carringford. " I knew Ward casually : I doubt very much if his name *was* Ward, and I'm quite sure the various stories he's told me of his origin were untrue, because he was always contradicting himself—but I enjoyed his company. He was a wit—undoubtedly an educated man and originally a well-bred one, and he had that quality which, for want of a better name, we call charm. Incidentally, I am employed in an advisory capacity by the Superb Film Company : I vet their historical sets—as far as they'll allow me—and I'm always ready to pick up information. Ward was undoubtedly an Irishman—southern Irish—and he knew a lot about the history of his country. That happened to emerge one evening when we got arguing about Sinn Fein : Ward knew the history of every act of oppression perpetrated by the English against the Irish. But that's not going to help *you*, I am afraid."

" Every item of information may help me," replied Macdonald. " Miss Willing, who lives upstairs, told me that Ward said he had been wounded during the Black and Tan period."

" ' The trouble,' " quoted Carringford, with a half smile. " Ward always called the Easter Rebellion ' the trouble.' Yes. I should think that was probably true. He was a typical rebel—authority was always wrong in his eyes. He maintained some contact with his friends in Ireland, that I know through some unguarded remark he let slip in my hearing—and I shan't be at all surprised if his sudden end was connected with his compatriots."

" Could you enlarge on that, sir?" inquired Macdonald, who was beginning to get interested in his companion.

Carringford shrugged his shoulders, and the slight movement made Macdonald realise the immobility of the man. Carringford had ben sitting absolutely still—a striking contrast to the perpetual-motion habits of Mr. and Mrs. Rameses.

" I don't want to mislead you by laying claim to information I do not possess, Inspector. All that I can tell you about Ward is in the nature of conjecture. You see, he was a liar. He didn't lie for utilitarian ends, he lied simply because he had a slipshod lazy mind, an able mind gone to seed. He said whatever was the easiest to say at the moment. Stop me if I'm wasting your time."

" You're not," said Macdonald promptly, " so please go on. I'm interested."

" Ah—you have one trait in common with me, you're interested in what's called human nature," said Carringford. "You

42

might be sufficiently interested to wonder why a man like my-self—dull, respectable, academic and elderly—should have bothered to entertain a fellow like Johnnie Ward, an unstable, unreliable, whisky-swilling Irishman. You see, he interested me. To me, he became a living symbol of what we used to call the Irish Problem. He had the wit, the versatility, the charm and the good looks of the real Southern Irishman—and he had the illogical, rebellious, thriftless lying habits of that type. Correct me if I offend you."

Macdonald chuckled. "I'm a Highlander by extraction," he said.

"So I surmised. We shall understand one another," re-joined Carringford. "Just as Ward was by nature a rebel, so also was he by nature an intriguer. He couldn't go straight because he was by nature devious. I think he kept in touch with some of his old Irish boon companions. One evening when he was three parts drunk he boasted that he was on to some information which the Ministry of Information would pay a lot for. It might have been true—it might not—but if he made a habit of spying on his friends—well, a knock over the head in the blackout seems a not illogical termination to his career."

Macdonald nodded. "I quite agree with you—but my de-partment exists to deal with terminations of that kind. Now can you tell me when you saw Ward last?"

"Certainly. I saw him yesterday evening, shortly before 7 o'clock. He called to borrow some money—he was chronic-ally short of change. I may say I did not oblige. He told me he was meeting a friend who was repaying a considerable debt. I congratulated him. Actually I felt a little ashamed of myself. On occasions Ward went hungry—and he had the look of a hungry man last night. I was going out to dine with a friend at Canuto's, a friend who orders a good dinner in advance. While eating pheasant I admit I thought of John Ward with something like a pang of regret. I shall always be sorry I didn't let him have that pound note—for the last time of asking." There was a moment of silence, and then Carring-ford said: "I'm afraid I've talked a lot without giving you any real assistance. You want to know 'Who were the man's associates? Had he any enemies, anyone who bore him a bitter grudge? What were his origins, his kinsfolk, his past history?' Frankly, I can't tell you. I saw him infrequently. I never asked him questions, and I never encouraged him to talk about himself. It was a waste of time. He always lied.

43

I knew that he lied. He knew that I knew he lied. On this basis of mutual understanding, Inspector, I studied the Irish Problem.''

CHAPTER FIVE

i

BRUCE MALLAIG worked in a laboratory equipped by the Ministry of Supply in a big modern building in Bloomsbury which had been intended for very different purposes from those to which it was now being put. There was a canteen in the building, but Mallaig often went elsewhere for his mid-day meal, to vary the monotony of the fare obtainable at the canteen. On the day after his exciting evening in Regents Park he made his way to the Grill Room at St. Pancras Station, experience having taught him that he could get a good meal there. The Grill Room was pretty full, but he saw an empty seat at a table for two where another man was sitting waiting for his lunch to be served. Mallaig, before sitting down, inquired:

" Are you keeping this seat for anybody?''

" Oh, no—it's vacant—thanks for asking,'' returned the other.

Bruce stared. " Good Lord! How funny!'' he exclaimed. ·

" What is?—an empty seat?'' demanded the other.

" No. The long arm of coincidence,'' replied Mallaig as he seated himself. " I heard your voice in Regents Park last night. You're the doctor who rolled up when the Bobby was wondering what to do next. I suppose ' funny ' may not be an appropriate word, but you must admit it's odd.'' ·

" Damned odd,'' replied the other. " I recognise your voice now, I hardly saw your face. The constable was holding on to you with tender care. They let you go, then?''

" I should think they damn well did,'' said Bruce indignantly, and the doctor replied:

" Obviously I'm hoping you'll tell me all about it. I don't know what happened. I was taking my dog for a walk and I heard the chemozzle in the distance. By the time I arrived there was a corpse on the ground and two chaps in the arms of the law so to speak. I was asked to produce my Identity Card, and when the second constable arrived was given to understand that my immediate presence was no longer required.''

The doctor surveyed Bruce with keen humorous eyes, half

44

smiling behind his big horn-rimmed glasses. "Who batted who?—no offence meant," he concluded.

Bruce laughed and turned to the waiter. "Soup, roast beef and all that, and a Bass." He turned again to the doctor, deciding he liked the look of him—a lean well-built fellow, round about fifty, with grizzled reddish hair and grey blue eyes.

"Incidentally, my name's Ross Lane," said the doctor, producing a card. "I've got rooms in Wimpole Street, and I take my dog for a stroll round the Outer Circle most evenings—though I don't generally meet any excitements en route."

Bruce rejoined with his own name and then said: "If you want the yarn, here it is," and gave a neat précis of his previous evening's experiences.

"It's a fantastic story—but fantastic stories do happen in London," said Ross Lane. "Incidentally, now the excitement's over, in the cool judgment of the morning after, do you suppose the chap under the bridge was the guilty party?"

"No. I don't," said Mallaig. "At the time it happened I did: that's why I grabbed him. Thinking it out later I'm certain he couldn't have done it, because I should have heard him climb that bridge. He was a clumsy goof."

"Well, what was he doing under the bridge? Innocent folks don't generally hide under bridges."

"I know. I felt that, too, but after the police had finished asking me questions and had let me go, as you put it, I hung around deliberately because I wanted to talk to that bloke who was under the bridge. Of course I didn't know if they'd detain him, but I thought they'd probably make him have a look at the chap in the Mortuary, as they did me. I was right over that—and they let him go afterwards. I waited around and had a talk with him—took him into a pub and we had quite a chat."

Ross Lane raised his fair eyebrows. "Very unwise of you, you know. The police are bound to suspect collusion."

"Well, let 'em! Damn it all, I've got nothing to be afraid of. I'd never seen the bloke before—Claydon his name is, a seedy sort of customer. By the same argument the police might suspect you and me of collusion."

"Quite true—so what?"

"Be damned to them," said Mallaig. "I don't know what you feel about it, but it's the first time in my life I've ever tumbled across a mystery, and I damned well wasn't just going to go home and pretend I wasn't interested. Besides, I wanted to tell that chap I was sorry I'd man-handled him. I

45

realised he couldn't have done it, and I was a bit sorry for him."

"Sympathy's an amiable attribute," said the doctor, "but before I expended any on the seedy-looking Claydon I should have wanted to know what he was doing under that bridge."

"Good Lord! Do you think I didn't want to know, too? It was because I wanted so much to know that I hung around in a damned cold street outside an infernally cold Mortuary waiting on the off-chance of seeing the other chap. Actually the story he told me was the rummiest business—it was worth while waiting for."

"Was it, by jove. Well, I'm waiting, too—ears flapping, so to speak."

"This is the size of it," said Mallaig, and related Claydon's story in full, while Mr. Ross Lane listened intently. At the conclusion of Mallaig's narrative, the doctor gave a prolonged whistle and looked around him with an expression of whimsical consternation.

"D'you know, I don't quite like it," he said. "The whole thing has too much of what the youngsters of to-day call ' pattern-making ' in it. The story begins with a telephone conversation overheard in St. Pancras Station: it goes on with the murder of a man unknown to any of the other participants. The next instalment is a chance meeting between two of the witnesses, previously unknown to one another, also in the purlieus of St. Pancras Station. What's the betting that the seedy Mr. Claydon isn't strolling around in the booking hall somewhere, haunting telephone booths on the off-chance of hearing more? I don't know if Scotland Yard wastes time on what the detective writers call ' shadowing ' but if anything of that kind's going on, the shadower must be getting his money's worth. I feel another drink's indicated. What's yours?"

"Oh—thanks. Gin and dry ginger appeals to me at the moment. Yes. I said ' How funny ' the minute I saw you." Mallaig paused a moment and then said "It's not really so improbable as it sounds. I work in Bloomsbury. I often come here to eat."

"So do I. I attend one day a week at the Collegiate Hospital and this place is conveniently placed. Also I often take the dog into Regents Park. Still—it's a rum go, taking it all round. Now look here: assuming that Claydon did *not* bump deceased off, and that you were merely a contemplative onlooker, what do you make of the doings? Any great thoughts to proffer?"

Mallaig pondered a moment and then said: "It occurs to

me that the chap who did the Irishman in wasn't the man Tim was expecting to meet."

" Why not?"

" Well, it was quite obvious from the way Tim behaved that he wasn't anticipating any violence. Far from it. He was full of confidence. When he arrived on the bridge he asked 'Anyone here?' in quite a matey tone of voice, as though he was prepared to go on ' Glad to see you, old chap.' He then struck a match and lighted a cigarette, making a deliberate target of himself. If he'd thought there was any chance of rough stuff, he wouldn't have done that."

" Yes. I think that's quite sound reasoning," agreed Ross Lane. " That being so one has to assume that Tim told somebody else of his projected rendezvous, and they took advantage of it to eliminate him hoping that a third party would be left to hold the baby. You've left out one point. Who was the party whom Tim expected to meet at the bridge? Are you certain there wasn't anyone else in the offing?"

" I can't be sure, can I?" said Mallaig. " It was as black as pitch and you couldn't see a thing. It was true I listened pretty hard—but that proves nothing, because I didn't hear the third chap arrive. I should never have known he was there if I hadn't seen his face in the matchlight."

" You can swear to it that you *did* see a face?"

" Oh lord, yes. I saw the face all right. It was the face of a dark high-coloured merchant : he'd got rather bulging cheeks, a black moustache, bushy eyebrows, and he'd got a purplish chin as though he needed a shave. I saw him all right— although I didn't hear him. Not a sound."

" Well, in a way it's lucky for Claydon that you were a witness, although you were the means of his being copped. If you stick to it that you saw the face of the real aggressor—and it was quite unlike Claydon's face—the latter's safe enough. You're his witness for the defence."

" Yes—but I've wished once or twice I'd got a witness for my own defence. I know quite well that when I told my story to the Inspector bloke at the station, he didn't believe a word of it—and it *did* sound pretty thin. Why did I choose to sit down by Regents Park lake on one of the foulest November nights you could wish for? Did I often walk in the Park?— and all that. Have you ever been to listen to a case at the Law Courts or the Criminal Courts?"

" And heard a skilful counsel cross-examining, making a witness contradict himself and tie himself up into knots? Yes. I have—and I tell you it's made me sweat in sheer sympathy

47

for the bloke who was being badgered. But I'd say this: if you haven't any idea who the dead man was, and if your story is true throughout, you've no cause for apprehension. Our English police may be slow, and their manners a bit surly, but they're not out to convict any man but the man who commits a crime."

Ross Lane paused for a moment, turning round to call the waiter, and Mallaig was silent as they settled their bills. Then he said:

"What you say about the police is quite true—I'm sure of that. There's one other point I've been pondering over: I've got a queer feeling that I've seen that chap Tim somewhere before. I never knew him—I'm sure of that, and I haven't the foggiest idea who he is—was—but I still believe I've seen him somewhere. You had a look at him—did he remind you of anybody?"

"No. No one at all. I've never set eyes on him before. When you say you think you've seen him before, can you place the occasion? Was he by any chance a fellow you knew at school, or college, or have you seen him in the dock or witness box when you went to hear a case at the law courts or police courts?"

"I don't know," said Mallaig. "I can't place him—but I still feel that his face is vaguely familiar. It'll come back sometime: it may be just that he resembles somebody I've known or seen."

"I don't suppose you want any advice, or that you'll take it if I offer it," said the doctor quietly, "but it does seem mere common sense to avoid giving the police food for suspicion by involving yourself unnecessarily in this case. Don't try to see any more of Claydon for instance. The chap may be a rogue—he's obviously a busy-body—and he might tell lies about you that you'd find it difficult to disprove."

"Yes, I see that—but I can't help being interested. For instance when I saw you sitting here, if I'd been as cautious as all that, I suppose I should have gone and sat somewhere else—whereas I've enjoyed talking to you. I feel I've got my ideas straightened out a bit by talking them over."

"I'm jolly glad you didn't go and sit somewhere else," said Ross Lane. "I've been enormously interested in hearing you talk. As you can imagine, I wondered what the deuce had happened. Well—I expect the Inquest will be held to-morrow, and you'll have to say your piece. You'll make a good witness because you express yourself clearly."

"Will they call you?"

48

" Yes, I expect so—to testify to the fact that the man was dead when I first examined him. It's probable that proceedings will be very brief. In any case which promises a prolonged inquiry the police prefer the original sitting of the Coroner to be as brief and formal as possible. Well, I must be getting back to my job. Good-bye—and thanks for a very interesting lunch."

Mallaig sat on at the table for a few moments more feeling vaguely uncomfortable. He had liked Ross Lane: there was something about him which was both sensible and sympathetic; he had a very pleasant voice and the easy confident way which is a characteristic of all successful doctors. Mallaig's feeling of discomfort was due to the doctor's rather abrupt termination to their talk. He had not said " Are you going my way?" or waited for Mallaig to get up and accompany him out of the grill room: neither had he said " I hope we'll meet again "— a very usual termination to a chance meeting which had given pleasure to both parties. " Does he believe I did it?" Mallaig asked himself the question uncomfortably, and then poured himself out another cup of coffee and sat pondering deeply, oblivious of the fact that he ought to have been back at his job. A sudden idea struck him, and he sat worrying away at it in the same manner that he worried at his problems in the laboratory.

ii

When he returned home that evening, Mallaig had a call from a constable who left a document demanding his presence at the Coroner's Inquest the next day. A few minutes after he had studied this unfamiliar document a telegram arrived from Pat saying that her leave was off as she had got 'flu. Bruce began to feel unreasonably depressed. There was yet another ring at the front-door bell and his landlady, with a long-suffering expression on her face, opened the door of his room announcing " A gentleman to see you." The visitor followed her into the room, and Bruce found himself face to face with a tall, dark fellow, lean, well-built, well-balanced: a man with dark hair brushed back hard from a good forehead, and a tanned nut-cracker type of face lighted by pleasant grey eyes.

" I'm sorry to bother you at the end of your day's work when you're probably looking forward to a spot of peace and comfort," said the visitor. " My name is Macdonald. I'm a C.I.D. Inspector——"

" Good Lord! The Irishman again," groaned Bruce, and the newcomer laughed.

" That's about it. Has he been haunting you?' '

" That's exactly what he has been doing," rejoined Bruce. " As a subject for thought I'm about fed-up with him. Sit down, won't you."

" Thanks. Perhaps a talk on the subject will de-haunt you. It often helps. I expect the fact is that this is your first experience of murder, and you don't like it."

" Perfectly true," said Bruce. " I keep on thinking about the beggar, even when I'm trying to balance equations. I suppose I was an ass: I got talking to that chap Claydon last night—I hung about outside the Mortuary waiting for him."

" Why did you do that? Just intelligent interest, or had you met him before?"

" No. I think the fact was I was a bit ashamed of having let him in for a poor time—he was a seedy down-at-heels sort of blighter, and I was pretty certain he hadn't anything to do with the actual murder: at least, that's how I felt when I'd had time to think it over. When I copped him it was a sort of reflex action—stop thief. I hadn't time to think, I just jumped at him. Then—oh, I just wanted to know what on earth he *had* been doing under that bridge. He told me about the telephone business—and the rest was natural enough, I suppose, when you realise how bored the chap was."

Macdonald had been letting Mallaig talk on because it gave a good opportunity of studying him. Bruce was a thin fellow, pale faced and not very robust looking; he had a pleasant face, though he certainly wasn't good looking. A low square forehead, short nose and obstinate chin, with blue eyes set well apart and a thatch of dark reddish-brown hair. Macdonald judged him to be impetuous and obstinate, naturally straightforward and honest—a young man of little finesse but of good character. Mallaig would have been surprised had he known how the other was summing him up. Rumpling up his hair (which was naturally intractable and stood on end if not firmly dealt with) Bruce went on: " When I went into the St. Pancras grill room for lunch to-day, I happened to sit at the same table as the doctor who turned up when the Bobby blew his whistle last night. That was just chance—one of these rum things that does happen occasionally. Of course we talked—chewed it over right through lunch. Wouldn't have been human nature not to. Then at the end he got up and sort of said, ' Thanks so much, that's that,' and beat it. I've felt ever since that he was convinced I'd done the dirty work—and it's a beastly sort of feeling because it's so difficult to disprove."

Macdonald laughed. "I hope you feel better now you've got all that off your chest. Don't think your reaction is an abnormal one. It's hardly ever that an innocent person doesn't feel uncomfortable when questioned by the police: the more innocent they are, the more likely to get agitated and imagine we're suspecting them. If it's any comfort to you, I can assure you that the D. Division men—the local police—know their stuff. They went over the ground by the bridge most conscientiously before I got on the job at all. They observed what shoes you were wearing—the same ones you've got on now, I take it. They found the traces of your shoes by the seat where you said you'd been sitting: they found one set of your footprints, made when you'd obviously been running, between the seat and the bridge. They found no return traces of those particular shoes. In short, the statement you made was corroborated by your own footprints as well as by the chap under the bridge."

"I say, it's jolly decent of you to tell me that," said Bruce. "Stops that sinking feeling."

"Good. Having got you on to an even keel as it were, perhaps you won't mind answering a few more questions."

"Anything you like—if I happen to know the answers," said Mallaig, "but there's one thing I'm simply bursting to tell you. The Inspector made me go to the Mortuary last night to see if I could identify the chap who was killed. I couldn't, of course: I'd no idea who he was, but I thought I'd seen him somewhere before. His face was familiar in some vague way. I've been worrying all day about where I'd seen him before and I believe I've spotted it."

"Good. Where was it?"

"In a film studio. I was taken to the Denham Studios once—they were doing a film which had a scene in a lab. and I was taken along by a chap in our lab. who was giving an opinion about the setting. We saw another film being shot, and I believe the Irishman, as I call him, was in one of the crowd scenes. The film was ' The Night's Work.' I saw it when it was released in the West End. I'm almost certain the Irishman was in the railway station scene in that film. Did you go to see it?"

"No—but I expect I could get it run through for us. It might be useful if any other contacts in this case appeared on the same film. I hope your recollection turns out to be correct.

Why do you call John Ward—deceased, that is—the Irishman?"

"Because he looked like one—and sounded like one, even though I only heard him speak a couple of words. Was his name really John Ward?"

"I don't know—probably not, but I haven't been able to find out much about him. What I really want to ask you about was the third man in the case—the man whose face you saw by matchlight. Are you perfectly certain you saw a face and that you didn't imagine it?"

"I'm perfectly certain."

"Then will you describe to me, in the most detailed way, everything that you can remember from the time the Irishman threw his first cigarette away."

"I'll do my best. I was sitting at the end of the bench by the lake—the end farthest from the bridge, I mean, and I was sitting in such a way that I faced the bridge. I was watching and listening for all I was worth. I knew somebody was underneath the bridge, and what I was really expecting to happen was that a girl friend would turn up and join the Irishman, in which case I intended to warn them about the blighter under the bridge. It all made me very inquisitive, because it was such a rum set-out, with one chap on the bridge and the other immediately below it. Anyway I was listening and watching, too—although it was pitch dark and I couldn't see anything except when somebody showed a light."

"During the time the Irishman was on the bridge can you remember hearing anything at all? Did you notice anybody walking on the path on the other side of the lake, or along the Outer Circle, or up York Gate?"

"No. Again I'm perfectly certain of that, because I was *expecting* to hear somebody. It was obvious the chap on the bridge was waiting for someone, and I wondered which path they'd come by. There are a lot of ways of approaching that bridge, aren't there? You could get to it by the way I did—walking along the north side of the lake by the college railings, or you could come up by the road bridge over the lake from York Gate and Marylebone Road, or you could come down from the Inner Circle. I put my money on someone coming from York Gate—because not many people are mugs enough to walk in the park on a night like last night."

"Can you remember hearing the footsteps of the other two arrivals—Claydon and Ward?"

"Oh, yes, I heard them all right. They both came from the York Gate direction. No one passed along the path I'd come

52

by, I'm certain of that, and no one came down from the Inner Circle. I remember thinking how uncannily quiet it was: I didn't even hear any cars or taxis in the Outer Circle."

" How long had you been sitting on that bench before Claydon arrived?"

" About five minutes I suppose, not more."

" Were you smoking?"

" No, not while I was on the bench."

" Right—then go on, telling me every single thing you can."

" There's so little to tell. The chap on the bridge threw away the fag-end of his first cigarette. A minute later I heard the rattle of matches in his box as he shook it—as though he were wondering how many matches he'd got left—and then he struck a light: it seemed a surprisingly big light for a match—but I'd been in the dark for a goodish while. I could see his face bent down over his cupped hands—and then I realised there was someone just behind him——"

" Let's go over this very carefully. How was the Irishman standing?"

" He was leaning on the handrail of the bridge, facing towards the lake : the other chap was facing me, more or less, but he was very close behind the Irishman. I didn't have time to notice much, but I remembered wondering how the deuce the third chap had got there without my hearing him. It was like a peep show, all over in a flash. I didn't actually see any blow struck: I heard a thud and a tumble. That was all. I certainly didn't hear any one running away. It was just fantastic. If I hadn't caught sight of the other face I should have believed Claydon was right in guessing that the Irishman had been hit by something dropping from a plane."

" What do you remember about the height of the man whose face you saw, comparing his height with the Irishman's?"

" The chap must have been very tall. His head was a lot above the Irishman's. Thinking back he seemed grotesquely tall. You see I only saw his face. He must have had a dark coat fastened right up to his chin and something like a dark beret on his head: the only thing that caught the light was the face—fleshy and dark with rather bulging cheeks and very black eyebrows. It's no use pretending I made that up," declared Mallaig. " I didn't. I shall never forget it. It was just a disembodied face seen for a split second against the blackness. You see, I think the Irishman had finished lighting his cigarette, and he waved the match as one does to put it out. It was a very still night and the flame burnt steadily."

" Yes. It was a Swan Vesta—we found it afterwards."

" Look here, how on earth do you account for the fact that the third man got on to the bridge without Claydon hearing him underneath?"

" Claydon's a bit deaf. We got a report from his doctor. He can hear most things, but his hearing is not at all acute. Now you have described the third man to me as having a dark coat right up to his chin and perhaps a dark beret on his head. Does that put you in mind of anything?"

" Yes, of course. Civil Defence uniform. That'd just about fit the bill—but I couldn't *see* it. If I told you the man was in a Warden's uniform I should be telling lies—but he might have been."

" Well, I think you have done pretty well to remember as much as you have," said Macdonald. " Now I've got two requests to make. The first is this: I want you to come along to Regents Park to witness a reconstruction of what you saw last night, so that you can tell me if I've got the idea right."

" All right. I shall dream of this for the rest of my life—but I'll do my best."

" Good. Some time later—you can fix a convenient time yourself—I want you to have a look at John Ward's neighbours—some men who live in the same house as he did, just to see if you recognise them. An identity parade, in short."

" All right. Any evening will do."

" Good. I'll fix it up. Now if you're game we'll go straight along to Regents Park. I shall drop you at Clarence Gate and you can saunter to your seat by the lake, just as you did last night."

" All right—but I do wish to goodness Pat hadn't got 'flu and I'd never gone into Regents Park last night," said Mallaig.

" I'm sure you do—but there's this to it. You can be grateful you didn't interfere too soon," said Macdonald. " There was a man on that bridge who knew how to hit, and who aimed extremely accurately."

" Good Lord!" said Mallaig. " I hadn't thought of that."

CHAPTER SIX

i

MACDONALD drove Bruce Mallaig as far as Clarence Gate, and there he bade him cross the iron bridge as he had done the previous evening and saunter round to the bench where he had sat before. All that he was to do then was to watch and listen.

"When proceedings are finished I'll join you again," said Macdonald. "Of you go—and don't stumble into the lake en route."

Macdonald himself drove on round the Outer Circle to York Gate, where he met three men of his own department to whom he had telephoned orders when he set out with Mallaig. They knew the parts allotted to them and went to their positions, while Macdonald went and waited a yard away from the bench Bruce had occupied last night.

It was a very dark night, misty, windless, moonless—a replica of the previous evening's conditions. The chill dank air seemed to soak into a man's bones, and Macdonald reflected that no one but a man with urgent business, or a man very much in love, would choose to linger by the lakeside under such conditions.

A few minutes after he had taken up his position Macdonald heard leisurely footsteps approaching along the path which led along the lakeside to Clarence Gate. A moment later Mallaig switched his torch on, throwing its small beam downwards towards the bench. He seated himself at one end of it, and switched the light off. Though he was not more than a yard from Macdonald the latter could see nothing of Mallaig at all. There was a few minutes silence, and then footsteps approached from the direction of York Gate, and someone with a slow shuffling gait walked on to the little bridge and turned a faint torchlight downwards: next came the sound of someone scrambling rather clumsily over the hand-rail and dropping with a thump on to the ground below the bridge. To Mallaig the whole proceeding had a nightmare quality: it was exactly as though he were re-living the experience of last night. Macdonald, close at hand, could hear Mallaig's quickened breathing and the abrupt movement he made when the "bridge man" did his stuff. Again came a pause and then the sound of footsteps: Macdonald was listening intently and he counted the steps as soon as he was conscious of them—fifty steps he heard before a man halted on the bridge and enquired "Anyone about?" Then a match was struck: it was Detective Reeves who stood on the bridge and lighted a cigarette: his cupped hands shielded the flame, but his lean dark face, seen profilewise, seemed to be brilliantly lit by the spluttering match. He threw the match away, extinguishing it by waving it in the still air, and leant on the bridge hand-rail. As he inhaled his cigarette, the tiny glow of the cigarette end was enough to show up the contour of his face against the darkness. Macdonald was now listening intently. He knew what was happening—Detective Sergeant

Little was guiding a bicycle cautiously on to the bridge. His hands were gripping the handlebars of a very specialised machine, one foot was on the pedal, the other ready to brake his machine cautiously by touching the ground. Macdonald knew all that—but he could hear nothing at all. The bicycle had been borrowed from a trick rider who often gave highly hilarious shows on the variety stage, and Macdonald contrasted its silent performance with the click and rattle of the bicycle he had borrowed the previous evening. Reeves threw his cigarette away and a few seconds later lighted another match. As he bent over the flame his face was brilliantly lighted, and then he lifted his head and waved the match in the air. Instantly, like some fantastic illusion, another face appeared, some twelve inches above Reeves', and Mallaig suddenly shouted, as though his strung-up nerves impelled him to give voice. "There's the third chap ... look," but even as he spoke the match went out and there was a dull thud and a heavy fall. Mallaig jumped up, dropped his torch, fumbled for it and at last turned it on. In the beam of light a man could be seen astride the bridge rail and another lay on the ground. Mallaig sprang forward, but Macdonald's voice came out of the darkness:

"Steady on, laddie. It's only a reconstruction you know."

Mallaig halted with a rather uncertain laugh. "That was pretty grim, you know. It was *exactly* what happened last night—except the faces were different. The third chap—he was the same in a way—dark coat and cap—but his face wasn't like the one I saw last night. What's so amazing was the way you could see just in the light of one match."

"Yes. No one would believe it unless they'd seen the performance," agreed Macdonald. "Now while your memory is fresh tell me this: was the third man about the same height as the one you saw last night?"

"Yes, just about the same: he looked ridiculously tall—about seven feet high. It was because one only saw his face without any body, I suppose."

"Just a minute," said Macdonald. "Put your torch out ... Are you fellows all there, by the gate? Right."

He switched his own torchlight on—a much more powerful beam than Mallaig's, and the latter saw three men standing in a row before him. One was dressed in a dark overcoat and felt hat, one in a raincoat and a tweed cap, and one was in Civil Defence uniform.

"Can you remember which was which?" Macdonald inquired, and Mallaig replied at once:

" That chap in the trilby hat played the Irishman's part, and the chap in the Civil Defence uniform was the third man. I didn't see the other."

" He was under the bridge. Did you hear anything, Brain?"

" Hardly a sound, sir. Little did his job well. I'd never have known."

Little chuckled. "I only moved about an inch at a time. That's a marvellous contraption, Chief."

" What is?" put in Mallaig eagerly, but Macdonald replied:
" You'll hear later. Thanks very much for coming to help us. Reeves will drive you home and not leave you to the mercy of infrequent buses."

" Oh dash it all—I mean thanks for the lift—but I think you might let me in on what happened."

" Think it out for yourself," replied Macdonald, " and don't go talking about it if you have any brain-waves. Sorry to be so abrupt, but I've got to get on with the job. Good-night."

And Mallaig, still mystified, was driven home by Detective Reeves, who entertained Bruce by a story of a chase which he had once enjoyed at a little shipping village called Mallaig, opposite the island of Skye.

ii

When Macdonald left Regents Park after his reconstruction scene he made his way to 217 Wimpole Street, to call on Mr. Ross Lane. Macdonald had learnt that Ross Lane was a well-known surgeon who specialised on throat, nose and ear cases. He had a flat at the top of the tall house which held many sets of consulting rooms. After climbing a great many stairs Macdonald was shown into a room after his own heart. It was a long low room with a good Adams' fireplace: the walls were deep cream, the curtains, upholstery and carpet dull leaf brown. There were bookcases all round the walls, and some deep comfortable-looking arm chairs were drawn up to the glowing fire. Ross Lane had been sitting reading, and the only light in the room was that of a standard lamp beside his chair, shaded so as to throw a strong circle of light downwards but leaving the rest of the room pleasantly dim. The room had a peaceful look, and it was pre-eminently a room in which a tired man might enjoy his leisure. Macdonald knew well enough the pressure at which all doctors were working during the war and the apology with which he started the interview was a sincere one.

" I very much regret having to bother you this evening, sir. I realise you've been working hard all day——"

" Well, I'm not the only one, Inspector. Everyone is working rather harder than he or she wants to—and I don't expect you're any exception. Sit down : at least I can offer you a comfortable chair. Smoke if you care to."

Macdonald pulled his pipe out of his pocket with a feeling that the man opposite to him—a tired man—would be easier to talk to if he were not hustled. Macdonald had had to interrogate a number of doctors and surgeons during his career, and he knew that a medical man of high standing was capable of terminating an interview exceedingly abruptly if his interlocutor made a false step. It wasn't exactly professional dignity, it was something more inherent, derived from the fact that a consultant was called in to give an opinion, and having given it was not going to argue about it or justify it. A distinguished doctor could, in Macdonald's opinion, be even more difficult than a barrister. The Chief Inspector allowed himself a glance round the pleasant shadowed room and then turned to the man who leant comfortably back in his big chair under the clear light.

" Yes," said Ross Lane, as though answering a question, " I enjoy my own room . . . I don't get a chance to spend too long in it."

" Something in that," agreed Macdonald. " I wish you could have seen some of the rooms I've been in to-day."

Ross Lane laughed. " I bet they weren't more fantastic than some of the rooms I have visited since I first qualified. I gather the chap whose body I saw in Regents Park wasn't exactly opulent."

" Not exactly. All I can say about him is that he is negative so far. Nothing to get hold of. He knows nobody, and nobody knows him, so to speak. His neighbours merely met him en passant and his Identity Card was originally issued to somebody else. The point I want to discuss with you is this." Here Macdonald gave a précis of Claydon's evidence, and then waited.

" I see your point," said Ross Lane placidly. " Deceased telephoned to a doctor, according to the evidence, and a doctor turns up shortly after the murder was committed—was in the offing, so to speak. To save you further trouble, I can assure you that I was not the doctor who was called up from St. Pancras Station. Incidentally, what time was that call put through ? "

" Half-past ten yesterday morning."

" I'm afraid I wasn't at home : I was operating yesterday

58

morning—it's my operating morning at the Collegiate Hospital. Incidentally—though it's not my province, don't you think the use of the title ' Doctor ' can be misleading? The term is often loosely used among certain types. I've heard the queerest birds addressed in that manner—palmists and astrologers, among others."

Macdonald nodded. " Yes. That's perfectly true."

" Isn't there any more data?" went on Ross Lane. " Couldn't your witness give any name, since he listened so intently?"

" The only names he heard mentioned were Joe and Tim. Tim, or Timothy, was the name of the man speaking, Joe was the name of the person spoken to."

" Not very helpful. My own front name is William. You'll find a number of Joseph's in the Medical Directory. Old Joseph Trotter has rooms a few doors along—but I doubt if you want to interrogate every Joe in practice."

" Quite true. I don't," replied Macdonald. " I'm hoping to get at the facts by less devious means. One of the lines I'm following is collecting information from everyone who was known to have been near York Gate last night. It seems that there were few pedestrians about. The point duty men can help a bit on that score. Would you tell me what time you set out for your walk, and if you can remember meeting anyone en route?"

" I left here just about eight, with my dog. I turned along Wimpole Street towards the Park and then cut diagonally across the streets—first left, first right—into Marylebone High Street. I crossed the churchyard of the Parish Church at 8.15. I know that, because I remembered that I wanted to call in on John Mountford—a colleague of mine who lives in Chiltern Court. He isn't generally in before 8.30 and I glanced at my watch to make sure of the time, but I went along there on the off chance. He was out, but I left a message with his servant and walked back to York Gate by the road running parallel with Marylebone Road—it connects Allsop Place with York Gate. Now up to that time I had met two or three people, all in the Marylebone Road: there were also groups of people by the bus stops. From the time I left Chiltern Court—8.25 that would have been—I met nobody. I turned up York Gate towards the Outer Circle and stopped to light my pipe while my dog fossicked around, and it was then I first heard someone shouting. I couldn't place the noise at first— it seemed to come from over the lake somewhere. I stood still and listened and heard someone running—that must have been the constable, because he went across the open piece of ground

59

to my right (where the barrage balloon used to be) and on up to the bridge. I started to cross the road and nearly collided with a cyclist—the chap was riding without lights and he went past me like smoke. I think he saw my pipe because he swerved when he was nearly on to me, and then I heard a police whistle and that made me get a move on. I ran for all I was worth— and the rest you know."

"About that cyclist," said Macdonald. "Which way did he come?"

"I can't tell you. It was pitch dark and I didn't see him: it sounds ridiculous, but I *felt* him: he was going so fast he made a wind as he passed me and I think I actually brushed his handlebars."

".Did you hear him coming?"

"No. I didn't. As a general rule before I step off the kerb in the blackout I look and listen: this time I didn't, because my attention was taken up with the fussation across the lake."

"Can you remember if the cycle made any sound at all— did it rattle, like an old machine, or was it noticeably quiet?"

"Again, I can't tell you. When your attention's fixed on a certain thing, you don't notice other things—at least, I don't. Thinking back, I should say the cycle made the average sound that such a machine does make when it's ridden on a tarmac surface. I was quite sure it was a bike that passed me. It was being ridden southwards—in the direction of Marylebone Road that is."

"Could you tell which direction it came from? I take it that you were standing at the corner of York Gate and the Outer Circle?"

"That's right—I hadn't crossed the road. I assumed the bike came along the Outer Circle from the direction of Albany Gate—but I'm not certain."

"Could it have come down from the Inner Circle and turned right just before it passed you?"

"Yes. I suppose so."

"You say it was being ridden fast: if it had come from the Inner Circle by the bridge over the lake it would have been coming downhill and the cyclist could have free-wheeled as he swung right in the direction of Clarence Gate."

"Quite possibly—as I said, I can't give a definite statement. Actually the events of the ensuing minutes put the incident out of my head. I didn't think of it again until you asked me if I'd met anybody on the course of my walk."

Ross Lane was studying Macdonald with a half-smile. "Do

you want to know if I own a bike myself? I don't—but I used to ride one a good deal."

" You're quite sure that you didn't meet anyone or anything—pedestrian, cyclist or car—between the time you left Chiltern Court and the time you stopped at the corner of York Gate?"

" To the best of my recollection I met neither person nor vehicle."

There was silence between the two men for the course of a few seconds, and then Ross Lane said: " You said that deceased carried an Identity Card which was not his own: I don't know if you're willing to answer questions, but do you mean that the card he carried had a different name on from the name he was known by?"

" No. His card had the name John Ward on it, and that was the name deceased was known by at the address where he had been living for the past six months—but the John Ward who had lived at the original address on the card and to whom the card was originally issued was certainly not the man who was killed last night. Deceased had contrived to change his name by acquiring another man's Identity Card."

" One thing's pretty certain—no honest man would do that," said Ross Lane.

Macdonald went on: " Does the name Timothy O'Farrel convey anything to you?"

" Timothy O'Farrel?" echoed Ross Lane. " That's a name in some play, isn't it? Congreve's or Wycherley's—one of the Restoration dramatists. I've never met anyone of that name, either as a patient or an acquaintance—but the name has a familiar sound. Why do you ask?"

" I'm asking everybody I come across. An identity disc bearing the name Timothy O'Farrel was found in the bombed shelter where the original John Ward was known to have gone after his home had been hit by incendiaries."

Ross Lane leaned forward in his chair and gazed thoughtfully into the fire. " I think I see," he replied. " You're working on the probability that John Ward was killed and that Timothy O'Farrel stole his Identity Card—the connection being the use of the name ' Timothy ' during the ' phone call."

" It can hardly be called a probability, but it is at least a possibility," said Macdonald. " In a crime of this kind, the first thing necessary is to establish the background of the murdered person. Up till the present I have only succeeded in finding out that the dead man carried an Identity Card issued to somebody else: he was living in a room lent to him by another man

61

—the latter being somewhere in Burma and therefore inaccessible—and none of his neighbours can give me any information of any value."

"And this nebulous person got his skull smashed in the blackout in the presence of two witnesses, neither of whom can tell you anything germane to the case," said Ross Lane. "It certainly is a teaser. Your positive information seems to amount to three words—Joe, Tim, and doctor. Incidentally —giving my own opinion for what it's worth—this crime doesn't seem to me the sort of crime a medical man would indulge in. I rather think a doctor would have had resort to more subtle means."

"I'm not sure that this was such an un-subtle crime as might appear from a bald description of the facts," said Macdonald. "We've got remarkably little to work on. A man was knocked on the head in the blackout: no house and neighbourhood to study, no finger-prints, no properties save an unidentifiable coal hammer—and finally, no real identity of deceased. It's a set of circumstances which may form a very difficult problem."

He got up, and Ross Lane said "You omitted to mention the bicycle in you précis of the properties involved."

"The bicycle is only a theory so far," replied Macdonald. "Could you swear to a bicycle you did not see, can not remember hearing—and did not actually feel?"

"I can swear to my impression that a bicycle passed me at full speed," said Ross Lane. "As to whether the jury will believe it, I can't say."

"We shan't trouble the jury with the bicycle yet awhile," replied Macdonald. "Good-night, sir—and thank you for your patience in answering my questions."

"I'm afraid I haven't helped you very far, Chief Inspector. You wanted to know if I met anybody near York Gate—and all I can supply is the unsubstantial and unconvincing bike."

"Unconvincing or not, that bike may lead to a conviction eventually—if I can find it," replied Macdonald, and Ross Lane replied:

"Well—good luck to your hunt, and good-night."

iii

When Macdonald left Ross Lane's house he turned southwards down Wimpole Street, cogitating deeply. Having had no dinner he turned into a pub behind Oxford Circus and ate some sandwiches with his glass of stout. Reflecting that wartime sandwiches were no food for a hungry man he continued on his way to Bloomsbury where he found the house he wanted to visit still standing—a reason for satisfaction in a neighbourhood which has many open spaces. He climbed a number of stairs and knocked on a fine solid door—for the house had been built in a period when joiners took pride in their work. The door was opened by a stout fellow whose massive head was becoming bald : this gentleman took off his horn-rimmed glasses and stared at his visitor.

" Dr. Crotton?" inquired Macdonald, and the other replied :

" By the lord, it's Robert! Come in, man. I haven't seen you for more years than I care to count. Robert Macdonald, by gad. Well, I'm pleased to see you—and that's saying a lot when a man's working. Come in and sit down."

Macdonald followed Crotton into a comfortable, untidy smoky room. Long years ago Crotton had had rooms in Pembroke College on the same staircase as Macdonald: that had been in 1918. The two had been contemporaries for a year at Oxford and Macdonald looked rather ruefully at the stout middle-aged man in front of him. Charles Crotton—recognisable, but only just.

" Well, *you* haven't changed much, Robert. I caught sight of you in the High once—1930 it'd have been . . . but I'd know you anywhere."

" And you're wondering what the devil brings me here to-night, Charles. It's quite simple. I'm out to cadge information, and you're a learned man. I read a review of your last book in the *Times Literary*. The critic said you were the foremost living authority on the Restoration dramatists."

" God save us—you've never taken to literature, Robert? I thought you were a policeman."

" I am. That's why I'm here. I've come for information. I've just been interrogating a distinguished surgeon. I had reason to ask him if he'd ever heard the name Timothy O'Farrel. He said he had, and he thought the name was that of a character in a Restoration drama—either Congreve's or Wycherley's."

" He lied."

" I thought he might have—or perhaps he was merely mistaken."

" Umps . . . as you like. Timothy O'Farrel . . . nothing like it in any work known to me."

" Thanks very much. That's all I wanted to know. I won't disturb you any longer."

" God almighty!—and you think you're going to walk out

63

on me like that, you unsociable blackguard. Damn all, Robert Macdonald, you can sit you down again in yon chair while I get some glasses and the last bottle of Scotch. You used to talk the night out with your hair-splitting pragmatical Paleyan system of corrupted philosophy. You can tell me what you've been doing these years. Didn't I say I was pleased to see you?''

Macdonald laughed and resumed his seat. " Thank you, Charles. I'm glad to see you, too. You were described to me once as the rudest Don in the University of London. It's good to see you again."

" Nothing like a reputation for boorishness to gain a man a little peace," said Crotton. " D'you mind James Menzies, a wee fellow with a big head . . .?''

And for the space of a brief hour or so Macdonald gave a truce to detection.

CHAPTER SEVEN

i

THE INQUEST held on John Ward was a more lengthy affair than was customary when the C.I.D. were handling a knotty problem. As a general rule, when it seemed probable that the inquiry would be a lengthy one, Macdonald and his colleagues often preferred the barest minimum of evidence to be put forward—identity of deceased, time of death, and in some cases cause of death, and then an immediate adjournment. On this occasion, however, Macdonald and the Assistant Commissioner, in consultation with the Coroner, decided to make nearly all the available evidence public because this seemed to be the most promising way of obtaining information which might lead to the fact of John Ward's real identity. Consequently, Bruce Mallaig and Stanley Claydon told their full stories in the witness box before an oddly assorted little group of the general public and an equally heterogeneous jury. There were a few press men present—mostly elderly men—and Macdonald observed the manner in which these sat up and took notice when they realised that the Inquest was going to be a really interesting one. Mrs. Maloney, the housekeeper at Belfort Grove, identified John Ward as a tenant at that address. Miss Rosie Willing testified to a slight acqaintance with her neighbour across the landing and denied all knowledge of his business or origin. Mr. Ross Lane testified that life was already extinct when he examined deceased, and the Police Surgeon gave a technical description of deceased's injuries. Finally, Macdonald entered the witness-box and gave evidence as to his investigation into the identity of John Ward of Dulverton Place. He also stated the facts concerning Timothy O'Farrel's identity disc being found in the ruins of the shelter.

After the Inquest was over, Macdonald went back to the Commissioner's Office to discuss the case with Colonel Wragley, the Assistant Commissioner. The latter had read Macdonald's report and found therein much food for thought.

" You have plenty of material to work on, Macdonald," said the grey-haired colonel. " There's no lack of suspects: you've got the conjurer with a circus training—the very fellow to bring off a crime of this kind if your assumption about the bike is well founded: you've got the Civil Defence chap who had a bike on the spot, you've got the surgeon who put in such an opportune appearance, and the man Claydon who prevented Mallaig from starting off in pursuit."

" In fairness one should surely include Mallaig himself, who gave the only direct visual evidence as to what happened," said Macdonald. " Any one of these could be regarded as suspect once we found any shadow of a motive or a connection with deceased. That's what is lacking. Until we learn more about the self-styled John Ward we're not going to get very far. I'm hoping the daily papers will find room to insert John Ward's photograph. The only trouble is that if Ward were mixed up with the Black Market racket no one will come forward to claim him as an acquaintance."

" How are you going to get round that, Macdonald? Wait and see if anything eventuates?"

" Provided waiting doesn't imply inactivity, yes," replied Macdonald, " but there are a number of questions to be considered immediately. One of the first is—why did a man who lived in the Notting Hill district go to St. Pancras Station to put a telephone call through at 10.30 in the morning? The same question applies to Claydon, but he can provide an answer. He lives near Euston and his sister lived near Bedford. If he meant to go to stay with his sister, it was reasonable enough to go to St. Pancras which is the station for Bedford trains."

" Are you assuming that John Ward also had relatives in Bedford?"

Colonel Wragley's question was in part facetious. He held with Kipling that the Scots are a great nation who cannot see other people's jokes. Macdonald was aware of the Assistant Commissioner's habit of thought on this subject, and he frequently infuriated Wragley by answering his rhetorical questions seriously.

"I have no grounds for assuming that Ward had relatives in Bedford, sir, but I have sufficient reason to think that he may have used the L.M.S. from St. Pancras. I think I made that implication in my report."

"Is that so? I am afraid I missed the implication, then."

"You will remember that Mallaig stated that Ward acted as one of the crowd in a film called 'The Night's Work.' I have not yet had time to substantiate this statement, but it seemed quite probable that a man like Ward who disliked and avoided regular work would have been glad of the occasional guinea to be picked up by casual film jobs. It's worth remembering that Elstree—which has a film industry—is on the L.M.S. line."

"I see. I see. A shot in the dark, Macdonald, but an intelligent shot."

"Less haphazard than a groundless assumption of relatives in Bedford," said Macdonald solemnly, and Wragley laughed.

"All right, all right—and so what? as my nieces and nephews are so fond of asking."

"I'm putting Reeves on to the St. Pancras job. He's trying to find any of the station staff who can recognise Ward's photograph. In the event of my guess about Elstree proving wrong, I want to find out what he was doing at St. Pancras and with whom he was doing it."

"Why not try the Elstree studios direct?"

"Reeves is doing that, but the St. Pancras end is important for this reason. If Ward travelled with a friend or acquaintance, he may have said something about his rendezvous in Regents Park. My argument is this: either Ward was killed by the individual he had arranged to meet at the bridge, or by some other person who knew that Ward was going to be at the bridge."

"Why the either-or, Macdonald? Isn't it safe to assume that he was killed by the person he had arranged to meet?"

"The principal argument against that is that Ward's behaviour at the bridge was not that of a man who expects danger. It's true, according to Claydon's evidence, that Ward was truculent over the 'phone: he spoke with confidence, like a man who knows that he holds all the cards, but his choice of rendezvous, and his behaviour when he got there, give the impression that he was going to meet someone from whom violence was most improbable. If Ward had had any idea that violence was going to occur, I don't think he would have chosen a dark and solitary spot for the meeting. It seems to me that someone may have learnt about Ward's appointment and used it for their own purposes. It's on that account that I am anxious to trace Ward's actions during the day."

" Yes. I see. To my mind, however, it's more fundamental to trace Ward's past history."

" Yes, sir. I hope to tackle that myself. It's an interesting point to consider. At some period in deceased's history he took the trouble to change his identity. That has been done by other men before, generally from one of two motives—the desire to escape from justice—keep out of the hands of the police, in short—or fear of an enemy. To the best of my knowledge the first motive doesn't apply. We have no record of any police conviction against Ward—his fingerprints can't be traced—neither does he resemble anyone for whom the police are searching at present."

" So you assume that he was hiding from an enemy?"

" Possibly—but he must have considered it profitable to disappear, so far as his previous identity was concerned."

" So profitable that he chose a particularly difficult time to change his identity. Wartime regulations don't facilitate that sort of thing."

" That's only partially true, sir. In one way, the chaotic conditions of to-day make such a thing easier. A man turns up from nowhere, possessing nothing : he says he has been bombed out and has lost his home, his family and his entire possessions. It's happened in so many cases. How many people bother to substantiate the story? Deceased was a man of considerable charm—can't you imagine how he would have made friends among similar casual gentry—those classed as Bohemians by the average respectable householder—and ' poor Johnny Ward —just been bombed out ' would have been accepted at his face value, having lost everything save his Identity Card."

" And Ration Book?" inquired Wragley.

" He lost that, certainly—but a new Ration Book was issued to John Ward of Dulverton Place after the bombing. They had to be issued to a number of people, and the clerks were too busy to challenge identities closely. The holder of an Identity Card got an emergency book if the original book was lost."

" By Jove, Macdonald, I'm beginning to get interested in this story. . . . It's got possibilities. . . ."

" Yes, sir," replied Macdonald, and his face was very thoughtful. " For the past twenty-four hours I've been meditating on this matter of poor Johnnie Ward. I assure you I've found it extraordinarily interesting. There's a story behind it : the story of a charming friendly scamp, a man who ' could only be relied on to be unreliable ' as little Rosie Willing said: a man who played about on the fringes of the Black Market, who had fought for Sinn Fein, who lived by his wits—and who finally became dangerous to somebody and was knocked over the head in the blackout. It may prove to be a sordid story, but I certainly find it an interesting one."

" Taking advantage of a particularly ghastly air-raid," grumbled Colonel Wragley to himself. " I find that revolting."

" I find it illuminating, sir—with regard to the man's character. I don't believe Johnny Ward stole a dead man's Identity Card on the spur of the moment. He must have planned to do it when he had the opportunity: he may have done it before. Here is a man too lazy to work—but he fought in the 1919 rebellion: a man given to cadging loans—but his neighbours said he did all he knew how to get into the Forces: a man who kept his nerve when a shelter was bombed and stole another man's Identity Card in the shambles of that shelter. It's a pity he was refused for the Forces. They ought to have put him in the bomb Disposal Squad—because he had just the qualities which would have enabled him to display his charm while straddling a live bomb."

" Really, Macdonald, you're giving way to flights of fancy," said Wragley severely.

" I apologise, sir—but admittedly I find this case food for one's imagination," replied Macdonald.

ii

It was in the early afternoon that Macdonald paid another visit to Belfort Grove. Most of the tenants were out, but Mr. Carringford proved to be at home, and he welcomed Macdonald cheerfully.

" I wanted to go to the Inquest, but a job of work kept me away," he said. " Did anything interesting emerge?"

" From my point of view, it was simply a recapitulation of known facts," said Macdonald. " What I'm panting for is something fresh—something that will give me a line on John Ward's origin, or at least on his way of life before he came to live in this house. You may well ask why I should come to trouble you again on this matter, since you have already told me that you can't help me."

" I hope you don't think it's because I'm not willing to help you, Chief Inspector," said Carringford. " Ask anything you like, I'm quite at your service. It's just possible that some-

68

thing may emerge—some small fact which might be meaningless to me might be significant to you."

"That's just it," said Macdonald. Studying his companion afresh he came to the conclusion that Carringford was a younger man than he had at first guessed—nearer fifty than sixty years of age. His hair was quite white and his face lined, but the contour of the face seemed too smooth for an elderly man: there was health and resilence in the lean muscular neck and hands: an interesting face, Macdonald meditated as he went on:

"Since the occupants of this house are the only people whom I can find at present who can tell me anything at all of John Ward, it is those same occupants I must badger. To put it quite simply, I come to you as the one person in the house who studies human nature intelligently and who is observant along lines which might be helpful to me. I'm not trying to be complimentary. I'm stating a fact."

"Well, I think you're being a bit optimistic—but fire away," replied Carringford.

"Right. To begin with, did you know the responsible tenant of Ward's flat—Mr. Claude d'Alvarley."

"No, I didn't know him except by sight. If you ever set eyes on him you'll understand why. He was of the gigolo type, the junior lead in the more fatuous provincial productions of musical comedy. A type I can't endure. Neither would he have have had any use for me, he'd have been bored to a degree if he had had to spend ten minutes in my company."

"How did you come to make Ward's acquaintance?"

"On the door-step, on the stairs, and in an air-raid shelter. Ward was gregarious: he liked company, he liked conversation, and despite the fact that he had wasted his ability through laziness and utter lack of application, he wasn't unintelligent and he wasn't uneducated. As I told you, he was a wit. He'd probably had a university education—or part of one. He may have been sent down. I don't know. As I told you, I never asked him questions. He called on me in the first place to ask for the loan of a book I mentioned. I lent it to him—but I never leant him another because he didn't return the first. I know he read it, and I suspect he sold it. However, if he called in occasionally when I wasn't busy I found him sufficiently entertaining to talk to."

"You mention an air-raid shelter. Was he nervous of raids?"

"Good Lord, no! The coolest of fish. We were all ejected from here one night by the Wardens because an unexploded bomb fell in the back garden. Ward was indignant about being

69

got out of his bed—I think it took something more than words to move him. I should say he was quite fearless: one of the fatalist type who believed that when his number was up nothing could save him, and that it wasn't worth while taking precautions of any kind. You'll generally find that men who hold that philosophy are mentally lazy."

Macdonald laughed. "Maybe. Personally I believe in taking shelter when I get the chance—which isn't often—but that's not because I'm mentally energetic. Do you know anything of Ward's associations with other members of this household?"

Carringford's angular eyebrows shot up. "Rather an awkward question, Chief Inspector. We're a rum lot here, as you may have noticed. This house suits me: it's cheap and you're not interfered with. In the evenings it's quiet, because the tenants are generally out. I don't want to do the dirty on any of my fellows in this menagerie. They reacted according to their several natures. Miss Willing is a shrewd little lady, but she has the everlasting kindness of her type. She nursed Ward when he was ill and gave him a bit of her mind when he was tiresome. My fellow tenant on this floor is one of the acquisitive kind, I should say—Miss Odette Grey. Have you met her?"

"Yes. I had a few words with her."

Carringford chuckled. "Then you'll understand me if I say that her association with Ward might be summed up in a few words I heard on the landing: ' I know your sort. Leave a girl to pay for the drinks, you do.' Miss Grey prefers to have her drinks paid for. I imagine Ward never paid for anything. Finally there is the strenuous couple on the ground floor—Mr. and Mrs. Rameses. I believe them to be an honest hardworking pair. I should rather like to know him better—but not her. So I leave it at that. I don't think that Ward got much encouragement in that quarter—I'm sorry to be so unhelpful, but I'm trying to stick to facts. I can't tell you about rows on the staircase or riots on the doorstep because there weren't any."

"Have you ever come across Ward outside this house—in the course of your film work, for example?"

"No. If I had done so I should have told you. Ward did get an occasional job, I believe—but very occasional. He tried to put it over that he'd played some good parts—but I knew he lied. Actually, I don't think it was very probable he got any engagement, because he was incapable of being punctual for anything. Agents get sick of that type."

" Did he ever offer to sell you anything?"

" Of course he did—but I never caught on. He'd offer to sell anything—whisky, silk underwear, pornographic literature —but as I always refused point-blank to have any dealings of that kind I can't tell you if he could really supply the goods or not."

" You're being very patient with me," said Macdonald, and Carringford replied:

" My dear chap, I'm only sorry I can't help you. I've returned a colourless negative to every question you've asked, but I never pretended to know anything about Ward. My attitude is live and let live and mind your own business. I thought him a very probable rogue—and left it at that. I could tell you some of his wilder stories: he pretended to be related to several noble Irish families—Lurgans, Listoels, Plunkets, and so forth—but it was always a different story."

" Talking of Irish names, did you ever hear him mention the name O'Farrel?"

" O'Farrel? That's an odd coincidence. No, Ward never mentioned the name to me, but a chap I got talking to at lunch mentioned the name to me only a few hours ago—Timothy O'Farrel to be exact."

" How did it come about?"

" I went into a snack bar for lunch—the one at Paddington station, and I got talking to a couple of fellows standing beside me—the place was packed and I couldn't get a seat. I should say one of the blokes I was talking to was a commercial traveller, the other might have been a writer or a journalist. The first one started cursing the Irish nation in general—he'd just had a raw deal from some Irish wholesaler. The other bloke joined in and talked very intelligently. We bandied a few names—famous Irishmen and so forth, and then he suddenly asked me if I'd ever met a chap named Timothy O'Farrel. I said no, and inquired why he asked. He said he believed the chap lived in the West End somewhere and he wanted to find him. It turned out that this writer—if he was one—was an Irishman. He'd been at Trinity, Dublin, in 1919, and O'Farrel was up with him for a term. Why do you ask?"

" Because I've come across the name in connection with Ward."

" Well, I suppose that's what you describe as a coincidence —one of those odd things which makes you wonder if the universe is more purposeful than sometimes appears."

" Maybe it is—but tell me what you learnt about O'Farrel— if you did learn anything."

71

" Oh I heard quite a lot—enough to be bored with the subject before I was quit. All Irishmen talk—they're the most garrulous nation under the sun. This Timothy O'Farrel read medicine at Trinity, and apparently he married one of the woman students—also a medical. This girl was named Josephine, and I suppose she was originally the fiancée of the chap who was talking to me—anyway it was Josephine O'Farrel my chap was really trying to find. I told him to try the Medical Directory, since he believes she qualified. That was about the sum total of the conversation."

" I should like to get into touch with the man you were talking to—or who talked to you. Can you describe him?"

" He was a big chap, dark, inclined to stoutness, with a high colour—the opposite of a romantic in appearance, but with the mind of a sentimentalist once he'd got some beer inside him. He was dressed in an old Burberry and a Trilby hat and he carried a suit-case."

" Any initials or labels on the latter?"

" I didn't notice. I have an idea he said he came from Bristol. He was certainly an Irishman and he was a very intelligent fellow—until he got reminiscing about his Josephine. Has it ever occurred to you that you get told some marvellous stories at railway stations? There's something about a station and train journeys which makes a certain type confidential to a degree."

" Yes. I have noticed that—particularly with regard to train journeys," replied Macdonald. " I've had a man's life history poured out to me between Edinburgh and Carlisle before now. Now isn't there anything more definite that you can tell me about the man who talked to you at Paddington—anything that would make it possible to identify him? You say he may have been a writer. Why did you assume that?"

" Mere guesswork. The chap was widely informed and expressed himself clearly. He had an unusually good vocabulary and he spoke correctly—which very few people do. A good writer gets into the habit of correct speech. Also—this chap didn't seem to have any job which tied him down to a time-table as far as I could gather. He'd all the time in the world. When you get talking over a drink most men have a tendency to mention their jobs, or it crops out in the course of conversation. Now as to identifying him—I can't remember anything outstanding. He had very big hands, well-shaped and well-kept . . . no ring . . . a soft collar and dark tie . . . a rather dark chin and jowl . . . wanted shaving twice a day at least

72

. . . a jutting out nose, dark eyes, rather beetling brows. I'm afraid that's about the best I can do."

" Will you describe the other chap—the bagman."

" A smallish fellow—colourless, dressed in a grey top coat and bowler hat . . . potato coloured face, string coloured hair and light blue eyes. A very unnoticeable chap. We were wedged in between a crowd of Tommies and Jacks—most of them hurrying to get a drink before they got on the West of England trains. The commercial gent hurried off to catch the 12.45 to somewhere. I stayed long enough to have a good lunch —you get an uncommonly good one at that place, and I left the other chap having another glass of beer. Sorry I can't think of anything which would identify him for you. Verbal descriptions are no good without some definite abnormality to aid them."

Macdonald had taken out his note book: " Let's see the best we can do. What was the man's height?"

" He was tallish—say five feet ten: stout build, large hands and feet, black hair—what I could see of it—dark eyes. High colour."

" Dressed in a raincoat and felt hat, carrying a suitcase," concluded Macdonald. " Similar, in short, to a few thousand other men who walked up and down Paddington platform to-day. Well—nothing's lost by trying. This is where I go to hand on a thankless job. Many thanks for all you've told me."

" Not at all. May it be counted unto me for righteousness that I forebore to ask all those questions I might have asked," replied Mr. Carringford.

CHAPTER   EIGHT

i

MACDONALD put Inspector Jenkins on to the job of doing his best to elicit information at Paddington Station, observing that it was quite unlikely any information would be forthcoming, but forlorn hopes did occasionally bear fruit. The Chief Inspector himself set other wheels in motion. He rang up one of the police surgeons who was a personal friend of his own, saying " I've got to make inquiries about a chap in your line of country—a consultant at the Collegiate Hospital. I've no doubt you can find out what I want to know about him much more easily than I can—and he won't he annoyed by hearing that the police are collecting data about him."

" Umps . . ." said the voice at the other end of the line.
" Are you talking about Ross Lane? I noticed he'd had the
misfortune to come across one of your cadavers. He's a first-
·rate chap. What do you want to know about him?"

" Is he married?"

" That one's easy. Yes. He got married about four months
ago."

" Who's the lady?"

" A woman doctor—very competent one too: she specialises
on backward children—thyroid deficiency and the like."

" Does she practice under her maiden name?"

" Yes—Dr. Josephine Falton. She's kept her old consulting
room in Welbeck Street. Incidentally she's out of London at
the moment. I know that because they wanted an opinion from
her about a juvenile delinquent and couldn't get hold of her."

" Right. Can you oblige further with the date of their mar-
riage?"

" Beginning of August some time. They went to Skye for
their honeymoon. He's a friend of mine incidentally, so don't
go getting bees in your bonnet about him because he was
sufficiently public-spirited to go rushing in when he heard a
police whistle."

" I'll remember. Thanks very much for your help."

Macdonald meditated for a moment after he hung up the
receiver. Then he put a call through to Ross Lane's consulting
room and was answered by his secretary. Inquiry evoked that
Mr. Ross Lane was booked up with consultations until half-past
six that evening, and it was probable that he wouldn't get rid
of his last patient much before eight. If an appointment was
to be made with him, it could not be before the middle of the
following week. Macdonald rang off, deciding that he would
leave Mr. Ross Lane to his patients for the time being and con-
centrate on another angle of his case.

ii

None of the tenants at Belfort Grove had telephones in their
flats, but there was a call-box in the hall. This was answered
by the housekeeper, Mrs. Maloney, when she happened to
hear it. Mrs. Maloney disliked climbing stairs—a not unreasonable aversion since her age was nearer to the constable's
guess of eighty than the sixty-five years which she claimed
officially. In order to save her legs, she was careful to observe
when the tenants went out, so that she need not mount the stairs
unnecessarily if a telephone call came for them. Over the tele-

phone, as over much else, Mrs. Maloney ' obliged.' It was not part of her official duty to answer the telephone, but it was a profitable sideline for her, for the tenants were quite willing to pay a few pence for her trouble when she fetched them for a call or took a message for them. The afternoon was generally a peaceful time for her, for most of the tenants were out and she had the place to herself.

On this particular afternoon she was ' doing ' Mrs. Rameses' bedroom : she knew that everybody was out except Mr. Carringford, and when she heard the telephone bell she disregarded it. The bell went on ringing, however, with quite unusual persistence, and at last, in sheer exasperation, she went to answer it, and having grasped the purport of the message she toiled up to Mr. Carringford's flat and rang his bell.

" It's the telephone. The police want you," she announced when he opened the door. " Been ringing goodness knows 'ow long, and me on me 'ands and knees working. You'd better 'urry up. They sounded real mad the time you've kept 'em," and with that Mrs. Maloney stumped off downstairs. Mr. Carringford was not one of her favourites. " Fussy, 'e is, like an old woman with 'is bits and pieces and everlasting books, and never a word to spare." So she described Mr. Carringford, for his meticulous neatness " got on 'er nerves " ; and his terse rejoinders to her well-meant chattiness were not endearing.

Going back into Mrs. Rameses' flat, Mrs. Maloney pushed the hall door to and listened—her hearing was excellent. She did not learn very much from the one-sided conversation, save that Mr. Carringford was distinctly put out.

" What—immediately?" he demanded. " Oh, if it's urgent I suppose I must, but it's very inconvenient. Where? The first-class booking office? All right."

A moment or so later Mr. Carringford left the house, and Mrs. Maloney saw him go with considerable satisfaction. " That's the lot," she said to herself. " Now the blinking telephone can ring its 'ead off an 'oo cares—not me." She was a very honest old soul, as the tenants could testify, and she did her not very skilful best in the way of cleaning and polishing, working harder than many a younger woman would have done. Having brushed the carpet in Mrs. Rameses' bedroom, and retrieved the very varied oddments which had been kicked under the bed, Mrs. Maloney sat back on her heels for a breather, and uttered a heartfelt " Drat!" when the front door bell rang. " You get on with it," she said, producing a duster—but the bell rang again, and she peered carefully out of the window.

"Lawks! them police again. What did 'e want to go and do it for, there ain't a moment's peace for anybody."

Macdonald was standing on the door-step accompanied by a uniformed officer. Mrs. Maloney hurried to the front door: she might grumble about the police, but she had her fair share of natural inquisitiveness. She had, moreover, been rather taken with Chief Inspector Macdonald, who had talked to her " as a real gentleman does talk to a lady." She removed her working apron and went to the front door.

" Sorry I'm shore, sir, but it's all out they are—every one, and me doing a bit o' dusting for the first floor."

" Well, it's fortunate that you're in, Mrs. Maloney," replied Macdonald, quietly making his way into the entrance hall. " Shut the door, will you. I'll explain what we have come for." She obeyed, and Macdonald went on: " You know what a Search Warrant is, Mrs. Maloney?"

" Sure to goodness—you're never going to search here, and all themselves out? It's me they'll be blaming when they come back."

" There's nothing for you to worry about, Mrs. Maloney. You have the key to all the flats, haven't you?"

" Sure and I have, me doing the only bit of cleaning that's worth calling cleaning. I have to get in, don't I, and there's never been no complaints——' '

" I know that. All the tenants trust you. Now I have a Search Warrant which gives me the right to enter any of these flats. I shall get you to come in with me and this officer. We shan't disturb anything. I want to look round to see if I find one particular thing: it's quite a large object and it won't be in a cupboard or a drawer or anywhere like that."

" Well, I can't stop you looking if you've got a what-you-call-it," replied Mrs. Maloney, " but seeing as I'm trusted with the keys I reckon I ought to keep an eye on you."

Macdonald was much entertained with this notion, but with a perfectly straight face he said: " By all means. Now you were working in the Rameses' flat, so shall we start there?"

" Dearie me, and a fine old mess it's in and all. Never you let rooms to no conjurers, sir. I'm always expecting to find snakes under the bed and I don't know what."

Macdonald's search was a very superficial affair. He glanced into each of the untidy rooms and stood studying it while Mrs. Maloney tried to guess what he was looking for. Macdonald was actually assessing the size of cupboards and other places of concealment, but as he went through each room of the different flats he saw at once how little space was allowed for any store room or box room. Originally this house had had very big rooms, but these had been sub-divided to make bathrooms and kitchenettes, and cupboards had been dispensed with. At the conclusion of his tour he turned to Mrs. Maloney.

" Do the tenants have any storage room in the basement?"

" That's right, sir. The ould scullery down there's been made into lock-ups. Shilling a week or two shillings a week according to size. Ten shillings a week that scullery brings in—that's 'ow to make easy money."

" And what about the keys?"

" The tenants all 'ave their keys, but I got keys too. You see people's that careless, always mislaying 'em. It's mostly trunks and old junk, save for Mr. Carringford, and 'is books— 'undreds of 'em. Ought to go for salvage I say. Down 'ere, sir. I've got me keys in me kitchen. I uses the kitchen for 'eating water and that."

Mrs. Maloney retrieved a bunch of keys from a tin which stood on the kitchen shelf, and she led Macdonald to the scullery door at the back of the house. The scullery was now sub-divided by matchboarding into narrow cubicles. Some were the full height of the room, others divided into an upper and lower storey, each locked, and a stepladder was provided for access to the upper ones. There were eight compartments altogether and Mrs. Maloney announced their ownership.

" One, two and three are the big 'uns. One and two belong to Mr. and Mrs. Rameses, three's Mr. Carringford's. Four and five are Miss Grey's. Six is Miss Willing's and seven's Mr. d'Alvarley's. Eight's to let. Keys is numbered according . . . Drat that bell! It's the front door again. I'll 'ave to 'op— and don't you go moving nothing."

The old soul hurried off, and Macdonald opened the Rameses' compartment. In front of the first lock-up was the object he had been looking for—a bicycle. It was a similar machine to the one he had borrowed for his reconstruction scene, specially built for trick riding on the stage. It was made in sections which would come apart at a turn. The sergeant who accompanied Macdonald chuckled as he looked at it.

" I've seen those trick riders pull their machines to bits till there was nothing left but the back wheel and the pedals and they still rode round like monkeys. It always makes me laugh —I've rocked till my sides ached over them."

Macdonald nodded. "So have I. I should like to see Mr. Rameses in this outfit . . . I've been thinking. A real trick rider could have used this thing scooter-wise on that bridge."

The sergeant nodded. " I reckon he could. My hat! it'd

have been a queer sight if anybody could have seen it. Do you think it was this Rameses did the job?''

'' According to the manager at the Surrey Met, this Rameses was on the stage from 8.15 till 8.40 on the evening of the murder—and the manager's prepared to swear to that.''

'' Yes—but I was talking to Bill Thwaites—he's seen that turn at the Surrey Met. He says the Rameses are made up as Egyptians—a sort of mummy outfit, they hardly look like human beings at all. Who's to swear it was really Rameses and not one of his pals?''

'' I know. That's a point—but here's the old lady again.'' Mrs. Maloney came thumping down the area steps.

'' 'Aven't you finished? I don't like you being 'ere and that's a fact. Reflects on me, it do. I've never 'ad no complaints before.''

'' And you shan't have any now,'' replied Macdonald. '' I haven't moved a thing. The only thing I'm going to move is that trunk of Mr. d'Avarley's. I want to look through it to see if there's any letters mentioning Mr. Ward. You see we can't find out who his people are.''

She gave him a shrewd glance. '' P'raps his people aren't that anxious to claim 'im. I liked 'im meself—but 'e wasn't everybody's money. Always cadgin'. I've paid 'is taxi for 'im meself when 'e was stuck.''

Macdonald leaned against the door of Mr. Rameses' lock-up.

'' You're old enough to know better, Mrs. Maloney,'' he said, and the old woman bridled.

'' But 'e'd got a way with 'im, he was a boy, he was! I shall miss 'im. Brought a bit o' fun into the 'ouse with 'im, 'e did.''

'' But you say he wasn't everybody's money—and you're right. He got shown the wrong side of the door by some folks here sometimes.''

'' And I'm not saying 'e didn't. That Rameses couldn't abide 'im—Mr. Ward talked too pretty to Mrs. R. But there wasn't nothing in that, bless you. Them too—Mr. and Mrs. R., love birds ain't in it. Dippy, they are. Lady Bird 'e calls 'er. Some bird—but she's generous. The Variety folk is all free with their money.''

'' Would you say Mr. Rameses was generous?''

'' Bless you, yes. Very good 'e is. Never expects nothing for nothing. 'E's all right. ' E didn't go wasting 'is money on Mr. Ward—'e'd too much sense, but 'e's open 'anded if you works for 'im.''

"On Thursday—the day Mr. Ward was killed—you were in the house all day, Mrs. Maloney?"

"I was—same as I told the other policeman until 'alf past eight when I went out for me usual."

"Did any of the tenants come in during the afternoon or evening?"

"Everyone was out all afternoon. Quiet as a grave it was. Mr. Ward came in about 'alf past six. I 'eard 'im in 'is room. Mr. Carringford was in some time, because I 'eard Mr. Ward speak to 'im before they went out. I didn't 'ear no one else. Mr. and Mrs. Rameses, they don't generally come in at tea time. They got matinees to do and once they go out they stay out—but I never 'ear Mr. Rameses when 'e comes in. Quiet as a ghost 'e is, a great big chap like that. Still, I reckon 'e was out Thursday. Mrs. R. told me they 'ad a fish tea at the Corner 'Ouse between shows."

"What time do you generally knock off work?"

"Depends what you call work. I reckon to finish me cleaning by five o'clock, and I'm on duty with the front door till six. Then I goes up and stays up, and I don't take no notice of nothing."

"But you heard Mr. Ward speak to Mr. Carringford on Thursday evening?"

"Me hearing's all right, sir. I 'eard Mr. Ward go downstairs from 'is room, and I popped out to the you-know-what, on the landing outside me room that is, and not wanting to meet Mr. Ward on the landing, tho' 'e always disregarded, 'aving nice manners and not being vulgar like that d'Alvarley 'oo I couldn't stomach. I 'eard Mr. Ward stop on the first floor and there wasn't no one else 'e could've been talking to but Mr. Carringford. They both went out almost immediate—Mr. Ward first Mr. Carringford a little later, 'cos 'e always slams the front door, so I knew."

"I think you're a very observant person, Mrs. Maloney. There's not much you don't notice. I wonder how often Mr. Ward took advantage of your good nature when he was particularly hard up."

"As to that, 'e always was 'ard up. Lost all 'is bits and pieces in the blitz, *so* 'e said. I reckon some went to Uncle. I'm not denying I lent 'im a bob 'ere and there. Silly—but there it was."

"Did he ever pay you back?"

"Sure and he did—when he put it on the right one which wasn't often. 'E told me 'e was coming into some money— but there, I've 'eard that one before. If you want to know

79

what 'e was talking to Mr. Carringford about that evening I'd say it was the usual, because I 'eard Mr. Carringford say ' Sorry, old chap, can't be done ' and Mr. Ward, 'e said ' But it's the last time!' It always *was* the last time with 'im. I've 'eard that one, too, lots o' times. Well, dearie me, if I don't go and wash up them plates of Mrs. Rameses I shan't be done till morning. 'Ow much longer are you goin' to be 'ere? I'd rather you was out of the place before any of 'em come in. Sure to cause unpleasantness, no offence meant, and unpleasantness I can't abide."

" We shan't be much longer," rejoined Macdonald imperturbably. " You go and finish your washing up and we'll get on with our job quickly."

" One thing, you're trustworthy—I'll say that for you: not like some o' the police I've known in me time, dearie me . . ." and the old soul took herself off still talking.

" Just go over that bike for fingerprints," said Macdonald to the sergeant, " while I tackle Mr. Claude d'Alvarley's trunk . . . I wonder why he chose the name Claude."

He produced a key-ring as he spoke and heaved the trunk forward while the sergeant opened the door of Mr. Rameses' cupboard and got busy on the bike with an insufflator.

" I knew a boy called Claude once: nasty little nipper he was, too," said the sergeant meditatively, " but what could you expect with a name like that."

Macdonald gave a whistle: he had opened Mr. d'Alvarley's trunk with one of his own peculiar outfit of keys.

" Somebody's been through this trunk recently," he said. " Look at the creases in this coat—some old, some new . . . Do you suppose that Johnnie Ward borrowed Claude's clothes? Anyone could open this lock with a bent hairpin."

The sergeant looked round at the open trunk.

" Don't know," he replied, " but someone's cleaned this bike jolly carefully. Not a print on it. Well, well."

Macdonald was on his knees lifting out Mr. d'Alvarley's clothes: the ex-actor had a lively taste in shirts, ties, and pyjamas, to say nothing of socks.

" Just go through the pockets," said Macdonald.

A few moments later he said " That's that. If Mr. d'Alvarley ever packed any letters or other documents in this outfit, somebody has removed them for him. They say two negatives don't make an affirmative, but the number of negatives in this house induces a few positives in my mind. Help me fold this stuff up. If ever Claude *does* come home it'll be nice for him to find his clothes neatly packed."

The two men worked quickly and deftly, and in a very short time the trunk was repacked, locked, and returned to its home.

"We'll go and say good-bye to the old lady," said Macdonald. "She's yearning to see the last of us. I think she feels personally responsible for any misdemeanours we may commit."

The two went upstairs to the hall again where Mrs. Maloney was awaiting them.

"Finished, 'ave you? Glad to hear it. I shan't say nothing. Least said's soonest mended." She looked at Macdonald knowingly. "Lucky they was all out, wasn't it? Mr. and Mrs. R., they've got a matinee job as you knows: Miss Grey ditto. Rosie Willing's always out on Saturday as you could guess—and Mr. Carringford was rung up by the police and they told him to go to the first-class booking office. You're thorough, I'll say that for you."

Macdonald laughed. "So are you, Mrs. Maloney. You ought to join the C.I.D."

She chuckled—a cheery wheezy sound: "Sez you. I'm not so young as I was though you mightn't believe it. Some people looks older than their years—and some looks younger. Well, it's been nice to see you—though it's not everyone might agree."

"Priceless old girl," said the sergeant as they left the house, "no spots on her, either! Bright as they make them."

Macdonald nodded. "Yes. She's uncommonly shrewd. Now we'll see about that identification parade and see who spots who."

"A sort of double event," said the sergeant, and Macdonald nodded.

"That's the idea," he said.

CHAPTER NINE

i

MACDONALD had timed his identification parade for 5.45, that hour being reasonably convenient for all parties concerned. "Quite a circus you've got here, Jock," murmured one of his fellow inspectors and Macdonald felt that the comment was cogent. All the tenants of 5 Belfort Grove had been summoned to attend; Miss Rosie Willing, smiling and interested, looking quite remarkably young, stood beside Miss Odette Grey—the latter a platinum blonde of tonsorial perfection with an expression of calm disdain on her most efficiently painted face. Miss Grey wore a fur swagger coat over her brief petunia coloured house frock and she had an expensive posy of orchids pinned to her shoulder. Close to these two ladies stood Mr. and Mrs. Rameses, he with an expression of stolid indifference on his dark melancholy face, while his ' Lady-bird ' was suitably all of a twitter. Just behind them was Mr. Carringford, looking very much out of place among his theatrical fellow tenants. In addition were a few odd ' supers ' who had been collected to mingle with the principals in the indentity parade. In another room Bruce Mallaig and Stanley Claydon looked furtively at one another, both wondering who were the other men with them in the room.

Both groups of people were given similar instructions in their different rooms : the Belfort Grove collection was asked to study the men who would file past them in order that they could say if any of them had ever been seen in or near Number 5A. The group in which Mallaig and Claydon found themselves were told to study the people they would see in the other room and to say if they had ever seen them before. The doors were then opened and the Mallaig-Claydon group walked into the other room and filed very slowly past the Belfort Grove tenants.

Macdonald watched both groups, his eyes travelling over the various faces, studying them with an interest which never failed him when dealing with human beings. None of the Belfort Grove tenants showed any particular interest in the other group: Miss Grey maintained her pose of disdainful indifference, hardly bothering to study the tardy little procession: Miss Willing, alert and smiling, looked back and forth along the line, shrewd and entertained but showing no sign of recognition. Mr. Rameses stood stolidly and unblinkingly, looking at each face with the same immutable melancholy calm. Mrs. Rameses broke the silence with a twitter to the effect that the leading man (actually a plain-clothes policeman) resembled an acrobat she'd seen in Rio. Mr. Carringford, after studying the various types before him, began to look amused, as though the situation struck him as vaguely comic. Bruce Mallaig was evidently intent on doing his duty: he studied the whole group carefully and eventually halted in front of Mr. Rameses and looked at him with frowning intentness. The latter stared back in his stolid unblinking way and then quite suddenly winked. Macdonald was watching and he saw the flick of the heavy eyelid over the dark eye. A voice which appeared to issue from Mallaig's mouth squeaked '' Daddy . . . my Daddy . . .'' and Mrs. Rameses tittered. '' Don't you do it, Birdie,'' she admonished, while Bruce Mallaig jumped and looked over his shoulder for the speaker with the squeaky voice. Stanley Claydon tittered—a nervous sound which ended in a cough, and then the group of men filed back again into the other room.

Macdonald had Mallaig and Claydon brought to him seperately. Mallaig said immediately: " The only one who could have been the chap I saw in the matchlight was the dark bloke who winked—but I can't be sure. I wouldn't swear to him, but he *was* somehow like that other one. If I saw him again in the same conditions—just in the glow of light from a single match, I could judge better. Who on earth said Daddy?"

" The dark bloke you were looking at. He's a ventriloquist," said Macdonald, " likewise a conjurer and juggler with a circus training."

" Good Lord! When I first set eyes on him I thought he was a parson minus the dog-collar . . . he might be anything —but a circus would be my last guess. Come to think of it, we must have looked a pretty fair circus altogether while we stood there gazing at one another. We were a good mixed lot . . I wish I could be sure of that bloke's face."

" Don't worry too much about it. It's much wiser to say that you can't be certain than to give a positive or negative answer if there's any doubt in your mind at all."

Macdonald did not spend long on Claydon. He had had him brought to the ' parade ' more in order for him to be looked at by the Belfort Grove contingent than for any other reason. Claydon, sniffing and asthmatical, said " I don't know any of them—they looked a rum lot to me. The only one I've ever seen before was the white-haired bloke—leastways, I think I've seen him. It was a long time ago, when I was a nipper just before I left school. Sort of lecturer he was, came and talked to us about pacificism and that. League of Nations. Fat lot of good it did. Funny how much older he looks: suppose it's his white hair. He had black hair then and was quite a young chap."

Macdonald laughed. " Well, that's an odd coincidence, but it doesn't seem to have much connection with the present case. I wonder if he recognised you."

" Likely, ain't it? I was only fourteen then. 1930 it was, the year I left school."

" What school were you at?"

" Euston Street: I wanted to go on to the Secondary School, but I couldn't get a free-place. Always this ruddy asthma. Kippers me whatever I do."

83

Macdonald sent Claydon away, still grumbling to himself, and then interviewed the Belfort Grove contingent. Miss Grey was positively, if acidly, negative.

" I have never set eyes on any one of them, Inspector, and I should be so glad if you could let me go immediately. Our show starts again at 6.30."

" Off you go then. Sorry you were troubled, as the exchange ladies say," replied Macdonald, and Miss Grey switched on a professional smile as she replied:

" Don't mention it—and thanks ever so for seeing me first."

Next came Rosie Willing. " Nothing doing. Never seen any of them at our abode of bliss. Sorry. O.K. then, and ta ta!"

Mr. and Mrs. Rameses followed on her heels, and Mr. Rameses proceeded to give a remarkable demonstration of his own powers of observation.

" One, a fellow in shoddy tweeds and a rubberless mack. Fair hair, grey green eyes, false teeth and large feet—probably a C.I.D. man, bored stiff with the whole show. Two, a fellow with asthma and a cold in his nose and a face like a poor potato. Nervy and all hett-up. Three, another police bloke, brown hair, brown eyes, and a wart on his chin: very sure of himself. Four, a chap who goes to a decent tailor, reddish hair, short-sighted, ultra-conscientious, probably a first-class Civil Servant. Five, a funny little twirp, five foot nothing, left eye green, right eye blue, probably a cleaner on the premises brought in to oblige. That's the lot—don't know any of them, never seen any of them before to my knowledge. Number four fancied he recognised me. Maybe he did. I've been on view twice daily since before he was born. All I can say is, I don't know him."

The deep voice ceased abruptly and Mrs. Rameses gave voice. " Isn't he a marvel, Inspector? Fancy remembering all that. Beats me how he does it. I remember one day we were in Glasgow——"

" Cut it out, Ladybird," boomed Mr. Rameses. " This chap's only interested in one thing—have you ever seen any of those blokes at Number 5A or hanging around the neighbourhood? Make it snappy—we've not got all the time in the world to spare."

" I've never seen any of them, anywhere, unless that man with the false teeth—the first one—was the same as that acrobat you quarrelled with in Rio . . ."

" Well, he wasn't. Take it from me," said Mr. Rameses. " Satisfied, Inspector? She'll go on talking till morning if you give her the chance . . . Right. Good-evening."

84

Carringford was the final witness. He walked in slowly, like a tired man, his white head looking very venerable and his aspect schoolmasterish in comparison with the previous witnesses.

" Well, Chief Inspector, I suppose that as a responsible citizen I've no grounds for complaint, but you've taken a pretty large slice of my time to-day. I don't mind trying to be useful, but that business at Paddington Station was sheer rank waste of time. I don't know what opinion you have of the amiable member of your department who kept me walking in circles round the booking-hall—but if I ever met an optimistic incompetent that was he."

" I'm sorry, Mr. Carringford. If it's any comfort to you, your time hasn't been wasted. Elimination is one of the most important elements in detection. You gave me a very important piece of evidence to-day and I had to try to follow it up. It was just bad luck that this identity parade business had to follow right on top of the Paddington episode."

" Provided I'm being useful I'm not complaining," said Carringford, " but a man of my age does feel an outsize in fools when he's asked to walk round a station looking for a man who had lunch there some hours previously and who's probably in Bristol or Cardiff by this time. I'm quite willing to squander my time when you're in charge Chief Inspector, for you're a man of common sense—a very uncommon quality, not shared, apparently, by your robust colleague at Paddington. Now about this identity parade of yours. I can't say with any conviction that I recognised any of the participants. The only one whose face seemed familiar to me was the second man who entered—a weedy pallid youth who had a filthy cold."

" Have you any idea where you've seen him before?"

" I don't know. I can't be sure. I'm only giving you an impression—and I may be quite wrong, but I believe I've seen him hanging about at the corner of Belfort Grove—near the pub in Belfort Place. I always go out for my lunch and I generally pass that corner about mid-day. There are several loungers—chronics, I call them. I have an idea I may have seen him there."

" It's a bit odd," said Macdonald. " The fellow you mention thought he recognised *you*—but he didn't mention a pub."

" Ah—but the fact that he knew my face indicates that I may have been right in saying that I thought I recognised him. Where did he say he'd seen me?' '

" He said that you once lectured to him concerning pacifism

85

and the League of Nations while he was still at school—in 1930.''

Carringford laughed. '' Good Lord! What an idea. I wasn't in England in 1930. I was in the West Indies. I was born there and I went back for a visit—so I think that that was one of those long shots which went very much astray.''

'' I'm interested to hear you were born in the West Indies,'' said Macdonald. '' I've got some friends in Jamaica. We must have a yarn sometime.''

'' Delighted—but it's a long time since I lived there. I came to England in 1890, when I was a kid of six——''

'' Are you really sixty years of age? No one would believe that.''

'' It depends. Some days I look ninety—and feel it.'' He got up from his place, adding '' Forgive me if I was irascible over that futile business at Paddington. I find irratability grows on me with age. You must often get exasperated with your job, but I envy you your serenity—I often say it's a mistake to be born in the tropics—we're all over irritable. Well—if there's any way I can be of service, command me, but not, for the love of Mike, to loiter in Paddington Station!''

After Carringford had left, Inspector Jenkins came into Macdonald's room. Jenkins was a stout rubicund fellow of fifty-five. Detecting was in his very bones and Macdonald considered Jenkins one of the most shrewd and able of his colleagues, despite the big man's air of simple good humour. A number of crooks had reason to regret the fact that they had assumed that Jenkins was a fool: nothing pleased him better than to give that impression. '' The bigger ass they think me the more confident they become,'' said Jenkins, '' and it's when a criminal feels confident that he gets careless.'' It was Jenkins who had occupied Mr. Carringford at Paddington Station that afternoon, and the inspector sounded almost contrite when he described their activities to Macdonald.

''' Poor old chap,'' he said—and it was to Carringford he referred. '' Not too good on his feet and he got tired. I was sorry for him, I was really. I got hold of the young fellow who waits in the snack bar—very nice lot of people in that place. Of course they didn't remember any of the chaps who'd been in that morning—how could they, with the crowd they get here —but the waiter—name of Jackson—came along to the booking office with me, and he recognised Carringford. Said he'd noticed what beautiful white hair he'd got. That was quite good for a start, and then Jackson said he did seem to remember a heavily built dark chap who was in conversation with

86

Carringford. Jackson had an idea one of the other waiters might know him, and this last chap said ' Oh, you mean that commercial who talks such a lot. I believe he lives at Reading —at least he travels by the Reading trains.' Well, that was worth following up. There are a lot of trains which stop at Reading and I'm afraid Mr. Carringford got rather fed up. We did our best—but I never expected any luck straight away. I kept on explaining that it was patience we needed. Why, I've worked Paddington Station for days in some cases."

" I know you have," said Macdonald, " but you can't expect Mr. Carringford to display the same enthusiasm. I'm afraid if we ask him to go to Paddington again he'll refuse point blank. Did he talk to you at all?"

" Oh yes. He was very friendly to start with. It wasn't till his feet got tired that he got terse. He talked a bit about Ward. That evening Ward was killed Carringford dined with a friend at Canuto's—man named Hardwell, lives in Bentinck Street. Hardwell's what they call a connoisseur—expert on antique furniture and china. Carringford's very well informed on that line—period stuff. He's an intelligent man. I quite enjoyed the bit of chat we had."

" I can't say he did. Mr. Carringford felt he was wasting time for nothing. However, I had a nice peaceful time at number five Belfort Grove. Mr. Rameses possesses a bike—a very fine machine made for a trick rider."

" Does he, by jove. Pity we can't tell Carringford that—he wouldn't have minded that station business so much if he'd known how helpful he was being by just keeping out of the house. I believe he suffers from corns. I'd have liked to have given him a bit of advice about footwear. You never get corns if . . ."

" I know, Jenkins, I know. All very well for you to talk, but aching feet spoil a man's temper. Now I'm going along to Wardour Street. The Flamingo Film Company have promised me a private show of the station scene in ' The Night's Work.' Would you like to come and see if you recognise poor Johnny Ward?"

" Now that's just the sort of job I like," said Jenkins. " Sit still and just use your eyes. No walking. Thanks, Chief. I'll come with pleasure. A private view's the very thing I should enjoy."

ii

The studio in which Macdonald and Jenkins were given a

" run through " of the section of film Macdonald had asked to see was very different from the vast cinemas in which films are usually seen. The studio was just long enough to enable a limited number of people to see the screen at a sufficient distance to get a good view. To Macdonald's mind there was something almost eerie in the fact of watching a film portraying a crowd of people waiting to meet the boat train at Charing Cross and himself watching for the appearance of a man whose body was lying in a mortuary. The star players in the foreground of the picture were arguing with passionate emphasis, and all around and behind them was a moving throng—rich men and poor men, guards, porters, inspectors; fur-coated women and well-dressed men, paper boys, buffet boys, couriers, chauffeurs —all the crowd of pre-war travelling days. Then suddenly, at the side of the screen, a man turned and faced the onlookers for a few seconds—a man with a dark whimsical face and a charming smile. He collided with a stout woman carrying a heavy suit-case and his expression and gesture of apology were curiously real. He drew back and stood on one side waiting, his face expressing an amused interest as he looked at the moving throng surging forward from the train—and then the scene flashed off and the white screen was left blank. "O.K.?" inquired a bored voice. " That's the only station scene in that picture."

" Thanks. That's all I want for the moment," replied Macdonald. He and Jenkins left the studio and went to interview one of the management staff. " We've spotted the man we're interested in," said Macdonald. " He was one of the crowd at the barrier—not a speaking part. Would there be any records of those employed for crowd parts in the studio where the picture was made?"

The reply was not encouraging: " You never can tell with these crowd scenes. The agents send along a job lot and a few odd ones may come in from nowhere in particular. That's an old film—I doubt if any records would have been kept of the supers. Tell you what—I'll put through an inquiry for you. Maybe we can find someone who was in that scene. If we can, we'll run through it for you again and see if we can get the guy located. Is he wanted?"

" No. He's dead. He was knocked over the head in Regents Park on Thursday evening. We want to get a line on his friends. The name he was using when he was killed was John Ward, but he may have been known as Timothy O'Farrel. He was an Irishman."

" Right. I'll see what I can do—but the trouble is he pro-

88

bably used another name at the Studio. They nearly always do."

" Where was the film made?"

" Engleton Studios. They were blitzed in 1941."

" I see. Doesn't look very hopeful, does it?"

" Well—there's always a chance. I tell you straight out it'll be a hundred to one against, but I'll do my best."

" Right—and thanks very much."

" Rum business," said Jenkins as they reached the street again. " The bloke's dead . . . and he looked so much alive in that picture. Come to think of it, they keep folks alive in a way these days. You can turn on a movie and see the way they walked and moved and looked—and hear their voices talking to you. It's a damned queer world we're living in."

" It's a damned sight too queer for my liking," said Macdonald. " If we go on being so infernally clever, homo sapiens will annihilate his own species. Sapiens on the wrong track."

Jenkins was following his own trail of thought. " That bloke —Johnnie Ward—or whatever he called himself—had got an interesting face . . . he'd got some quality."

" Yes. A quality called charm," said Macdonald. " He'd got a way with him, and when you've said that you've said all that there was to say in his favour so far as I can make out."

CHAPTER   TEN

i

IT WAS shortly after eight o'clock that Macdonald sent up his card to Mr. Ross Lane and he was taken straight up to the surgeon's sitting-room. Ross Lane got up from the same comfortable chair in which he had been sitting on Macdonald's first visit, but he was not alone in the room this time. A slim grey-haired woman stood with her back to the fire and studied Macdonald as he came into the room : her scrutiny was deliberate and impersonal and he was aware of an interesting face and a well-tailored figure as Ross Lane said :

" Good-evening, Chief Inspector. My wife has asked me to introduce you. Chief Inspector Macdonald—my wife."

Macdonald bowed, and was able to get a closer impression of a very charming face, thin and not unlined, with clear-cut features, sensitive close-shut lips and dark blue eyes, wide-set under arched black eyebrows. Macdonald said :

" How do you do. I believe that you practice under the name of Dr. Josephine Falton?"

" I do. It is customary for women doctors to keep to their professional names—but at home I am Mrs. Ross Lane. Will you sit down?"

" Thank you." Macdonald then turned to the surgeon. " Last time I was here I asked you if you had ever heard the name Timothy O'Farrel."

" You did. I replied that I knew the name and that I believed it to be that of a character in one of Congreve's or Wycherley's plays. I was quite wrong, of course—but the name Tim O'Farrel *does* occur in an old Irish play which I once saw produced at the Abbey Theatre in Dublin."

" I'm not prepared to dispute that—but would you like to reconsider your answer to my question?"

Mrs. Ross Lane promptly put in : " I think that suggestion is put with remarkable courtesy and lack of acrimony. In fact it shows much more consideration than we deserve."

" Quite true," said Ross Lane. " Well, Chief Inspector, having discussed the matter with my wife, who was away from home last time you called, I am prepared to make you a full statement, which can be supplemented by my wife later. Would you rather interview us separately?"

" No. I don't think that is necessary," replied Macdonald. " I may have my own opinion about the unwisdom of concealing evidence in the matter of a capital crime, but I have a high opinion of the integrity of your profession. In short, I should be very much surprised if you were to make any statement which you knew to be untrue."

" Your judgment is perfectly correct," said Ross Lane, and though his voice was dry and formal, there was a twinkle in his eyes. It was plain that the surgeon, though possibly embarrassed, was not in the least apprehensive. " Well—here is my statement—and a pretty kettle of fish it is. My wife, while still a medical student, married a man named Timothy O'Farrel. She left him three years afterwards. That is her part of the story. Mine begins later : I first met Dr. Josephine Falton in 1925. I did not persuade her to marry me until 1944, when she was informed of the death of Timothy O'Farrel in an air-raid shelter in Camberwell. We had had three very pleasant months of matrimony, and then my wife was asked to go to see her mother—who has since died. On the morning of the day my wife was to travel to Devon she had a telephone call purporting to come from Timothy O'Farrel."

Mrs. Ross Lane interrupted here. "The call *was* from Timothy O'Farrel. His voice was unmistakable."

Her husband continued: "You know the substance of the call. My wife told me about it, and I said that I would go and keep the appointment at the bridge. Obviously, if Timothy O'Farrel were alive, it was necessary for us to see him and consider what was to be done. I should in no case have allowed my wife to go to Regents Park alone to keep the appointment, and eventually she agreed with me that I should go and meet Timothy O'Farrel and hear what he had to say while she travelled to Devon as arranged." The surgeon paused a moment, studying Macdonald's face with the lively quizzical air which was so characteristic. "I might make an interpolation here. Obviously the resurrection of Tim O'Farrel was a confounded nuisance. It meant that Josephine and myself were bigamously married, and people of our profession have to reckon with a body called the General Medical Council. I should like to make it plain that I used the word ' nuisance ' advisedly. O'Farrel's reappearance was just that, no more. I am close on fifty years of age: my wife is forty-eight. We neither of us intended to wreck our lives because a rogue was hoping to exploit his roguery. If the Medical Council debar us from practising—well, it's a pity, but we are quite capable of leading happy and, I hope, useful lives along other lines. I want you to understand that. I intended to listen to what O'Farrel had to say: obviously blackmail was indicated—but I didn't lose my wool over it. I wanted to tell him to go to the devil his own way, and to assure him that his progress was not going to be assisted, financially or otherwise, by myself or my wife. I don't know if you can swallow that, Chief Inspector, but it's true. All I wanted to say was ' Publish and be damned. If you think you're on to a soft proposition—think again.' "

Macdonald nodded. "Yes. I think I can believe that—but I very much doubt if most people would do so."

"If the jury would do so," put in Mrs. Ross Lane tranquilly. "In other words, only a mature mind, which has evolved its own philosophy, would believe that we were not in a hair-tearing state."

"To continue," went on Ross Lane. "I set out from here on Thursday evening with my dog—and I haven't a word to add or delete from the statement I made to you previously about my progress to the bridge. There's a very important point I want to make here. I had never seen Timothy O'Farrel, neither had I seen a photograph of him. When I reached the bridge, the constable was in charge of three men—one dead, two alive. I had never seen any of them before. Later I was told that the dead man was named John Ward. I knew of no John Ward. Neither had I any knowledge of who caused the man's death, by what agency it occurred, or anything at all about it."

He paused here and Macdonald said: " Very good. The gist of your statement will be set down, and after reading it you will be asked to sign it."

" That's all right—but I'd rather go on a bit, if you're prepared to listen."

" It's my business to listen," said Macdonald. " As a matter of correct procedure, I ought to have another man with me, and had I anticipated a detailed statement such as you are making, I should have brought one. If, however, you are willing to continue your statement with no further witness and without the presence of a solicitor, I am only too anxious to hear that statement."

" Personally I'd much rather tell you the story, just as I'm doing now, than have a witness to take my speech down and a solicitor to check any garrulity," said Ross Lane. " At the beginning of our talk you said a very unexpected thing, to the effect that you were willing to accept the integrity of our profession and that you would not expect to be told lies. I respect you the more for saying that because you know I evaded giving you a straight answer last time you talked to me."

" From my recollection of what you said the word ' evasion ' covers it," said Macdonald. " You told me that the telephone call from St. Pancras was not answered by yourself. That was true. In reply to my question about the name O'Farrel you said that it was a name in a play. I noted the answer for what it was worth."

" Quite—and when you think the matter out now you can realise that my evasions had this to justify then: it was my wife who answered O'Farrel's telephone call, and I had no intention of telling you anything about her affairs until I had had the chance of talking to her."

Dr. Falton put in a word here. " You did a very unwise thing, Bill. The only sensible course would have been to refuse to answer. The Inspector would then have had no cause for complaint."

" Well—that's as may be. John Ward is dead and Timothy O'Farrel is dead. He gave you a lot of trouble during the course of his life. If I could have saved you any further trouble in the matter of his death I would have done so." He turned back to Macdonald and addressed him directly: " I think I've said all that's relevant. I went to Regents Park with the intention of meeting Timothy O'Farrel on the bridge. When I arrived there he was dead, and I know nothing about his death. I had never seen him in my life, so I could truthfully say I could not identify him. If I could have saved my wife from becoming involved in the inquiry about O'Farrel's death I should have done so. To be involved in it will cause her a great deal of trouble and will not assist the police at all. We neither of us know anything about the matter." He paused and then added: " I have spoken to you quite frankly, Chief Inspector. I realise that you must inevitably suspect me, and I don't resent the inevitable. I prevaricated to you when you first asked me for evidence, and, in the eyes of the average man, I had a motive to kill O'Farrel. The point which I think you will understand—though most people would not—is that I wanted to avoid trouble for my wife. I have wits enough to know that to commit a murder is not a trouble-saving course of action."

" I quite agree," said Macdonald, " though I wish you had employed your wits a little further, and considered the fact that to conceal essential evidence is not a trouble-saving course of action, either."

He turned to Mrs. Ross Lane. " Do you wish to make a statement, or would you rather answer explicit questions?"

" I would rather make a statement. If I am to tell you about Timothy O'Farrel it means giving you a large slice of my life-history. I don't like the prospect, but I'm prepared to go through with it—if only to make amends for my husband's behaviour in the matter of evidence. I was telling him, just before you came, that I can't understand how a man with a first-class mind could have been so stupid as he appears to have been."

" It's a type of stupidity which I frequently meet," replied Macdonald. " It's easy to say ' If I had been in the same position I should have done so and so.' Very intelligent people are capable of doing very ill-judged things under stress of circumstances."

" That's a two-edged comment," she said. " However— here's my statement concerning Timothy O'Farrel. We were fellow students at Dublin University. He was sent down in his second year. I married him in 1918, when I was twenty-two. Our married life was brief and difficult and we parted in 1921— though even in those three years we did not live together for longer than six months all told. I had a small income of my own and I paid my husband an allowance on condition that he left me alone and did not attempt to interfere with me or come to my house or make any attempt to see me."

" You must have had very strong reasons to follow such a course." said Macdonald. " It is my business to try to understand the type of man O'Farrel was. I realise it must be unpalatable to you—to say the least of it—to discuss him, but will you diagnose him, as it were—state his condition of mind as though he were a patient."

" I am quite willing to tell you all I can about him: it is twenty years since I had anything much to do with him at first hand, and he means no more to me than an illness which is past and over: a one-time misery which no longer has power to distress. Timothy O'Farrel was fundamentally dishonest and incorrigibly lazy. He would make no effort of any kind to work or to earn a living. When he was without money he borrowed or stole, first from me, then from my friends. He read private letters—and sought to profit from what he learned in them. He induced confidences—and exploited them. He was a very dangerous person because he was a very attractive one. Everyone liked him, men as well as women: people confided in him. He was a curious creature because side by side with his laziness and inertia, he was physically brave. He loved a scrap, and he got involved with the Sinn Fein extremists. I have no doubt at all that he had several murders to his credit, though he always got off scot-free."

She paused, lighted a cigarette, and then went on: " I had qualified as a doctor: I did my term in hospital and I wanted to practise. It was abundantly evident that I could not do so while my husband lived with me. Further, I knew that he cared nothing about me. I soon found out that he had married me because he thought I should keep him without any effort on his part. He admitted it—coolly and amusedly. It was then that I told him that I would pay him an allowance provided he kept away from me—and he agreed, still amusedly. That arrangement went on for seven years. I had come to England and I was practising. Timothy turned up at my house one day and demanded a larger allowance. I refused it. Then, by a stroke of good fortune for me, I learned that he had stolen from a friend of mine. We had the evidence. I told him he could clear out or else be handed over to the police. I was still willing to pay him a subsistence allowance— but he could subsist elsewhere. He went—I paid his passage to America. He drew his allowance until 1930. Then he disappeared. I believed he was in prison. In 1935 I heard from

94

him again—this time in Eire, in County Cork. I continued to pay him the allowance I originally promised, remitting to a firm of solicitors in Cork. In 1938 he ceased to claim the allowance. I heard no more of him until I had a letter from an address in Camberwell last February, saying that Timothy O'Farrel had been killed when a shelter was bombed on February 5th. The letter was signed M. Casey—you can see it. I went to the address on it—Dulverton Place—and found it was blitzed. I went and examined the names of those killed in the shelter. Timothy O'Farrel's name was down as ' missing, believed killed.' I made further inquiries and learnt that a cigarette case had been found in the shambles. It was Timothy's cigarette case. It was that which convinced me he was dead. He had pawned that cigarette case dozens of times and always redeemed it. I believe that he would never have left anything on which he could raise money in a shelter. I was wrong. That was casting his bread upon the waters. Perhaps he had been ' observing me ' and thought I might get married again if I knew he was dead. I did—and it must have seemed to him the chance of a life-time. He was at last in a position to blackmail his wife. That's the story, Chief Inspector.''

'' Thank you for being so frank,'' said Macdonald quietly. '' There are one or two questions I must ask. First, in that conversation over the telephone, O'Farrel mentioned the bridge in Regents Park. Why should he have assumed that you knew it?''

'' He knew that I did. I have twice talked to Timothy in that spot—once during our honeymoon when we stayed in London, and again in 1925 when he tried to get more money out of me. It was on that bridge that I told him that I would tell the police about his theft if he persisted in bothering me. I didn't mince words, and it was an occasion which he could have remembered with no pleasure at all. He wanted to turn the tables on me. I understood that all right. He always had a sense of the picturesque.''

'' It seems to me an odd place to have chosen to talk—in November and in the blackout.''

'' Yes, I suppose it was odd—but so was Timothy. He was a fantastic creature in many ways. The oddest part of it all is that I didn't hate him. I hardly even resented him. I made a fool of myself over marrying him and I paid for my foolishness, but the thing I shall always remember about him was that he was capable of being the most delightful companion. Even as a self-confessed rogue and shameless egotist he was charming. I'm Irish too, you see, and though I soon realised that life with

95

Timothy was impossible, I always admitted his attractiveness. Now having heard all that, Chief Inspector, are you really any nearer to knowing who killed Timothy O'Farrel?—for certainly I did not, and neither did my husband."

Ross Lane put in a word here, and his voice was whimsical.

" No. I didn't kill him. There's something bizarre in the suggestion that I should have done so. I've never seen Timothy O'Farrel. The idea of killing an unknown man in the blackout on the mere assumption that because he's in a certain spot he's unmistakably the man you want to kill strikes me as a bit chancy. Whoever killed him must have known him by sight sufficiently well to recognise him in the gleam of a matchlight."

" That's all self-evident to you and me, Bill," said his wife. " We both know that it's true that you didn't know Timothy by sight. Also, there's evidence to show that you did not make his acquaintance on the bridge—there was no conversation before the murder—but I fail to see how you could *prove* that you didn't know him by sight."

" That is perfectly true," said Macdonald. " From every point of view it is desirable that Mr. Ross Lane should try to find some corroboration of the facts concerning his walk to Regents Park on Thursday evening." He turned to the surgeon. " You can realise for yourself the importance of substantiating one point—that at the moment when the constable blew his whistle on the bridge you had just arrived at the corner of York Gate and the Outer Circle, having walked there from Chiltern Court."

" Yes. I see that all right," said Ross Lane. " I can only give you the same answer which I gave before—after I left Chiltern Court I met no one and I saw no one until I came to the bridge. The cyclist doesn't count, because although I was aware that he passed me I didn't actually see him." Ross Lane's shrewd humorous eyes met Macdonald's steadily, and the surgeon went on: " The last patient I saw to-day was a man who has only a short time to live. His doctor came with him and at the close of my examination that doctor said: ' You can feel perfectly safe with Mr. Ross Lane—trust him altogether.' I don't know if you see the appositeness of that, Chief Inspector, but I'm prepared to trust you, altogether. You're a sane fellow and a man of experience. I have told you the truth—and I leave it at that."

" And all that we have said sheds no light at all on the question the Chief Inspector is dealing with—who killed Timothy O'Farrel?" Mrs. Ross Lane looked at Macdonald meditatively: " If I knew the answer I should have to tell you, but, frankly, I'm glad I don't know it."

Macdonald turned and faced her. " I can see your point, but I take it that you agree with me on this point—murder and assassination can never be justified: the society which allows them to go unpunished is likely to suffer for its omission."

" Yes. I grant you that."

" Can you tell me anything at all about any of O'Farrel's acquaintances?"

" Nothing at all. His friends came and went—no one trusted him for long and without trust there is no friendship. As for acquaintances, he picked them up easily. I've told you—everyone liked him at first, but his acquaintances did not mature because he asked everything and gave nothing."

" Finally, what may seem to you an odd question," said Macdonald. " Did you ever see a film called ' The Night's Work '?"

" No. I hardly ever go to pictures. I loathe them."

Ross Lane put in: " I saw ' The Night's Work.' Why do you ask?"

" Because O'Farrel played in the station scene—not a speaking part, he was just in the crowd, but Bruce Mallaig remembered O'Farrel's face from seeing the picture."

" Then Bruce Mallaig has a better memory than I have," replied Ross Lane.

Shortly after this Macdonald took his leave. Mrs. Ross Lane stood by the fire and lighted another cigarette.

" Before I married Tim one of my friends said to me ' If you *do* marry him, you'll never leave off regretting it: O'Farrel is one of those permanent nuisances!' It looks as though she were right. Tim's dead this time . . . but he still has nuisance value."

Her husband nodded. " Quite true—but not *permanent* nuisance value. Cheer up, Joe. I did not bat Timothy O'Farrel over the head."

" I know you didn't—but will a jury believe that?"

" It won't come to a jury—not so far as I'm concerned."

Josephine Ross Lane's face lost its equable expression for a moment: " My dear, exactly what do you mean?"

Her husband chuckled. " Not that, Joe. I mean I'd put my last penny on that detective: he's the type who'll worry away at a problem until he gets at the truth. I've nothing to fear from him."

Mrs. Ross Lane pondered and replied at length: " That detective is a remarkably nice person and we're uncommonly lucky to have a man of that type in charge—but if ever I felt afraid of anybody it is of Macdonald. It's his quietness—and you can't tell what he's thinking.''

" Maybe, but there's no woolliness in his mental make-up, he's clear and to the point. What about some coffee, Joe? I feel it'd help.''

" Yes: coffee: clear, black and hot . . . oh dear . . . *damn* Timothy O'Farrel.''

" Amen,'' agreed a distinguished surgeon.

CHAPTER ELEVEN

i

MACDONALD'S work for the day was not done. When he left the Ross Lanes he returned to Scotland Yard to see Detective Reeves and Inspector Jenkins and to hear their latest reports.

It was Reeves who had been given the job of trying to trace O'Farrel's movements at St. Pancras Station and he had been very successful in his quest. Armed with O'Farrel's photograph he had tackled the unpromising job of questioning the station staff about a man who might have travelled on a stopping train to Elstree two days ago. The fact that O'Farrel was remembered was due to his talkativeness. The driver of a horse van who picked up goods at St. Pancras regularly every morning remembered the dead man's face because O'Farrel had come and chatted to him about his horse, patting the beast and showing a lively affection for horses which nearly made him miss his train. He had jumped into the rearmost compartment just as the guard blew his whistle, and consequently the guard also remembered him, O'Farrel having leaned out of the window and chatted to him at the many stops between St. Pancras and Elstree on the 10.50 train. From the guard Reeves learned that O'Farrel had been alone in his compartment until Cricklewood when a couple of railwaymen joined him and travelled with him to Elstree. At Elstree Reeves went to the studios and produced his photograph. Here he was told that O'Farrel had gone to the office to enter for a crowd part, saying that an agent had sent him. Apparently he had mistaken the date—the job had been for the previous day and he had to return to town having wasted his railway fare. The clerks in the office to whom Reeves talked did not know the name Timothy O'Farrel though they recognised the dead man's photograph—neither did they know him by the name John Ward. He was simply one of the unknown supers who turn up for crowd parts. ' That Irish bloke ' was the description given of him by a weary office manager, who asked Reeves how the blazes he was to remember the names of every guy who blew in to cadge a job?

" Try the agents. They'll have some sort of name to label him by—a dozen names more likely," said the manager. " Daphne, who sent that guy along on Thursday?—is he one of Flicket's lot?"

" Search me!" replied Daphne. " I was busy—I just shoved him off. There wasn't a show for him and I couldn't be bothered with him."

Another girl in the office, addressed as Jill, produced some further information about the Irishman.

" When he left here he went with John Merrilees—he's had a small part in ' The Girl I Left Behind Me.' John Merrilees often goes to lunch at that place in Covent Garden—the Scarlet Petticoat. It's a snack-bar. Perhaps your boyfriend went there with him."

Reeves thanked his informants politely and asked them to report anything they could concerning the talkative Irishman, after which he returned to London, learning from a girl ticket-collector at the station that two film chaps had travelled together on the 12.50 London train on Thursday. The train had been late (even later than usual) and they had beguiled their wait by talking to ' Doris,' telling her she had just the sort of face for the flicks. In London Reeves had gone to the Scarlet Petticoat and had eventually run Merrilees to earth. The latter remembered Ward all right (' Johnnie Ward ' was the name in use again on this occasion.) " Amusing chap—real Irishman and a dirty dog at that," said Merrilees. " Tied himself on to me for lunch and then left me to pay the bill, blast him . . . Never saw such infernal cheek. Ate a good meal, lowered a couple of Lagers and asked for the bill—just before the bill appeared Ward jumped up, saying, ' Excuse me a second . . . I want to catch that chap . . . you ought to meet him.' "

Merrilees saw Ward make for a crowd by the door—and that was the last he did see of him. A waiter had told Merrielees that Ward had played the same trick before.

" That was two-thirty," said Reeves. " Deceased walked out of the Scarlet Petticoat with another chap—and the rest is silence. Maybe I'll pick up his trail later. I'm going to eat at the Scarlet Petticoat for a week and try all the habituees."

" Experience worketh hope," said Macdonald. " You've done jolly well to trace him so far. Now what about Jenkins? Been on the trail since our private view, old sobersides?"

Jenkins, who had apparently been taking a nap, settled deep in an uncompromising government chair, nodded his head and came-to immediately, cheerful and alert.

"Yes, Chief. Been improving my education both ends so to speak. I went and had a chat with a gentleman named Hardwell—a connoisseur and epicure to use high-sounding terms. Nice chap. He dined at Canuto's on Thursday in company with his friend Mr. Carringford. They met there at 7.15 and parted at 9.20. A long sitting, but they had some other friends to join them for coffee at 8.30. Carringford's an interesting bird, I gather. Historian, bit of a journalist, and an expert on certain periods—costume, furniture and china. It's that sort of knowledge which earns him a fee from the Movie magnates. Hardwell finds him useful in other ways. For instance if there's some historic stuff for sale at Christie's or Sotheby's, Carringford works out the history and lineage of the owners of the stuff. That sort of thing enhances its value to the Yanks, I'm told."

"It seems Mr. Carringford is more original than most historians then," said Macdonald. "As a rule a history degree implies a teaching career—but not cinemas and sale rooms. However, the point is he was at Canuto's from 7.15 until 9.20 on Thursday evening. Better check up with the waiters of Canuto's, Jenkins."

The stout man chuckled: "I get you, Chief, I hadn't forgotten. Now for the rest of my evening. I had a nice chat with a little pro. at the Mayfair Palais de Dance—it's in Earl's Court. Her name's Elsaby Vere—professionally. Mabel Harris at home. She was 'crackers' on Johnnie Ward—always game to stand him a drink and a meal. She doesn't know anything worth while about him—she's a dancing partner and picked him up on the dance floor. The point which seems to emerge about Johnnie Ward is that all his acqaintances were recent ones. No one seems to have seen Johnnie Ward before January of this year. He just appeared, tagging round with his pal d'Alvarley. I've talked to several little girls—some of them shrewd, some of them foolish—but they're alike in one thing, they first saw Ward some time this year. I can't find anyone who knew what he was doing previous to this year."

"It seems quite probable that he wasn't in England prior to this year," said Macdonald. "In 1938 he was in County Cork, and he suddenly ceased drawing an allowance from a solicitor empowered to pay him. The answer may be that he got himself into prison in Eire, or else got involved in some of the I.R.A. disturbances that are always brewing: in any case it must have been something which made it inadvisable for him to claim his allowance under his own name. It's fair to assume that he contrived to get himself into England on some-one else's papers and that once in England he watched out for an opportunity to establish a new identity."

"If we could only get in touch with Claude d'Alvarley he ought to be able to tell us something about the blighter," said Reeves.

" 'Ought' doesn't equal 'would '," said Macdonald. " I should think the probability is that d'Alvarley lent his room to O'Farrel under compulsion, arguing from what we know of the latter. Gentle blackmail seems to have been his recipe for earning a living."

Jenkins chuckled, the deep amused sound of a good-natured man enjoying a private joke.

"That's about it, Chief," said Jenkins. " I'm almost sorry that O'Farrel isn't here to enjoy the joke. Here are three of us, respectable, reponsible, not to say high-minded servants of law and order, concentrating on finding some chap who took it into his own hands to do a bit of social scavenging by ridding the world of a blackmailer who lived on other people's worries."

"All right: laugh you old pillar of respectability," said Macdonald. " I've said this before and I'll say it again—just as soon as a society tolerates private vengeance, that society is allying itself to Nazism and opening an avenue for every abuse which exists."

"I know, I know—and don't think I disagree with you," said Jenkins, " but let a man have his joke."

Reeves sat regarding his superior officers with a thoughtful air, and Jenkins said, " A penny for your thoughts, young fella-me-lad."

"Well, if you want an honest answer, I'd like as big a helping of roast beef and Yorkshire pudding as I could put down," said Reeves, " but since I'm not likely to get any-thing nearer to it than what's *called* sausages I'll say this: murder's murder and once a chap's been murdered I'm out to get the other chap who did the murdering, and that's all there is to it."

"And quite right, too," said Jenkins soberly.

ii

Macdonald sat writing his report after the other two had left his office, wondering as he wrote what the Assistant Com-missioner would make of Ross Lane's evidence when a message came through that a witness had called asking to see the officer responsible for the Regents Park case.

"Man of the name of Veroten—says he couldn't call earlier in the day on account of his job. Looks like a fat man at the fair," reported the officer on duty below.

"Send him up. I want a little light relief," said Macdonald.

Mr. Veroten was duly sent up and entered the door just ahead of a constable. The latter was a stout massive fellow well on into his fifties but for once he looked slim. The witness called Veroten was fat to the verge of the ridiculous, a tall, preposterously cylindrical creature with rosy cheeks and yellow hair, and a smile which switched on an off with disconcerting swiftness.

"Sit down, Mr. Veroten. I have been working on this case for fourteen hours already to-day," said Macdonald. "If you have anything of value to say, my time is at your service. If not, you may end by wishing you hadn't come here. What about it?"

"I think I am justified in asking to see you, Inspector," boomed the yellow-haired man. "I will put my evidence briefly. Yes, briefly. I am an artiste, employed by the Flodeum Company, songs and patter with a juggling act. My turn at the Surrey Met precedes that of a couple known as Rameses."

"I see," said Macdonald—who also saw some prospect of the 'light relief' he desired. "I have not seen your show, but I have had a private view of Mr. Rameses practising . . . prestidigitation, shall we say?"

"Practising my hat," said Mr. Veroten. "The man has no more finesse than a rhino—but let that pass. It came to my ears that inquiries were being made about Mr. Rameses' presence on the stage on Thursday evening. As you may guess, being, as I can see, a man of intelligence, such inquiries, though made in private, spread rapidly in a company such as ours. The whole company is discussing the matter."

"I can well believe it," said Macdonald. "Your manager has assured me that Mr. Rameses performed his act between eight and nine o'clock as usual on Thursday evening."

"Meaning his act was performed," said Mr. Veroten with a rapid wink. "Now I, sir, was in a position to see more than most on this occasion. I told you that my act came earlier in the programme than the Rameses'. Between my act and theirs is a dancing turn—a very pretty little turn done by a very pretty little girl." Here Mr. Veroten winked again and his lightning smile flashed on. "I tell you this to explain my presence in the wings, Inspector. I stood there to watch this dancing turn.

Just as it was over, I saw Rameses standing beside me. As you may have heard theirs is a costume turn—Egyptian costume, very elaborate indeed. When they are made up the pair resemble mummies or dead Pharaohs, with bronze-green faces and pretentious headdresses. I tell you, Inspector, I assure you, that no average person could have recognised those two when they are made up. Actually you can't tell if they're going or coming, because they wear masks on the back of their heads at times and get a laugh by turning round and round so that the audience doesn't know which is which or what is what. Now I ask you, how can anybody—any average person—swear to an identity in those conditions?"

"It must be very difficult," said Macdonald solemnly: he was enjoying this conversation. "Assuming that *you* are not an average person, Mr. Veroten, could you swear to Mr. Rameses' identity during his act?"

The fat man puffed out his cheeks, winked rapidly and held up an incredibly fat pink podgy hand as though for inspection.

"You listen to me, sir," he said earnestly. "There are more ways of identifying a man than by his face. Yes, sir. I am an artiste and my hands are part of my stock in trade. Same with Rameses: I don't call his stuff high-class: very poor some of it is, but he's got skilful hands. Yes. I'll admit that. He's got skilful hands. He insures them—for he'd be in the soup without his hands."

"He certainly would—up to the neck in it," agreed Macdonald and the other winked again.

"You're a man of great perception, Inspector. You'll understand the point I'm going to make. I stood in the wings beside this Rameses. I noticed he was fidgeting—and that's unusual because he can stand as still as a graven image. He does a deception stunt along those lines—sits as still as a statue, but this time he was fidgeting. Now I happened to glance at his hands. Ever seen Rameses' hands, Inspector?"

"Yes, I have. He's got remarkable hands with very supple fingers, and double-jointed thumbs."

"Quite right," beamed the other. "It's a pleasure to speak to you, Inspector. Now I wonder if you can go any further. Can you tell me any way in which you could identify those hands of Rameses?"

"I think I could identify them anywhere," said Macdonald, and the other went on:

"Maybe you could, but I wonder if you noticed that Rameses had a wart on his right hand—on the back of it, just below the knuckles."

"Yes. That's quite true," said Macdonald, and the other went on gleefully:

"Excellent! excellent. Now believe me, Inspector, on that Thursday night when Rameses stood beside me in the wings, he had *not* got a wart on his right hand."

"Perhaps he had had it removed: it's quite simple to have a wart burnt off," said Macdonald, interested to see how far his visitor's intelligence went.

Mr. Veroten winked rapidly. "True. True. In fact he has had it burnt off. It's gone. Yet though you saw his wart on Friday morning, Inspector, the hand I saw fidgeting with Rameses' robe on Thursday night had got no wart on it. It wasn't Rameses' hand, Inspector."

Macdonald sat very still and looked hard at the pink shining face of his obese visitor. "You had better think this out very carefully, Mr. Veroten," he said. "It is a very serious allegation you are making. It's one thing to make a statement light-heartedly, it's quite another to repeat it on oath. You know what perjury means?"

"Yes, Inspector. I know. Anyway, it's my word against any one else's. I saw Rameses' hand—and the wart wasn't on it on Thursday night. You say you saw it—on Friday morning that'd be? I heard Ladybird singing your praises on Friday afternoon. She's a talker, that one."

Macdonald was thinking hard. If this evidence was true, it looked like settling this case out of hand—but was it true? Mr. Veroten described himself as doing a 'song and patter with juggling' act, and his turn preceded the Rameses' turn on the programme—that was to say Mr. Veroten's turn was not re-garded as such a valuable performance as the Rameses'. Con-sidering the two men, Macdonald guessed that Veroten would not be in the same street as that 'graven image,' Mr. Rameses. There was much bitter jealousy among variety players.

"There are other talkers to be reckoned with in addition to Mrs. Rameses," said Macdonald. "Have you ever heard an able counsel cross-examining a witness? They're very for-midable talkers, these learned gentlemen."

"Let 'em talk," said the other, with his lightning wink. "Think I'm likely to go back on you, Inspector? I shan't. What I saw, I saw."

"Other issues will be raised. Apparently you don't think highly of Mr. Rameses' skill, but it's not many people who could take his place on the stage and do his stuff sufficiently well to deceive everybody."

" Not many people, no—but Rameses has a son. Did you know that, Inspector? Well, you ask."

" I will," said Macdonald, " and meanwhile, there are one or two things I should like to ask *you*, since you've been so obliging as to come and see me. About those masks you mentioned : are they the usual theatrical properties you can buy at the dealers?"

" No. Nothing of that kind. They're very remarkable productions, that I'll admit—life-like. Rameses won't say where he got them. Personally I believe he made them. He's as clever as hell in some ways. He's got a pair for himself and his missis that were made from casts of their own faces. He can put that mask on on the stage before a gaping audience without 'em ever seeing him do it. One second it's not there, next second it is—and once he's got it on, you can't tell which way he's facing. Damned funny : childish, but funny all the same."

" I'm sorry that I haven't seen the Rameses doing their act," said Macdonald. " I can imagine I should get my money's worth. Can you tell me where Mr. Rameses keeps his masks, Mr. Veroten? Would they be in the dressing-room at the Surrey Met?"

" I can't tell you, Inspector. I've never been into their dressing-room. As a rule variety artistes are a friendly lot—matey and generous. You may know it's difficult to buy make-up materials now—very difficult. Generally speaking, if I'm short of a liner or cream somebody obliges if I mention it—just as I should in the case of a fellow artiste—all friends together is our motto."

" Yes : all things in common—like the early Christians," observed Macdonald, and Mr. Veroten stared a moment.

" Ha ha !" he chuckled : " early Christians . . . very good indeed."

" But I gather the Rameses don't share this amiable attribute," went on Macdonald, and the fat man snorted—a fine loud snort which would have carried to the back of the pit, so that the attendant constable jumped in surprise.

" You're right, Inspector. Mean? You'd hardly believe the meanness of that man ! However, that's neither here nor there. You asked me about the masks. I don't think Rameses keeps them in his dressing-room. He sets great store on those masks. They're made of some queer plastic—rubbery, so that the masks aren't rigid like the usual stage properties. I should say Rameses takes 'em home with him in that case he always carries about."

" Does he take his make-up box home with him, too?" queried Macdonald innocently, and the other replied:

" Believe me, that's just what he *does* do. Suspicious, that's what he is. I hate suspicious characters. All out of place in the profession."

" Yes—open-handed friendliness such as yours seems more becoming," said Macdonald gravely, and Veroten stared, his mouth open to reply, but Macdonald went on: " I'm afraid I shall have to keep you here for a little while, Mr. Veroten, just until the main part of your statement is typed, and then you can sign it. Booker " (turning to the constable) " take Mr. Veroten to the waiting-room and send me a typist."

The fat man, looking distinctly less happy than he had done a moment ago, was ushered from the room. Macdonald, after a glance at his watch, (it was now half-past ten) took up his telephone receiver and put a call through to a number on the Flaxman exchange.

" Is that Mr. Borrington,. the Flodeum manager? Chief Inspector Macdonald speaking. Could you put me in touch with somebody who has enough knowledge to swear authoritively that Mr. Rameses' act last Thursday could not have been performed by anybody other than Rameses himself?"

" Good God! Are you still barking up that tree? I tell you I'm fed up with all this nonsense. Rameses *was* doing his stuff on Thursday. Look here, tell you what. I'll send you old Potter. Potter does the lighting effects for Rameses, and has to synchronise his changes with the act. Potter knows Rameses' stuff backwards. To-morrow morning do? He lives out Morden way."

" To-morrow morning will do. Thanks very much," said Macdonald, and as he hung up the receiver Constable Booker reappeared. " Got the gist of that statement,. Booker? Good. You'd have made your fortune as a Press reporter—terse and to the point. What did you make of Mr. Veroten, Booker?"

The constable scratched his thatch of greying hair absent-mindedly: he had been attached to Macdonald for years, and though he was one of the stupidest men in Cannon Row in many respects he had the native shrewdness of the real London Bobby—and he loved Macdonald with an almost maternal affection.

" If you ask me, sir, I'd say Veroten's a dirty dog. Jealous, that's what he is, trying to do the dirty on that Rameses. The awkward part of it is that it's going to be difficult to bowl him out over that wart story. Cunning it was: **very** cunning indeed."

"Very cunning," agreed Macdonald. "If it's true, that wart might hang Mr. Rameses. If it's not true, and I can prove it's not true, I'll see to it that Mr. Veroten loses some of his adipose before he's heard the last of it. However, apart from the wart, he gave us some interesting information. Those masks sound suggestive to my mind."

"You ought to go and see that Rameses, sir," said Booker. "'E's a marvel! I went when I was off duty this afternoon and 'e fairly got me moithered. Clever? you'd hardly believe it. Clever as the devil 'imself!"

"Well, well! Mr. Rameses is getting the attention of this department in more ways than one," said Macdonald, and Booker said:

"Seems to me if that Rameses wanted to murder anyone, he'd do it so neat no one'd ever guess how. I was almost frightened, sir—and it takes a bit to get me rattled."

It was at that moment that Macdonald's telephone rang and after a terse "Put him through," Macdonald said:

"Good-evening Mr. Rameses," and Booker's eyes goggled. "Well, I'll take your word for it, and I'll be along with you shortly," said Macdonald. He turned to Booker. "Would you like to see Mr. Rameses in private life, Booker? It won't be much like fun for you—waiting about, probably in the dark, while I do the chatting."

"Would I like . . .? Not 'arf! Yes, sir. Thank you, sir," said Booker.

CHAPTER TWELVE

i

IT WAS very dark when Macdonald turned his car under the arch at Cannon Row and set out westwards. Booker, sitting in front, was glad that it wasn't his lot to be driving in the murk of that solidly black November night. They went along Birdcage Walk, past Buckingham Palace and up Constitution Hill and Booker was glad to see the traffic lights at Hyde Park Corner: his eyesight was poor in the dark at any time, and it seemed to him that they were alone in the world—not a car on the road and nothing to break the blackness save the blur of a searchlight hazed by the London mist. Marble Arch, then a left turn at the Bayswater Road, then a right turn and Booker was lost again in the dark maze of streets near Notting Hill.

Just as the car slowed down in Belfort Grove the sirens sounded, wailing in hideous cacophony.

"The bastards!" muttered Booker, (he had never got over his dislike of sirens) and he heard Macdonald's placid voice inquiring:

"Which, Booker—sirens or Jerries?"

"Both, sir," replied Booker, somehow glad of the unruffled calm in the other's voice as he got out and stood in the blackness.

"Five steps up here—steady on," said Macdonald, grabbing Booker's tunic as that worthy turned blindly away from number five as the first guns thumped in the distance.

"Hullo, we've got company," said Macdonald, and a shrill cheerful voice replied from the neighbourhood of the front door: "So it's you again. Can't say I'm glad to see you cos I can't see you, but you're welcome. Someone's left the front door open. Silly the way they all loses their heads. Ought to be used to Wailing Winnie by now."

It was Mrs. Maloney, just come home after her evening "usual."

"Now that's funny—bulb must have gone," she went on conversationally, and Macdonald heard the click as she worked a switch up and down: "That bulb was all right when I went out," she continued, and a heavy thud shook the ground and set the doors vibrating. "Oh, go on, you!" she said contemptuously, as though addressing the distant explosion, "take more'n you to frighten me."

Macdonald had let go Booker's arm, and they were standing on the doorstep when the Hyde Park guns roared out.

"Go on! Give 'em beans!" said the undaunted voice as Macdonald went inside and put his hand in his pocket for his torch. At that second he was aware, amid the racket of the guns, that someone had run across the hall of the house to the open door and Booker gave a sudden grunt and a heavy thud told its own story.

"Be damned!" exclaimed Macdonald, believing that he had brought out an elderly constable to get him killed by shrapnel on a doorstep in Notting Hill. "Booker, are you there?"

"Here sir," grunted a voice from the pavement. "'E landed me one in the wind . . ."

"And he's gone with the wind, too," said Macdonald, whose quick ears had caught a sound of running footsteps during a second's lull. "Can you manage, Booker? I can't show a light until the door's shut."

"O.K., sir," grunted the constable and Macdonald guessed

108

from the sounds that followed that the heavy fellow was mounting the steps on all fours to avoid tripping up again. Mrs. Maloney's voice chirupped on:

" It's one o' them from upstairs. Always runs when the guns go. Dippy I call it. I wouldn't demean meself like that."

A second later Macdonald closed the front door and switched on his torch.

" Now we're all cosy," shrilled Mrs. Maloney. Her hat was very much askew and her cheeks flushed. " Well—I'll be off to me bed. Don't 'old wiv late hours."

" I say, hadn't you better stay downstairs until things are a bit quieter?" shouted Macdonald, but she shrilled back with gusto:

" Not me. Take more'n that 'Itler to keep me out of me bed. I'm not going to get meself killed running out to no shelters—like that silly boob as did a bolt just now. Put me 'ead under the clothes and takes no notice. Good-night all!"

A line of light from a cautiously opened door seemed to throw a brilliant illumination on the dreary lobby and a deep voice inquired:

" Is that you, Chief Inspector? Rameses here. Sorry to have brought you out in this racket."

" Not at all. We ought to be used to it," replied Macdonald. " I'll bring my man inside—he'll feel more cheerful somewhere with a light on. The fact is he doesn't like air-raids."

" Don't blame him. Damn' silly business it all is—like small boys chucking stones," said Rameses. " There's a cup of tea if he'd like one—and something in it."

A moment later Macdonald was sitting in Mr. Rameses' practice room, while Booker occupied a chair in the little lobby and gratefully accepted a cup of tea (which smelled pleasantly of rum) from the illusionist who had " nearly frightened him " that afternoon.

" Like a cup yourself, Inspector?" inquired Rameses and Macdonald said:

" Thanks. I should. It's against regulations—but on occasions like this regulations seem silly."

" Silly? You've said it. Everything looks silly—and the silliest thing of all is for a chap like you with first-class brains and physique to be bothering about who killed Johnnie Ward last Thursday. However—if you're still interested I've got a few things to tell you."

" Good. I'm like Mrs. Maloney—at least I try to be," replied Macdonald. " I decline to be put off ' by *'im* '."

" That old woman's pure gold," said Rameses unexpectedly.

" I hope for her sake she'll go out with a direct hit, knowing nothing at all about it—and if there's anything in the philosophy of any religion at all she ought to wake up in her own idea of heaven. That may be nothing to do with your case, Inspector, but I admire courage when I see it, and by the lord, I lift my lid to her!"

Sitting as immobile as some squat Buddha, Mr. Rameses regarded Macdonald with mournful inscrutable eyes while the London barrage roared overhead. There were shutters at the windows, and the heavy curtains—which quivered now and then—helped to reduce the racket so that Rameses' deep slow voice sounded distinctly against the muffled clamour.

" There have been some damned funny things going on in this house, Inspector," he went on. " Whether they're due to people inside the house or outside it, I don't pretend to know, but you may as well hear about them. Incidentally, have you had a visit from an outsize in fat boobs, a yellow-haired son-of-a-gun named Veroten? Thought so," he added, before Macdonald had made any reply at all. " That bloke's asking for trouble—and he'll get it in God's good time. Now I take it you've been round this house and know the amenities—including the storage-room downstairs." He paused a second, staring with his unwinking eyes. " The old lady didn't split," he went on. " She's a rare one to hold her tongue and she's taken a fancy to you. I don't know if you've gone through all the junk down there—but someone has."

" No. I haven't gone through it all," said Macdonald. " I didn't open any of your boxes, for instance."

" So I imagined. If you're anything like the chap I take you for you'd have done it more neatly than the merchant who did do it . . . That one was somewhere close Marble Arch way," he added. There had been a thud and reverberation which told of a near-by " incident " and Macdonald moved his cup farther on to the table for safety as the saucer bounced a little on the bare wood. When he looked at Mr. Rameses again he thought at first that the " something " in the tea had affected his vision. The man's face had completely changed: in place of the high shining forehead with shinning hair brushed back from the temples was a low bumpy forehead fringed with thick oily hair, and the chin had coarsened and thickened, while the black eyes seemed to protrude under bushy eyebrows.

" Look out! look out! it's coming," wheezed a voice behind Macdonald as another thud shook the room. For the life of him he could not help looking round, and when his eyes sought

Rameses' face again the illusion had passed, and the stolid melancholy-eyed Rameses faced him as before.

"Look here," protested Macdonald. "If you *must* practise your technique, will you kindly wait until the All Clear goes. I'm willing to regard air-raids as all in the day's work, but if you throw Guy Fawkes stuff in too, I'm liable to lose my temper. Now about that mask——?"

"Yes, about this mask," said Rameses, holding the thing up by its black wig. "What do you bet me that if that young Bruce Mallaig had been in here when that last bit of iniquity exploded somewhere in Kilburn, he'd have identified the man he saw on the bridge in Regents Park?"

"We can ask him about it later on," said Macdonald, "for the moment will you kindly tell me just what you're getting at?"

"Right. There's a storage room below and I keep some of my properties there—including this mask and a few others. Somebody has been through the boxes in which I keep the masks. Somebody has had this one out and put it back out of its place. Nothing to make a song about, is it?—nothing stolen, nothing broken."

There was a second's pause, and Macdonald was so much interested in what Rameses was going to say next that he didn't even notice the guns."

"Nothing to make a song about," went on the melancholy voice. "I heard the evidence at the Inquest—Ward was killed by somebody who got behind him so quietly that even the man under the bridge didn't hear a footstep. A face was seen in the matchlight—a dark heavy face with bulging eyes. Now how could you get behind a man so quietly that another just below the boards of the bridge didn't hear a footstep? By avoiding footsteps, eh? You've looked in that cupboard of mine downstairs. What did you see? There's a stage cycle down there. Don't tell me you didn't see it."

"Yes, I saw it—because I looked for it," said Macdonald.

"Yes, you've got the wits to see the connection," growled Rameses. "The bike, and then this——" dangling the mask. "Both mine . . . and I've only got one neck, same as other folks . . . and that fat buffoon is cooking up some story about my show on Thursday night. Says I didn't do my own stuff. Says my boy did it. My boy's in the Commandos . . . got a week's leave after coming out of hospital. There it is. If I know an honest man when I see one, I'd say you're an honest man. That's why I'm telling you. Matter of common sense. If you took me before a jury to-morrow with only the evidence

III

I've given you to-night I should be committed for trial. I see that."

"Yes. I see it, too," said Macdonald. "I take it you're pleading ' not guilty——' "

"Pleading? I'm not pleading anything. I've seen men shot: I've seen men stabbed. I've seen a knife thrown so that it slashed a man's wind-pipe and cut through his jugular—but I've never killed a man yet, nor done any dirty trick I've cause to be ashamed of. I've played the clown—on stage and off. I've laughed and made crowds laugh and I'm proud of the skill I've worked to attain. Plead?—the word makes me mad. . . ." The man's voice was extraordinarily impressive: low and deep, it rumbled on and yet the words were curiously distinct against the background of gunfire. Macdonald was hard put to it to find an answer—and then came an interruption, as someone hammered on the outer door.

ii

It was true that Constable Booker disliked air-raids, but it was the actual shriek of the sirens which penetrated to his nervous system, and as the raid went on he became more and more phlegmatic in the face of danger. After he had put down that very comforting cup of tea he sat down in the dimly-lighted lobby of Mr. Rameses' flat and had a comfortable rest, reflecting that things might be much worse—he was well under cover, on the ground floor at that: Booker accounted himself lucky and even felt halfway towards a comfortable nap. His heavy head was showing a tendency to nod when his ears—which were still on the alert—picked out a different sound from the uproar without—someone was clattering down the stairs and running across the entrance hall of the house. "The old girl's got the wind-up after all," he thought, and then realised that someone was banging on the Rameses' front door. He opened it and saw Mrs. Maloney, her grey hair in curlers on one side and straggling down to her shoulders on the other.

"Now don't you get worked-up, mum. Things is quieting down nicely," said Booker.

"*Me*, worked-up? an' you the Bobby that fell down my front steps in a funk?" she retorted. "You look after your own business, and I'm telling you it's not sitting in an easy chair on the ground floor you ought to be. There's something 'appening upstairs in the late lamented's flat—sounds like 'e's come back and is makin' a real old racket. 'Eard 'im through the guns an' all I did."

" What's that you're saying, Mrs Maloney?" inquired Macdonald who had come out into the lobby, and she said joyfully:

" You come and listen yourself, sir—you're the one to settle this. Not 'im " (indicating Booker): " not safe on 'is feet, 'e isn't. You come upstairs and listen. Bombs I don't mind, but ghosts I never did fancy, and if so be Mr. Johnny Ward's rumpusing about up there, 'tis no place for me to be."

" I'll come up," said Macdonald, and began racing up the dark stairs, holding his torch half-covered in his hand. Booker made a spring after him, but Rameses was quicker: slipping past the constable he gained the stairs just behind Macdonald while Booker rushed behind and Mrs. Maloney panted in the rear shrilling breathless encouragement:

" Go for 'im—you're the one to do it," she shrilled.

Macdonald had just got to the bottom of the last flight when a crash sounded above his head which had certainly nothing to do with ghosts: there was a rending sound of cracking wood, and a rumble of plaster as the ceiling over his head came down in a shower of dust and pulverised fragments.

" That one's a dud," said Mr. Rameses calmly. " If it weren't none of us'd be left to chat on the stairs."

" It wasn't a bomb—not big enough," said Macdonald, as he shook the plaster from his head and shoulders. " It was either a shell or a good large hunk of shrapnel. I'll go on up—tell Mrs. Maloney to go and look after the basement——"

" Not me!" shrilled the old lady. " I don't mind bombs and bits, I'm goin' to see yer cop that ghost."

Macdonald began to negotiate the top flight, kicking aside the plaster fragments. He was shaking with laughter despite the racket of the guns. The whole situation had a quality between a farce and a nightmare and no ordinary common sense regulations seemed to apply. He doubted very much if ' the ghost ' had been anything more than the patter of shrapnel on the roof—but if old Mrs. Maloney were not afraid of sleeping on the top floor during an air-raid, Macdonald was not going to funk investigating her ghost for her, crazy though the whole proceeding seemed. He reached the top floor and found the door of Ward's flat, remembering that he had still got the key in his pocket. Rameses was just behind him, and Booker's voice panted:

" 'Ere, you stand back. This is none of your business," as he endeavoured to elbow the " illusionist " farther back on the narrow landing. Macdonald found the door was unlocked, but it refused to give to the pressure of his shoulder. Turning his torch upwards, he saw that there was a bolt on the top of the door . . . had that bolt been there before, he wondered? . . . and as he drew it back another crash resounded on the roof and more plaster came down.

" Incendiaries—heard that sort of thing before," said Rameses.

Macdonald got the door open at last, pushing back a heap of plaster and splintered wood. Rameses was right, he realised—incendiaries, somewhere in the bathroom. His torchlight showed him something else—a man's figure lying on the floor, pinned down by a beam which had fallen from the roof.

Rameses pushed in beside him. " I can help here . . . I'm as strong as both of you put together," he said, and bent to the beam.

iii

It was some minutes later that Macdonald and Rameses got the limp body down into the hall of the house. Booker had been sent to call up the Fire Post and Mrs. Maloney screeched like a banshee at the door of each flat while she opened the front doors with her own keys. The incendiary bombs had crashed through the top floor and reached the kitchenette on the second floor. Macdonald had to make up his mind quickly whether to act in his capacity as a Detective Officer or as a Civil Defence worker. He decided to deal with the casualty first and help the firemen second.

Rameses was as good as his boast—he was a phenomally strong man and he proved capable of lifting a beam with what seemed like half the roof on top of it so that Macdonald could get the limp body clear. Then, together, they carried the body down the stairs while smoke began to swirl round the upper part of the house. Whether their burden was a corpse or not Macdonald had not had time to decide, but his instinct was to get the man into safety. By the time they had reached the ground floor Mrs. Maloney had produced a stirrup pump and Mrs. Rameses—her hair more than ever resembling a home-made wireless set—was intent on helping to fire-fight.

" Give me the pails, dearie, and we'll have a real go at it," she said to Mrs. Maloney. " Not the first time I've played fireman. We had the big top alight one night we were in Rio—there's no elephants here, that's one thing. I never could manage elephants . . ."

" My God, Ladybird, come off it!" roared Rameses. " Here you—do what you like with this one, I'm going to stop my missus committting suicide," he shouted to Macdonald.

Booker had done his part well: he came panting up to Macdonald.

"'Phone's all right, sir. I got through to the Post. Fire engine and ambulance coming. I'll go up and see what I can do . . . Another wave of 'em coming over, the bastards . . . ought to get the old girl out of this."

Macdonald bent over the figure on the floor, his torchlight directed on to the pallid face. Stanley Claydon. "And what the devil you were doing in Johnny Ward's flat you'll probably never be able to tell us," said Macdonald—and heard the clang of an ambulance bell outside.

"Quick work," he said to the volunteers. "This chap has probably got a broken back . . . I haven't had time to find out."

"Right oh, we'll see to it," responded the man with the stretcher. "Any more casualties here? We're wanted further along. The N.F.S. chaps are just coming."

Stanley Claydon was carried out feet first as the firemen came in, and for the next few minutes Macdonald was busy going into every room in the house to make certain no one else needed assistance. When he came up the basement stairs again he heard a weird sound on the staircase. It was Mrs. Maloney, sitting on the bottom step, singing in a strange cracked voice, and an Air Raid Warden, who had just come in, was shouting:

"Now then, you've got to get out of this into the shelter along the road."

"Not me," yelled Mrs. Maloney, and Macdonald interposed:

"If you won't go quietly I'm going to carry you, Mrs. Maloney—stop in this house you shan't!"

He bent and lifted the old lady up as though she had been a child and she cackled with glee.

"Arms o' the law . . . well I'm blessed . . . Abraham's bosom."

"You stop being funny. I won't be called Abraham, not even by my friends," protested Macdonald. "Where's Mrs. Rameses?"

"Don't you worry about 'er. 'Er Birdie's doing the strong silent man I don't think. Can't carry two of us, can yer?"

Macdonald set her on her feet at the front door and listened for the next lull in the gunfire. He reckoned it was a hundred yards to the shelter.

"You stay here, old lady, and none of your jokes," he said. "My car's still there. It'll get you to the shelter faster than I can run—and this house is going to fall down any minute.

Now when I say ' jump ' you jump—straight into the car."

" All correc', Cap'n," she retorted, and at Macdonald's word she was down the front steps with the agility of a cat.

" You're a wonderful woman for your age," said Macdonald cheerfully. " Here we are: in you tumble—and don't let me find you've been up to any tricks when I come back. I want a nice long chat with you."

He pulled up at the shelter and hustled her in, left his car where it was and raced back to number five. No more bombs had fallen since the cluster of incendiaries came down, and the Fire Service seemed to have got things under control. At least, there was no big outbreak. At the front door Mr. Rameses was giving orders to his Ladybird:

" Right along there to the shelter and don't argue," he commanded. Macdonald raised his voice:

" I've just taken Mrs. Maloney along there. Won't you go and look after her—the poor old soul's all shaken up."

" Oh, that's different," said Mrs. Rameses cheerfully. " I'm always glad to oblige, but my husband . . ."

" I'll look after him," said Macdonald and steadied her down the steps.

" One thing, I never was frightened of the dark," she called back, " and if a girl was brought up to step dance on liberty horses she never loses her balance. . . ."

Her voice trailed off as she ran towards the shelter and Rameses said " Frightened? My God! I don't know what she *is* frightened of, barring burglars under the bed—and she could strangle any burglar with one hand. What's next on the programme? Go up and help the fire wallahs?"

" That's about it," said Macdonald.

CHAPTER THIRTEEN

i

" WHAT'S the time?" asked Mr. Rameses some time later, and Macdonald found that his wrist-watch was still intact.

" Half-past twelve—to-morrow in other words," he replied.

" ' To-morrow and to-morrow and to-morrow,
Creeps in this petty pace from day to day,
To the last syllable of recorded time;
And all our yesterdays have lighted fools
The way to dusty death '."

Amazingly, Macdonald thought that he had never heard those lines more impressively spoken—or more beautifully spoken, either. Drenched with water from the hoses, filthy, torn, Mr. Rameses stood in a fire-drenched room amid the reek of soaked charred furniture, his deep voice declaiming immortal lines with never a quiver in the superb bass. He turned to the window, from which glass and black-out had long since gone and stared out at the flickering skies, where a grim light shone on the under sides of the barrage balloons: " ' . . . have lighted fools the way to dusty death ' " he reiterated, half under his breath. " Can you beat it! You'd have thought he knew . . . there's many a fool found the way to dusty death this night."

" Don't stop here, old chap. If you want to spout poetry, go and do it in the shelter."

It was one of the N.F.S. officers who spoke. " This house may be standing to-morrow or it may not—so you get, while the getting's good."

Standing behind Mr. Rameses, he patted the massive shoulder. "Good old Samson!" he said. " I don't know who you are but you're a grand chap. Off with you! Our outfit's moving on, we're wanted south of the river. Get a move on! I'm evacuating this . . ."

Rameses chuckled: the unprintable words fitted his mood.

" All right—but I'm going to pick up some dunnage from my coop on the ground floor. What d'you think I sweated for? sheer goodness of heart? You think again. There's some tripe I don't want burnt."

" I give you three minutes then. Can't spare you, Samson, you might come in useful another day."

As they went down the reeking stairs the fireman spoke to Macdonald. "Who are you, by the way? You know your stuff."

" Inspector, C.I.D.," was the reply.

" Good God . . . and who's he?"

" Conjurer and illusionist, name of Rameses—knows *his* stuff, too."

" Cripes! I've met some odd couples on this job, but you two beat the band. See that Samson doesn't outstay his leave, Inspector. Three minutes I said—and I meant it."

" He won't lose me," said Rameses profound voice. " I'm the hangman's prize. He's here on a job. Funny, isn't it?"

ii

Macdonald followed Rameses into the flat on the ground

floor. Some of the ceiling had fallen down in the practice room and the place looked even more demented than before, but strangely enough the big brown tea-pot still stood intact on the table.

" Thank God!" said Mr. Rameses. " I'm as thirsty as hell. Tea for me—every time."

He poured out a cup of the cold dark liquid, and added some milk, saying " Help yourself . . . cold tea's a good drink."

Macdonald realised that he was very thirsty too and followed the suggestion. Mr. Rameses, having gulped down his tea, pulled a box from under the table and closed the catch carefully. It was the box which contained his masks. Seeing Macdonald's eyes on him he said:

" Most of the other tripe I can make again—but not these. There's nothing in the world quite like them . . . Wait a jiffy, I want something else." He darted across the passage and Macdonald followed, saying:

" Can I help. Time limit's running out."

" If you'd be so kind . . . these in your pockets . . . thanks, this lot over your arm . . . I'll take these . . . quick march. . . ."

To add the last touch of grotesqueness to a grotesque night, Macdonald found that his share in the final rescue act (probably made, he reflected, at the risk of both their lives to judge from the creaks of the old house) was the salvaging of Mrs. Rameses' silk stockings (in his pockets) and a quantity of her clothing (over his arm). Mr. Rameses had snatched the entire contents of a wardrobe, frocks, fur coats and trailing chiffons and thrown the lot over his shoulder.

" Never forget the wife," he boomed. " She'd have hated to lose this lot. Where are we going now? Condemned cell?"

" Not with these," said Macdonald, hitching up the trailing garments on his arm, and Rameses laughed—a laugh full of genuine amusement.

" You're a decent chap, Inspector," he said. " Whatever happens, I'll never bear you any resentment. Shake hands. We had a damned good show up there with those firemen."

Freeing his hand from some of Mrs. Rameses' garments, Macdonald shook hands. " Well played, Samson," he said, " and now I think we'd better go and see how many of the party are in the shelter."

" The shelter, eh? Well, I haven't heard the All Clear go yet," said Mr. Rameses. " I expect we shall find some of them there."

" I shall be very disappointed if we don't," said Macdonald.

As they went out of the front door of the house (it was jammed and would no longer shut) they saw a small group standing on the pavement. Booker was there, a Civil Defence man and a Special Constable. The guns still sounded in the distance, but it was almost eerily quiet after the preceding uproar.

" That was a good bit of work," said the Civil Defence man. " I thought the whole crescent would burn out—and no casualties to speak of."

" We're not through with the night's work yet," said the Special. " If I know anything about Jerry we shall have another wave of 'em over—it'll be H.E. next time."

" Always look on the bright side, as the devil said when he raked up the ashes a bit," boomed Mr. Rameses, and the Civil Defence man chuckled.

" What I'm really dying to know is if old Sam Stillman's got his back door open along at the Duke of Clarence. He's a lad is Sam—open house to the Civil Defence on nights like this. He's saved my life before now."

" Fancy you drawing my attention to a thing like that—I should have thought you'd more sense," chuckled Booker. He'd got over " that siren feeling " and was his cheerful self again. He drew nearer to Macdonald.

" You'll find them all in the shelter, sir—the old lady and Mrs. Rameses, and Miss Odds and ends and the gent from the first floor. He's looking poorly, poor old chap."

" Right. I'm going to join the shelter party myself," said Macdonald. " The wardens will tell me if there's any more excitement."

" You're going to the shelter, sir?" asked Booker, as though he couldn't believe his ears.

" That's it. You can go back to the Yard if you like, Booker. You're on duty there by rights."

" I'd like to stop and see it through here, sir," said Booker, and Macdonald laughed.

" As you like. If the All Clear goes come and report to the shelter."

Macdonald turned along the pavement, with Mr. Rameses beside him.

" Pity you're so well known, Inspector. If a Special turned his torch on us we might get run in for looting. I should enjoy that—getting run in for saving my wife's clothes. Once a clown, always a clown. I've spent my sinful life enjoying the comedy of the ironic."

" I know just what you mean," said Macdonald, " though I couldn't have put it so neatly myself."

Rameses paused as they reached the shelter, as though he were assessing the distant gun flashes, away to the north.

"You want to know what Turnip Face was doing in Johnny Ward's room," he said. "Someone locked him in. . . . Rum business. They couldn't have *known* a dud shell would gag him for good. Pity he's a goner. It would have been interesting to hear his story. What d'you bet he'd have told you a chap called Rameses invited him to a party?"

Macdonald paused. "Anything you'd like to add to that?" he inquired. "I'm listening."

"Nix," said Mr. Rameses.

iii

Macdonald blinked in the bright light of the shelter: he lifted his load of clothing on to Mr. Rameses' other shoulder and saw the big stout man waddle away towards his wife—she was having a comfortable snooze in a corner. Mrs. Maloney was a little farther away, nursing somebody's baby. She grinned up at Macdonald when she saw him.

"Never been in one o' these places before. I like 'ome comforts," she said. "What about me feather bed? You didn't bring it along by any chance?"

"Sorry—I'm afraid I didn't: actually there wasn't anything left to bring, not even the smell of roast feathers. We shall have to get you a new one."

"I shan't never fancy a new one. 'Ad that one ever since I left the old 'ome. Tell me—was Potato Face dead—'im as played ghosts in Mr. Ward's flat?"

"I'm not sure. They took him off to hospital." Macdonald sat down beside the intrepid old lady. "How did he get up there, Mrs. Maloney?"

"Ain't I been asking meself just that ever since I saw 'im?" she replied. "'E wasn't in the 'ouse when I went out, that I'm certain. Quiet as the grave it was after you left. I finished me bit of work for Mrs. Rameses and made a nice cup-er-tea in her kitchen—that's by arrangement, I'd tell you, me not bein' given to liberties—then I went upstairs to posh meself up a bit, seein' I was expecting to meet me boy friend as old Sam Stillman says. About 'alf past six it was when I went upstairs, but I left me door open—so's I could 'ear if you come back again. I thought we 'adn't seen the last of you."

"Very thoughtful of you," said Macdonald, and she went on:

"I should 'a been glad to see you, too. It was that quiet.

No one in the 'ouse at all—that was along o' you, wasn't it?
She and me's been 'aving a nice quiet chat."

She nodded towards Mrs. Rameses. "And nobody recker-
nised nobody, in spite of all your trouble," she added sympathetically. "Potato Face—'e was the one that 'id under the
bridge, wasn't 'e? I saw 'im at that Inquest. Wonder what
'e did it for? Well, *as* I was saying, I went up to me room and
changed into me black what I was given after me friend died
and I 'ad a bit of supper—tinned salmon. That reminds me:
'alf a tin was left and that's on points that is. That an' me
feather bed. Can't be 'elped. Then I started worrying about
me keys. I'd never worried about 'em before—just popped
'em in the tea-pot and trusted to luck. This time I 'id them
under me feather bed."

"But you lock your room when you go out?"

"I do and I don't. The lock ain't no good. Won't catch,
some'ow. I'd meant to get it seen to, but it's too late now.
Them locks in that 'ouse is a poor set-out—done cheap.
It's like this," she went on confidentially. "That lock on me
door was all right till Johnnie Ward went and got 'isself done in
—I'd 'ad a bit o' trouble with it at times, but it did. I wouldn't
'a left my door open when Mr. Ward was in the 'ouse. Com-
munist, 'e was. 'E'd 'elp 'isself to anything, I knew that—
but these others they're honest. I'll say that for them. There's
Mr. and Mrs. R. over there—never met the like of them, but
decent, I'll say that for 'em. No pokin' their noses into what's
not theirs. Then there's that Odette Grey as she calls 'erself.
Stuck up, and a face wot'd have made Jezebel die for envy,
but she'd never go pinching nothing. I know her sort: come
from a good 'ome, she did. 'Er pa's a grocer out Waltham
way. She's mean and she'd let anybody stand 'er a drink to
save 'er paying for it, but she'd never do no pokin' or pinchin'.
See 'er sitting over there doin' 'er face up—she'll be busy doin'
that when the last trump sounds, but she's got 'er good points.
Then there's that Carrinford. See 'im over there? I reckon
'e was the one knocked your copper flat on the doorstep. 'E
always foots it when the siren goes. Blue funk. Looks shocking, don't 'e? I always say 'e'll frighten hisself into 'is grave.
Got a weak 'eart, 'e says. ' You and yer weak 'eart,' I said
to 'im once when 'e ran past me in the 'all. ' I know what's
weak about you—you can't take it. Why can't yer take it in
your stride, same's Churchill and the rest of us? ' I says—
but I know 'e wouldn't demean 'isself comin' up to my room
pinching keys. Besides, 'e wouldn't 'ave the spunk." She
drew a deep breath and concluded " So if the key on me door

wouldn't turn proper, I didn't worry. I knew it was O.K. with all of them—besides, who'd 'a wanted to go into Johnnie Ward's room?"

" In any case, I've got the keys of that room," said Macdonald.

" Oh, maybe you 'ave—but Miss Willing's key opens that door. I found it out by accident and I didn't say nothing because Mr. Ward's key wouldn't open Miss Willing's door. I wonder where she is? 'Ope she's all right. She's one o' the best, Miss Willing is."

" You remember before I could open Mr. Ward's door this evening, I had to draw back a bolt at the top of it, Mrs. Maloney? Was that bolt always there?"

" Now you're askin'. I been wondering about that. Maybe it was, because that was only an old cupboard door done up—I told you they did things cheap in that house. I never used the bolt, and I can't say as I'd ever seen it before—but it stands to reason it must 'a been there all along. What's the sense of putting a bolt on that door?"

" To lock someone in."

" Jiminy . . . did someone do 'im in first before . . . No, that don't make sense. When I went up to bed, there wasn't no one in the 'ouse barring Mr. and Mrs. R., and you wiv 'em."

" How do you know?"

" If there's a raid on, I often goes in to Miss Willing in case she likes a bit o' company and a cup o' tea, and I went down into Miss Grey's room in case she'd left 'er light on. She's done that before, and 'er blackout's not all that. I just pops in to see it's O.K. I knocks first of course—wouldn't do to let 'er know I pop in and out. I knew Mr. Carringford was out—it was 'e 'oo knocked the Bobby down. I know the way 'e pants —so you see there wasn't no one in the 'ouse, and that's why I got the jimmies when I 'eard Johnnie Ward's ghost—knocking awful, 'e was. Sorry I didn't go in now—but I don't 'old with ghosts."

" What time was it that you went out this evening?"

" Just after eight—and there wasn't nobody in then, that I'll swear. I should 'a 'eard the front door open, 'cos I was listening." She paused and then asked suddenly, " Are yer married?"

Macdonald was surprised. " No—and not likely to be."

" Well, you do surprise me. Good 'usband wasted, that's what you are. D'you want an 'ousekeeper? Seems to me I've lost me job at Number 5."

"We'll soon fix you up for a job," said Macdonald and she replied:

"Oh, I'm not afraid of being out of a job—they'll queue up for me at the Labour Exchange, but I've taken a fancy to you, some'ow."

"Thank you very much—very kindly put," said Macdonald. "Now while I've got the chance I'd better go and have a word with Miss Grey and Mr. Carringford."

"Rightey oh. See you later," she replied cheerfully.

iv

Miss Odette Grey was feeling distrait. Although the noise of the guns was dulled by the shelter walls, it was evident enough that the second wave of bombers prophesied by the Special Constable had come over, and Miss Grey felt she'd had as much as she could stand.

"I wish I hadn't come into this place: I ought to've stayed in the tube," she complained.

"What time did you get home? Before the sirens went, I expect," said Macdonald.

"Of course—or I shouldn't be here," she replied querulously. "I got in at ten o'clock. I'd just got into bed when the sirens went and I got up and dressed as I always do, though I hoped it'd be over quickly. Then when it got so awful I came out here. I do hope Miss Willing's all right. She got in before I did and she was just going out again to see a friend who's ill . . . oh goodness, I do wish they'd leave off. I'm fed up with it. . . ."

Macdonald persisted tactfully: "People feel better if they talk, you know. It's sitting listening that's so upsetting. When you got home this evening, do you think there was anybody else in the house? Did you hear anybody moving about?"

"I know the Rameses were in," she replied. "I told you—just as I opened the front door Miss Willing came out. I couldn't see her because the light in the hall had gone and my torch had given out, but she said 'Who's that?' and I told her . . . I'm sure they're coming nearer. . . ."

"Only our guns," said Macdonald patiently. "I want to find out if there were anybody in the house when you came in because somebody got up into Mr. Ward's flat this evening."

"Goodness! Whatever for? I'm going to move away from that house, I can't stand it any longer . . . (That one *was* farther away, wasn't it?) If you want to know if anybody else

123

was in the house, ask Mr. Rameses. Someone came to see him just before I came in."

" How do you know that?"

" Because Miss Willing told me. She let him in. She was in a hurry to get to see her friend and she said to me ' I've just let a fellow in who wants Mr. Rameses. If he's still in the hall, show him the right door. I've got to rush.' I said ' Let me have your torch then. Mine's died on me and the light's gone in the hall.' I didn't fancy going into the house all in the dark with a strange man in the hall. She gave me her torch, but there was no one in the hall when I went through. I knew the Rameses were in because I could see the light under their door and I could hear them moving about—making an awful row."

" What sort of row?"

" Oh I don't know—pushing things about. They're awful people—really common."

" I shouldn't call Mr. Rameses common," murmured Macdonald. " I think he's the most uncommon person I've ever met. Tell me—did you stand in the hall for a minute or two, wondering what the noise was?"

" Yes, I did," she admitted. " So'd you have, if you'd been me. It's enough to give a girl the shivers to go into that dark house those days. I hate going upstairs by myself. I wanted someone to talk to," she went on in a burst of confidence. " I thought of knocking at the Rameses' door to ask what the time was—anything rather than be all by myself. I never used to be nervous, but these days I'm all of a jitter. When I first went to that house, Mirette Duncan was in the flat next to mine, but she's gone touring with Ensa. Miss Willing's all right—but I knew she was out, so there was only the Rameses in, and that Mr. Carringford—he's about as cheerful as the British Museum."

" Are you sure he was in the house?" asked Macdonald and she retorted tartly:

" No, of course I wasn't, but anyway he didn't count. Mrs. Rameses may be common, but at least she's cheerful, and if I'd said I was nervous she'd have come upstairs with me. But I went up by myself and turned the wireless on. I felt better once I'd got my light on—it was that dark hall made me nervous."

" Did you hear anything as you went upstairs, or was it quite quiet?"

" Apart from the row in the Rameses' flat it was quiet, and

once I'd turned the wireless on I didn't hear anything till the sirens went. Who was it in Mr. Ward's flat?"

"Someone who'd no business to be there," replied Macdonald.

"Is the house all right?" she asked.

"The top floor's burnt out and I'm afraid your flat's damaged a good deal—but it's not so bad as it might have been."

"Oh dear . . . I do hope I haven't lost all my clothes," she said mournfully. "I'd got some lovely things and you can't get anything now. . . ."

Macdonald left her to brood over her lost possessions between spasms of fear when the guns swelled to a crescendo—silk stockings and high explosive, an oddly assorted pair of thoughts. He went and joined Mr. Carringford, who was hunched up in a corner, his white head sunk between his shoulders.

v

"I'm sorry to bother you with questions: you're feeling pretty cheap, Mr. Carringford."

The other looked at him with sunken eyes. "D'you think the raid's going over? I can't stand much of this sort of thing. What about the house? Anything left of it?"

"Most of it was standing when I came away," replied Macdonald. "A few incendiaries got going—they went through the top floor and brought down the ceiling and beams, so it was difficult to deal with them. The top floor is burnt out. I'm afraid Miss Willing and Mrs. Maloney have lost everything."

"Anyone hurt?"

"The only casualty was a man who had got into John Ward's flat. He was hurt when the roof came down."

"John Ward's flat? Who the devil was in there—and how did he get there?"

"That's just what I want to know myself, and I'm trying to collect all the information I can. What time did you get in this evening?"

"Just before the sirens went. I opened my front door and went into the passage—and then that damned alert sounded. I came straight out here . . . that old house isn't safe. It'd tumble down as easy as a pack of cards. I can't stand the thought of being buried."

"I expect you passed me on the doorstep then: you knocked a police constable down the front steps as you ran. Did you realise that?"

Carringford shook his head. " No . . . I think you're mistaken. I didn't meet anybody on the steps. Were you in a car? It drove up just as I slipped out. There was someone behind me—I heard their footsteps on the stairs, running. Afraid I didn't wait to see who it was . . . My God, what's that. . . .?"

" That " was the last effort of a German bomber that night. The bomb fell in the roadway, halfway between number five Belfort Grove and the shelter. The blastproof walls stood up to the shock, but three old houses swayed, rumbled and fell: a clatter and uproar of falling bricks, cracking timber, breaking glass . . . clouds of dust and a reek of fumes: an Air Raid Warden poked his nose cautiously out of his sandbagged post: " That's that. Might have been worse. No one left in those houses . . . got 'em all out. . . ."

A few minutes later the All Clear screamed its message of relief to London's dauntless millions.

CHAPTER FOURTEEN

i

MACDONALD woke up unwillingly the next morning: he had had four hours of sleep and felt that he could have done with fourteen. He yawned and had an uncomfortable feeling that his lungs were still full of smoke: the reek of last night's fire seemed to hang about him. Then he realised that a thick fog brooded over London and he wished for a moment that he was anywhere else in the world—anywhere, away from fog and bombs and barrage and shelters and demolitions and all the rest of it. Then, as his brain cleared of sleep he found himself getting interested again. There was Mr. Rameses and his Commando son . . .; there was Stanley Claydon. still precariously alive: there were Mr. and Mrs. Ross Lane and there was Bruce Mallaig, Mr. Carringford and Rosie Willing—and Mrs. Maloney. Sitting up in bed and stretching, Macdonald began to laugh. He had done some odd jobs in his time, but finding a job for Mrs. Maloney was going to be funnier than most.

There had been some lively moments after the All Clear had gone last night: those who had been bombed-out of their homes were recommended to the Rest Centre—and a lively argument had developed. Odette Grey said she wasn't going to any Rest Centre.

" I'm going down the tube: I don't care if the All Clear's

gone or if it hasn't . . . I've lived through this and I'm not going to get done in . . . I'll go and get a job in the country somewhere to-morrow where there aren't any sirens. I'm going to get out of London if I have to walk. . . .''

Mrs. Maloney also declined a Rest Centre. '' Not me. I'm going to me friend Mrs. Stillman, she'll be glad of me—and I don't want no 'elp from no one. I never did like this 'ere ' community ' stuff.''

Mr. and Mrs. Rameses said they could go to their son and his wife. '' He's got a nice little house out Sudbury way, and if the Bakerloo's not running, we'll just wait on the platform until the first train,'' she assured Macdonald. '' I don't like the idea of these Rest Centres, I like to be independent and so does my Birdie.''

Mr. Carringford had said that he would go to his friend Mr. Hardwell. The authorities, who had quite enough homeless people to deal with, were far from anxious to dissuade those w..o had an alternative shelter from seeking it.

Macdonald yawned again after his contemplation on the dispersal of the tenants in number five and began to formulate his plans for the day. There was Rameses junior to see: there were the Ross Lanes: there was Rosie Willing. Mrs. Maloney had had a word about the latter. '' I never was no good at remembering names: she told me about 'er friend—name of Alice, but Alice what I can't tell you. Lives in one o' them Pembridges—dozens of 'em aren't there—but I'll tell you this —if so be Miss Willing's alive, she'll be at her the-ayter this afternoon. If she's been took, it don't matter to you where she is—Kensal Green or 'Ighgate makes no hodds.''

ii

It was between eleven and twelve that Macdonald arrived at the '' little house in Sudbury '' where Corporal Nightingale, son of Mr. and Mrs. Rameses, had made his home. The front door was opened by Mr. Rameses himself, with the clown's greeting on his lips—'' Here we are again.''

He closed the front door after admitting Macdonald and beckoned him into the little front sitting-room. The house was full of lively sounds: somewhere Mrs. Rameses was singing '' Somewhere a voice is calling '' (her own voice was unmistakable). Elsewhere another voice was singing '' There'll always be an England,'' and from upstairs a man's voice was rolling out '' Shenandoah.'' (It was a fine voice, Macdonald noted—undoubtedly the Commando son.) In a cage in the window canaries were singing. Mr. Rameses faced Macdonald squarely.

" You want to see my boy, to ask him about Thursday night. Well, you can. I tell you this straight. I haven't mentioned the matter to him. I don't know what he was doing, and he doesn't know anything about this Johnny Ward racket or that dam' fool Veroten. You're bound to believe that I've told him and warned him to give me a leg-up—but I haven't. I'll send him along to you."

A moment later Corporal Nightingale came into the room: he was a fine specimen physically—as are all the Commandos, a tall lithe dark fellow, with humorous dark eyes and something in the set of his head which marked him unmistakably as Rameses' son. He looked at Macdonald inquiringly:

" You want me? I don't know you, do I?"

" No. My name's Macdonald. I'm a Scotland Yard inspector, C.I.D."

" Cripes! What the hell do you think you want *me* for?"

" Only to answer some questions. I'm on a job, and your name has been mentioned by another witness. I want you to be good enough to tell me what you were doing on Thursday evening."

" That's easy. I went to see the old boy's show—my father, you saw him when you came in. He's a conjurer and all that. Cleverest old devil I've ever seen."

" So I've heard," said Macdonald. " I believe you can do a bit along the same lines."

Corporal Nightingale sat down and lighted a cigarette: there was something about his leisurely movements which reminded Macdonald more than ever of Mr. Rameses.

" Do you?" he replied. " Now perhaps you'd like to answer a question of mine before we go any further. Exactly why are you interested in my doings on Thursday night? I don't bear you any ill-will, in fact you seem a decent bloke, *but* I don't care for liberties—and it seems to me a bit cool for a C.I.D. man to walk into my home and ask me what I was doing on Thursday evening."

The deep voice was absurdly like Rameses' own and Macdonald couldn't help being amused, but his own voice was serious as he answered: " Yes, I can quite see that—but I've got justification for doing so because your evidence is very important. What *you* were doing on Thursday evening is going to matter a lot to the case I'm working on. It's been suggested that you took another man's place."

" It has, has it? You'd better go on and tell me the whole

story—otherwise I tell you straight you're going to be shown out of here pretty quick—no offence meant. They don't teach us to be patient in my present trade."

" That isn't quite true," replied Macdonald. " I happen to know a bit about Commando training, and if patience isn't achieved the rough stuff wouldn't serve its end. If you show me out of the door you'll be doing somebody else a very bad turn. I know you're justified in asking for a full explanation, but your evidence would be of much more value if you gave it on the strength of the explanation I gave you just now— that your name has been mentioned by another witness. I'm trying to be fair and I want an unbiased answer."

" You've got it, haven't you? I told you I went to see my father's show. If you won't say any more, I won't say any more."

" All right. Say if we have your father in, and tell him just how far we've got—and ask his opinion about it."

" I don't see that. He's had bother enough with being bombed out and all that without having Scotland Yard pestering him. . . ."

The young man broke off and stared at Macdonald, as though an idea had just percolated into his mind.

" I say, if you're trying to fix anything on my dad, you're for it."

" Why not do as I suggest and ask his advice? He's got more common sense than you have, because he's older and has more experience of life."

Again that deliberate stare and then the young man got up and went to the door.

" Dad," he shouted. " Come in here a minute."

Macdonald heard Mr. Rameses walk quietly across the little passage from the kitchen.

" I'm here, George. What is it?"

Macdonald answered, speaking to the son : " Tell your father exactly what I've said and see what advice he gives you."

George Nightingale drew his father into the room and then shut the door, standing with his back against it.

" This guy sails in and asks me what I was doing on Thursday evening, and I told him straight. He says it's been suggested I took another man's place. That made me a bit mad— sounds like hokey pokey. I asked him to come clean with the whole story and tell me what he was getting at, and he hands me out a lot of vague dope about getting an unbiased answer. I told him if he wouldn't tell me straight out what it was all about he could get out and stay out. Then he suggests I shall ask you to come in and give your opinion. What I say is, if he can't put his cards on the table, I've nothing to say to him. That's fair, isn't it?"

" Yes, it's fair enough, George—but you'd better see the cards and think again. They were dealt to me, so I've the right to call them. You just sit down and listen."

George sat down, on a little hard chair beside the door, his long legs seeming to stretch half across the little flowered carpet.

Rameses began: " There was a chap living in the top flat at Belfort Grove. Name of Ward. A lazy good-for-nothing son of a gun. I'd no interest in him except to see he didn't swindle me or sell Black Market stuff to your mother. On Thursday evening Ward was murdered—knocked over the head in Regents Park—8.30 it was when he got his ticket. The Inspector here comes along to our place to find out all that he can about Ward. He had to find out what everyone in the house was doing at the time Ward was killed. That's all right—if you've got laws in a country you've got to have police to see they're administered. The Inspector asked my management if I did my turn as usual on Thursday evening. The manager said that I did—but being a cautious chap he made a few inquiries. The story got round. There's a song and patter merchant who does a juggling turn early on in the show. He's see fit to put it around that I didn't do my own turn but that it was done by somebody else wearing my costume. Done by you, son. Now you know."

George sat still and swore, vigorously and persistently, uttering many strange colourful imprecations, most of them new to Macdonald, for the Commando brand of speech is peculiar to his own kind. Mr. Rameses cut in on the flow:

" Maybe—but all that's getting us nowhere. It's just waste of time. What were you doing on Thursday evening, George?"

" Me? I was at the Flodeum show, dad—the old Surrey Met, watching your turn to see if I could spot that stuff you did with the bananas."

" The hell you were!"

Then Rameses laughed. He laughed until his sides shook and tears ran down his wide cheeks.

" What's so funny about it?" growled George. " You diddled me every time, and I tell you I was watching you pretty close."

Mr. Rameses wiped his eyes. "And I never knew. You never told me you were there." He turned to Macdonald. " This just about puts the lid on it—puts the black cap on it. You'll never be able to prove anything now. George was there

. . . What did I say? The comedy of the ironic. I never knew he was there."

" What if I was?" shouted George. " Is this bastard going to say you committed a murder?—Say it!" He turned fiercely to Macdonald. " You just say it, and the . . ."

" That's not going to help, George. You use your wits." Rameses turned to Macdonald. " He's got some wits somewhere under that thick skin of his, though you mightn't think it. You tell him what happened to Ward on that bridge. You'll say it in fewer words than I shall—and you listen, son. Listen with your ears skinned and think it out."

Macdonald's statement was a model of brevity and clarity and when he had finished Rameses said:

" Very nicely put. Now then, George. How did the murderer get on to the bridge without his footsteps being heard by the man underneath? You think it out. I did. The Inspector did."

" Climbed a tree?" hazarded George.

" Won't wash. The Army's not improved your brains. The first witness saw the murderer's face, not in a tree, but just *above* Ward's standing there. Seems likely to me he was standing on the step of a bike or a scooter. Remember our cycling turn, George? The one we did in 'Frisco? Pretty wasn't it? We did a boxing turn on those bikes. I've still got that bike. Stored in the basement. The Inspector found it. He's thorough, and he's got some imagination." Rameses turned to Macdonald. " If I'd had you to train when you were a nipper I'd have made a good conjurer of you, Inspector. Better than George here. You've got more sense of detail."

George was silent now, his black brows contracted across his face so that he looked a younger replica of his father.

" Yes. I see," he said slowly. " I did your show for you, and you went to Regents Park to kill Ward, using your l'il old bike to stalk him. Very pretty. What did you kill him for, dad?"

" Search me . . . but that makes no odds. Ward was the type of skunk any man might be proud to kill. Perhaps he blackmailed me."

" But that bloke who saw everything said he saw the murderer's face," shouted George. " Was it your face he saw, dad?"

" No, son, but he gave a very good description of the face he *did* see: I reckon it was Ananias. Remember Ananias? I've got him here. Quite safe. Saved him from the fire along with your mother's silk pants and her best stockings. The

131

funny thing is somebody borrowed Ananias just lately and put him away upside down. No sense of detail. Well. That's the story. If it can't be proved I was doing my show, if there's the least doubt as to whether I was doing my show, then it's all handed to him on a platter like John the Baptist's head.'' He nodded towards Macdonald and George said:

" Sorry if I'm being slow but I want to get this straight. You went to Regents Park and I did your show. Without rehearsal. So that no one knew. Never a slip-up. Thanks very much everybody. No idea I was such a swell.''

Rameses chuckled. " Yes. You know that—but it'd take an expert to appreciate that little point.''

George stretched his long limbs and lighted another cigarette, slowly, contemptuously. He turned to Macdonald: " You're pretty smart. The dad says so, and he knows. You've only got one little bit wrong. I didn't do that show. I'm not up to it. Dad did his own stuff. I went to Regents Park and batted the bastard over the boko. I wasn't going to have my dad blackmailed. Killing folks so's they don't even notice is my long suit. I've been trained to it for four bloody years. Got that?''

" Well, I'm damned,'' said Mr. Rameses indignantly.

iii

" Now say if we all calm down a bit and ask Mrs. Rameses to make some tea.''

It was Macdonald who voiced this suggestion. For the past ten minutes Rameses and his son had been having an argument, and they had argued with a fury and verbosity which had left Macdonald almost speechless. Rameses had an extensive vocabulary and a capacity for non-stop exposition which rivalled his wife's when he got going. George had his own peculiar lingo, a mixture of Commando slang and Yankee back-chat which was incomprehensible to the average person. George stuck to it that he had been to Regents Park: having produced the statement he enlarged it and emphasised it until his father was roaring at him in exasperation. Then, quite suddenly, Rameses changed his tactics.

" You're a sanguinary liar, George. I did it myself. I killed Johnny Ward, with my little sword, I killed Johnny Ward. . . .''

It was at this juncture that Macdonald suggested a cup of tea, feeling that if the excitement continued at its present pitch, father or son—or both—would explode. Mr, Rameses heard the suggestion and performed another of his rapid *volte faces* and his voice modulated to the low bass murmur which Macdonald was always to connect with Macbeth.

"Tea? Not a bad idea. George, go and ask your mother for some tea. Three cups—and ask politely and tell her she's not wanted in here."

"Like hell I will," said George, "and leave you to tell the tale to the C.I.D. Likely." He opened the door and shouted: "Hi, Ladybird. He wants some tea. In here. Three cups. Sorry I can't come and fetch it but I daren't leave him. He's a shocking old liar."

"Tea?" chimed in Mrs. Rameses' fluty voice. "Coming, baby. I've got the kettle on. Quite a nice little chat you've all been having. Can I help?"

"No," roared father and son in unison. The tea was brought in by a smart young lovely whom Macdonald guessed was Mrs. George Nightingale.

"Glad you're enjoying yourselves," she said blithely. "If you make much more noise we shall have the police in."

There was a second's deathly silence and then Mr. Rameses said "Well, George, if you've forgotten your manners, allow me: my daughter-in-law, Mrs. Nightingale. Mr. Macdonald. This gentleman helped salvage your mother-in-law's best clothes last night, Belinda."

"Now wasn't that just sweet of him," she murmured. "Sorry I can't stay. George the second's in the coal-bucket."

Mr. Rameses applied himself to the teapot, stirring vigorously, and George turned nonchalantly to Macdonald.

"Going to arrest me?" he asked.

"No," replied Macdonald. "Not for the moment. I'm willing to accept one confession of guilt, but not two simultaneously. If you'll just get back to the matter in hand—which is version number one of your doings on Thursday evening—will you tell me which part of the house you were sitting in?"

"I wasn't in the house. I was in Regents Park."

"I wish you'd take your father's advice and use your wits," said Macdonald patiently. "You said you went in order to study his act and see if you could spot his methods, so I suppose you sat fairly well forward, in the stalls. You're a noticeable chap. Somebody must have sat next to you. Probably some of the usherettes noticed you—you're very like your father. You think things out. If you can't produce chapter and verse to prove that you were sitting in the stalls during your father's act, you're a duller chap than you've any right to be.

Now Mr. Rameses, it's time you and I had a quiet talk. You've still got that mask?"

" Ananias? You bet. If I'm going to appear in dock I'll wear it. Thinking of doing a reconstruction act?"

" Something of the kind. Next—about that wart you had on your hand. When did you get it removed?"

" Did it myself. Saturday morning. Burnt it off. Clean as a whistle. Heated a steel knitting needle in a blow-lamp. Learnt how to do it from a dancer in Buenos Ayres. Hate warts."

" During your act on Thursday or Friday night did you have any member of the audience on the stage to play up and spot the illusion?"

" Sure. A Jock. Seaforth Highlanders. Nosey Parker. Nearly spoilt the show."

" Good. I'll see if we can find him. He might have been an observant chap—they do exist. Next—what time did you get home last night?"

" Just after half-past nine. Finished early and came straight home."

" Was the front door open or shut?"

" Shut."

" Any idea if there was anybody in the house?"

" No idea. Perfectly quiet."

" Was the bulb in the hall all right?"

" It functioned—dim blue light, but enough for the purpose."

" Did you go downstairs to the basement?"

" Sure. Wanted to see about my masks."

" What did you do down there?"

" Took my torch—blackout's not too good down there. Went to see if the old lady kept her keys in the same place—keys of the storage rooms. She's got duplicates. She keeps them in a pail under the sink. Seen her go to get them. They were all there. Anybody could've borrowed them. I've never worried. The only thing of mine anyone could raise money on was that bike and I'd padlocked the back wheel."

" Had you. Someone had filed through the chain then."

" Yes. Noticed that. I got the box with the masks out and carried it upstairs."

" Light still on in the hall?"

" Yes."

" Did you hear anyone about?"

" No."

" Did you hear anyone come in or go out during the next half-hour?"

" I heard someone talking at the front door—Miss Willing I think it was. Didn't notice much. I was thinking."

" Miss Grey said that Miss Willing told her that a man had just gone into the house and asked for Mr. Rameses."

" Yes. That'd be Turnip Face. I guessed as much."

" Did he come to your door?"

" No. Nobody came to the door. No one came into the flat."

" What were you doing at ten o'clock, or around ten o'clock?"

" I unpacked that box of masks. Otherwise—I sat, thinking."

" What was the noise which was going on in your flat then?"

Rameses sat staring at Macdonald, still and inscrutable.

" There wasn't any noise. . . . At least, if there was I don't remember it. Never notice noise. I'm conditioned to it. Maybe the wife was busy—she can make a lot of noise when she's busy. Like to ask her? You're welcome. She's in the kitchen."

Rameses got up, saying, " You come along and find her. She'll be glad of a chat. She's like Mrs. Maloney—taken a fancy to you." Macdonald followed him into the little passage and Rameses breathed into his ear: " You leave me to talk to George. I'll make him see sense. He's never heard of Johnny Ward before I mentioned him to-day. His mother was too full of the air-raid to remember to mention it. Funny how women love talking about bombs . . . George didn't do it. Got that? You can say I did it—but you can't say George did it."

" Right. I'll remember," said Macdonald, and walked on towards the kitchen while Mr. Rameses returned to talk to George.

CHAPTER FIFTEEN

i

WHILE Macdonald was occupying himself with the complexities of the Rameses and Nightingale detachment, Jenkins was busy with another angle of the case. He went and called on Mr. Hardwell, the connoisseur of Bentick Street—the gentleman who gave good dinners in war-time. Jenkins was very much impressed by such an achievement, because it seemed to him a very long time since he had had what he would have described as a really good dinner himself. Pheasant had been mentioned as the piéce de résistance—and Jenkins sighed: he had not tasted pheasant since the war started.

Mr. Hardwell himself answered the front door of his chambers and he looked at the stout inspector with but little enthusiasm.

" I'm sorry to bother you again, sir," said Jenkins, in a voice so apologetic that no one could have resented it. " I understand that Mr. Carringford is staying with you and I hoped to have a word with him if it's not inconvenient."

" Well, if I were Carringford I should feel inclined to tell you to go to hell and stay there," replied the connoisseur. " I don't mean to me offensive, Inspector, but the poor chap was bombed out last night and he's got a weak heart anyway. He's resting in his room—I've no doubt he'll be willing to see you, but don't take him on another wild-goose chase. He looks shaky."

" Ah—he's feeling the shock . . . wretched business for him," murmured Jenkins sympathetically, " and between you and me he's not so young as he was. We feel these things more as we get older."

" Very true. I don't know how old Carringford is—never asked him—but I often wonder if he's not older than he admits, poor old chap. I shouldn't be surprised if he's getting on for seventy. Now what is it you want—anything I can help with? Come along in."

Jenkins was led into a room which he had the good taste to admire, even though he had not the expert knowledge to fully appreciate. Every piece, including china, pictures and *objets de vertu* were of that great period of English craftsmanship when Sheraton was building furniture, Gainsborough, Romney, Reynolds and Hoppner were painting portraits, and Robert Adams was designing some of the most graceful interiors ever achieved.

" Now what is it you want, Inspector?" demanded Mr. Hardwell, and Jenkins began to talk in that diffident gentle way of his.

" It's like this, sir. In our job we often come across what one might call curious coincidences. You'll have heard the main outlines of this case I'm working on?"

" Yes. Carringford has talked to me about it. Fact is, I'm a bit tired of the case. It seems to me that the fact that one ne'er-do-well has met a violent end is not a matter of supreme importance in a world which is in the throes of a convulsion which may destroy civilization itself before we're through. Take what happened last night: a few bombs, dropped haphazard

136

on London, a few lives lost, a few houses destroyed . . . no great matter, not worth a head-line, so to speak. The bombs which destroyed Belfort Grove might equally have fallen on this house—again, no great matter. If that had happened some perfect examples of a great period would have crumbled to dust. Quite unimportant perhaps—but posterity would have been impoverished far more than by the death of that Irishman you're making such a song about."

Jenkins always listened carefully to those whom he interviewed: his patience was a by-word among his colleagues.

" Yes, sir. I see your point—but I can't understand how it is you risk leaving all these beautiful things in London. I'm an ignorant man and I know it, but even a simpleton like myself can see the beauty of the things you've got in this room."

" Good for you, Inspector! You're a man after my own heart," said Mr. Hardwell. " I'll tell you a little secret. It's true I'm a collector, but also I'm a dealer. I tell you so frankly. I've collected this stuff in here to show to a particular purchaser. We've got some very big men in England just now— the cream of the American intelligentsia. I'm hoping to sell the contents of this room as it stands—furniture, fittings and all. Give me three days immunity from bombs . . . that's all I ask. I've got to show it as it stands, and I'm taking the risk. The man who wants it—I mustn't mention names—has no time to run down into the country: he wants to see the stuff here."

" Ah . . . I hope you'll bring it off," said Jenkins sympathetically. " I gather from what you told me that Mr. Carringford works up the history of these things?"

" That's right. He's a very able and learned man. No fake stuff, no imaginary pedigrees—all properly documented facts. He's an expert in his own line and he's valuable to me. That's why I don't want you to worry him into a heart attack. Now let's get on with your errand. You were talking about coincidences."

" Yes, sir. It's this. You remember a young fellow named Mallaig was present at the actual murder?"

" Yes. I remember."

" It so happens that he was meaning to have dinner with his young lady on the very evening that the murder happened. His young lady wasn't able to keep the appointment, and so Mallaig wandered off into Regents Park to walk off his disappointment."

" Very romantic—but what it's got to do with Carringford and myself, I just don't see," replied Mr. Hardwell.

" I wouldn't say it's got anything to do with you, sir—but

it's like this. The restaurant where Mallaig and his young lady were going to eat their dinner was Canuto's restaurant in Baker Street, where you and Mr. Carringford dined.''

'' Really? As you say, that's an odd coincidence—but Mallaig wasn't going to dine with us, you know. We neither of us knew him from Adam—never heard of him.''

'' Quite so, sir, and I'm very sorry to take up your time bothering you about it, but, between ourselves, we've got to look into Mallaig's story very carefully. At first glance it appeared that he and the other young fellow at the bridge—Stanley Claydon—had nothing to do with the case. They just happened to be witnesses—but as things have turned out, we can't hold that view any longer. In strict confidence I can tell you that Claydon is involved far more than appeared. He was found in John Ward's flat last night, just before the first incendiaries hit the house.''

'' Good lord! what a surprising business—but I still don't see what *I* have got to do with it.''

'' It's not you we're interested in, speaking officially, sir—it's Mallaig. If Claydon was mixed up in the murder, it's possible that Mallaig was, too—and Mallaig said he went to Canuto's. If you'll have a little more patience, sir, you'll see what I'm getting at. When I interviewed Mr. Carringford before we hadn't had that little identity parade. We had more than one idea there. If Mallaig had been waiting at Canuto's, as he said he was, he ought to have seen Mr. Carringford there, and if he saw him there, I should have thought he'd have remembered him.''

'' I don't quite see that. You might as well say that Carringford ought to have remembered seeing Mallaig.''

'' The circumstances aren't quite the same, sir. For one thing, Mr. Carringford is a noticeable person, if I may say so: that white head and dark eyes—what I'd call distinguished. Mallaig is a very ordinary-looking young fellow. Then there's this to it. Mallaig was looking out for someone who hadn't turned up: he'd have been studying all the other diners. I can't quite understand how it was that Mallaig, if he was at the restaurant as he says he was, didn't spot Mr. Carringford at that identity parade.''

'' Yes. I begin to see your point, Inspector. *Chacun à son métier et les vaches seront bien gardées,* as the French say. My *métier* is the study of antiques and I arrive at a judgment by detailed observation. You do the same thing in your trade —you consider the smallest detail to see if there are any discrepancies.''

" That's it, sir. Very well put."

" Now about this matter of the restaurant. There are two entrances, one in Baker Street, one in Paddington Street. Did Mallaig say which way he went in?"

" He went in by the Baker Street entrance, sir. There's a small lounge there, where diners often wait, or have a drink before their dinner. He waited a moment or two there, and then went in to ask about the table he'd ordered. The waiter he asked was an old man who didn't remember the name—it's a difficult name to get hold of—Mallaig—especially to foreigners —so Mallaig wasn't told at once that a telegram was waiting for him. He wandered round the restaurant looking for his young lady. Eventually, after he'd been given the telegram, he left the restaurant by the Paddington Street exit."

" You've evidently taken a lot of trouble over this, Inspector, but for the life of me I can't see what you're fussing about. You've got all this evidence to prove that Mallaig *was* in the restaurant and that he did get the wire as he says he did."

" Oh yes, he got the wire all right, but between you and me we're not absolutely satisfied with the evidence. This business about Claydon has made us reconsider things, and it's my job to sift the evidence again. We've got proof that a young man did go to Canuto's and did ask if there was a message for him, and that young man was given the telegram. What we haven't got is proof that the young man who was given the telegram was Mallaig himself. As I said, he's a very ordinary-looking young fellow and nobody at the restaurant remembers him well enough to swear to him."

" I see. You're certainly taking at lot of trouble over this," said Mr. Hardwell. " Is it so very important to prove that Mallaig was in the restaurant? You know he was at the scene of the murder—isn't that enough?"

" The real point is this, sir. If Mallaig's story is true throughout, it's probable that he's as innocent as he appears to be, but if we find he's been telling any lies the whole situation is different. If he told us he was at Canuto's at such and such a time and we find it wasn't true, it's fair to assume that he's hiding his actions—and that he made arrangements to secure an alibi for the half-hour previous to the murder."

" I see. All very interesting, Inspector—but if you're hoping that I can supply chapter and verse about Mallaig's presence in the restaurant I'm sorry to disappoint you, but I can't do it. He may have been there, but I didn't see him—at least, not to my recollection. That's not to say he wasn't there, though."

" Quite so, sir, but I'm not expecting *you* to prove his

presence there—that would be quite unreasonable. What I was hoping was that you would tell me if you recognised any other diners, and describe anyone you noticed yourself. Any lady with a striking frock, any arrivals, any incident which occurred. Then, if Mallaig can mention any of the same incidents—or recognise any of the other diners—it'll go a long way to prove he was really in the place when he says he was."

Mr. Hardwell nodded and seemed to be thinking the matter over: he produced his cigarette case and held it out to Jenkins, saying:

" You're interesting me a lot, Inspector. I hadn't realised the amount of trouble you C.I.D. men take over your job. I admire it, because I take a lot of trouble over my own job. You were pleased just now to describe yourself as a simpleton, and you've a very good technique. Just the simple, kindly hearty: if I wanted to put a fake piece past you, I'd reckon my chances were pretty poor. Now because you're intent on doing your job conscientiously I'm prepared to do my best to help you. Have a cigarette and listen to me."

Jenkins accepted a cigarette and Mr. Hardwell leant back in his chair and began: " You've given me a good demonstration of a man doing his job thoroughly, omitting no detail, taking no chance and hurrying nothing. I'm going to emulate your example. If I'm long-winded you can tell me yourself I'm only doing just what you've been doing—trying to be thorough."

" Very good, sir. I'm grateful to you for your understanding—and one thing at least I can claim to be, and that's patient. Patience is the basis of sound detective work."

" And of all other work for that matter. Now on Thursday evening I invited Mr. Carringford to dine with me for two reasons. First, he'd done a first-class piece of work for me in working out the history of the owners of that bureau you see over there. That piece has had a very interesting history. If you'd care to read about another sort of detective ' shop ' I'll lend you a copy of Carringford's script when you go. When a man has worked well for me, I like to show my appreciation of what he's done, apart from a professional fee. A good dinner is not to be despised these days—and I'd taken a lot of trouble to arrange as good a dinner as the law allows these days. Secondly, I'd invited two other men to meet Carringford: these men were fellow experts, acting as agents for my American purchaser. I thought it'd be interesting, as well as good policy to meet and discuss the work I'd done—and the work Carringford had done. He's a very good conversationalist when he gets going."

" Quite so, sir. In other words, your party was thought out and pre-arranged—not just a chance party on the spur of the moment."

" Quite right. I'd arranged to meet Carringford at the restaurant at seven fifteen: always dine early these days, Inspector. I'd ordered a table, set for two, which would be capable of taking four for coffee later in the evening. This table was in a recess, near the back of the restaurant; you remember the place is L shaped—one arm of the L ends at the Baker Street entrance, the other arm at the Paddington Street entrance. My table was in the corner, so that I could get a good view of both ends of the restaurant if I'd wanted to. We met there at a quarter past seven. At the next table to ours there was an Air Force officer and a Wren officer—both in uniform. At the farther side—towards Paddington Street—there were two elderly men, habituées of the place. I think one is called Parkman—you can ask the management about them."

Mr. Hardwell leant back and considered as he smoked his cigarette. " What time was it that Mallaig claimed he was in the restaurant?" he inquired.

" He was to have met the young lady at 7.45, sir. He says he got there about 7.30, and that he waited in the lounge until 7.45. Then he got impatient, and went inside to see if the young lady had come in by the other entrance."

" A quarter to eight . . . about the time we should have finished our first course. . . . There's only one incident I can remember which may help you. A telephone call came through for somebody named Manners and the porter called the name down the restaurant. If your man were in the place at the time he ought to remember that: the call was for a big stout chap sitting a few tables away from us."

" Thank you, sir. Can you remember anything else—no matter how small—which happened between then and eight-thirty?"

" I'd asked the other two for eight-thirty. Incidentally, if you're in any doubt about my own presence in the restaurant, the management knows me very well. Nothing like making sure, Inspector."

" Quite so, sir," replied Jenkins with his kindly smile, and Hardwell went on:

" I can't remember any incident during the later stage of our meal. I was very much interested in something Carringford was telling me about a Bhul cabinet which he thought was coming on to the market. Just before half-past eight I persuaded him to put through a telephone call to the owner—a chap he knows—to get fuller information and a moment or two later my other guests arrived and we all settled down for an hour's talk over coffee and liqueur—and a very profitable talk it was—always provided enemy action doesn't settle my hash.''

" Then you were sitting at your table from seven o'clock until nine-thirty, sir?''

" Barring a few minutes' break just before the other men joined us.''

" And you did not see a worried young man in glasses walking round the restaurant looking at the diners?''

" No. I did not—but that doesn't mean he wasn't there. When I'm eating my dinner, it's my dinner which interests me —not the other diners.''

" Quite so, sir. I'm very grateful to you for the trouble you've taken, very grateful, indeed. Now I wonder if Mr. Carringford feels well enough to spare me a few minutes? The Chief Inspector would have been here himself, but he's had to go out to Sudbury to interrogate another witness. There's a point he wanted Mr. Carringford to clear up for him about this fellow Claydon.''

" I've no doubt he'll see you. He's very much interested in the case—but do remember he's very far from fit. This bombing business can be very upsetting to a man with a weak heart.''

" I'll be very careful, sir. I won't keep him talking too long.''

ii

Jenkins had an admirable bedside manner. He found Mr. Carringford stretched in an easy chair beside the fire in his bedroom and the Inspector, after an apologetic opening, said:

" I'll put the matter as briefly as possible, sir. You told the Chief Inspector yesterday that you thought you had seen one of the witnesses at the identity parade before. This was a thin weedy chap of the artisan class—he was third in the parade.''

" Yes. I remember: he wore a cap and a shoddy raincoat. I said I thought I'd seen him hanging round the pub .t the corner of Belfort Grove.''

" That's a very odd thing, sir. Just before the incendiaries fell this same man was found in deceased's bedroom at Belfort Grove—the late John Ward's bedroom.''

" Found in his room?'' echoed Mr. Carringford. '' What explanation did he give of his presence there?''

142

" He wasn't able to give any explanation, sir. A dud shell brought part of the roof down, and this man, Stanley Claydon, was pinned underneath a beam. He was unconscious when he was found, and he has remained unconscious. The simplest explanation seems to be that he was involved in some of John Ward's questionable dealings and that he made his way into the house to look for something. There's only one point which makes this matter complicated. The door of John Ward's room was bolted on the outside when Claydon was found. Somebody must have locked him in.''

" Who the devil did that?''

" We can't tell, sir—not until Claydon recovers consciousness and tells us himself. He's got to give some sort of explanation of his presence there, but I'm willing to tell you, in strict confidence, that just before ten o'clock last night a man called at Belfort Grove and was admitted by Miss Willing. This man asked for Mr. Rameses. I can't say any more—but that piece of evidence is known to several of the inhabitants. Now do you think you've ever seen Claydon actually at the house before, or in company with Mr. Rameses?''

" No. I said I thought I'd seen him outside the pub—if I'd ever seen him at the house I should have said so. You say Claydon's unconscious. Does that mean he's in danger?''

" He got a nasty knock on the head, sir, but he's getting on nicely. We've got a man stationed by his bedside and we're hoping he'll be able to speak before long.''

" For your sake I hope he will—he may be able to simplify things. Did you ever trace the man we were looking for at Paddington Station?''

" No, sir—but the Chief Inspector has traced Timothy O'Farrel. It's a very complicated story and I won't bother you about it now. There's just one other point. When you were at Canuto's on Thursday evening you put through a telephone call, so Mr. Hardwell tells me. When you walked through the restaurant to the call-box did you notice a tall pale young fellow with glasses wandering about as though he were looking for somebody?''

" No. I can't say I did.''

" Do you remember what time it was you put your call through?''

" Yes. It was half-past eight. I glanced at my watch. Mr. Hardwell had got some other visitors coming and I wondered if they'd arrived. It was only a London call I put through—a matter of five minutes' conversation.''

" And there was nobody waiting by the phone?''

" No. Not that I noticed . . . I can't be quite sure, but I don't remember anyone."

" Very good, sir. I'm sorry to have bothered you, and I hope you'll be feeling better soon."

" Thanks very much, Inspector," replied Carringford.

iii

As Jenkins entered the hall of the house again he saw that Mr. Hardwell was waiting for him by the front door.

" Come in here for a moment, Inspector," said Hardwell and led Jenkins into a small room by the front door.

" I've been thinking this over, Inspector," said the connoisseur. " You've got me interested, and I was wondering if I could help you. Police work isn't in my line, but I admit that it's the duty of every honest citizen to help to uphold the law. You're trying to find out if this man Mallaig was really at Canuto's, as he claimed to be, or if he got some other chap to impersonate him. I've told you, perfectly truthfully, that I don't remember seeing him there, but I'm prepared to make an offer if it's any good to you. I always dine out, either at my club or at a restaurant—frequently at Canuto's. If I go there to dine this evening, could you get Mallaig to come in and to go through the same actions, more or less, as he did on Thursday? It's possible I may recognise him after all, or if I don't, some of my friends may. I know several people who dine in the place fairly regularly and I could ask one or two of them to co-operate."

" That's very good of you, sir," said Jenkins warmly. " I think it's an uncommonly good idea. I shall have to consult the Chief Inspector about it, of course, and see if we can arrange it."

" Certainly. My idea is this: if Mallaig is innocent, he'll have no objection to doing what you suggest. In fact he'll be glad to do it. If, on the other hand, he's guilty, he'll make any excuse he can to avoid going to the restaurant in case any of the waiters say ' That's not the same chap who got the telegram on Thursday night.' "

" Just so, sir. You've put it in a nutshell. I hope Mr. Carringford will feel well enough to come, too. His evidence would add corroboration."

" I've no doubt he'll come. We've got to eat somewhere—I have no one to cook a dinner here. Now look here, Inspector. I've made you a fair offer: I'm willing to do my best to co-operate and uphold the law as far as I'm able, but I think

144

you might tell me a little more. Have you any sound reason for suggesting that Mallaig may be guilty?"

"No, sir, It's a matter of elimination: if he's innocent, we want to count him out. In confidence, I'll tell you exactly what facts we've got. He was on the spot when the murder was committed, and he told us exactly how it was he came to be there. Atfer he had been interrogated on Thursday evening, he waited around outside the Mortuary and met Claydon. The next day he lunched in St. Pancras grill-room in company with the doctor who appeared in Regents Park when the constable blew his whistle. That's all we've got—but in view of Claydon's presence in John Ward's room it seems necessary to go into Mallaig's story very carefully."

Mr. Hardwell nodded. "Yes. I see that. My offer stands. Carringford and I will go to Canuto's this evening anyway—and if you get Mallaig to go there, we'll watch out."

"Thank you very much, sir."

"Thank yourself, Inspector. I told you I like to see a man do his job thoroughly—and I also like a man who is as patient and polite on the job as you are. Some of our young police could learn a lot from you: courtesy would get them further than the rather uppish hectoring manner they employ when they're asking what right a man's got to be driving a car on the King's highroad."

Surprisingly Jenkins blushed. He was a modest man. "Very kind of you, sir," he murmured. "I'm an old-fashioned chap myself, but I do like to avoid offensiveness as far as I can. Nobody likes having the police in the house and I know it."

Hardwell laughed. "Well, one day I'll do myself the pleasure of dining with an old-fashioned Inspector. I hope you'll come—and I'll promise you as good a dinner as circumstances permit. Good-day to you."

iv

Over a late and frugal lunch Macdonald and Jenkins compared notes about their morning's work, and Jenkins told of Mr. Hardwell's offer. Macdonald sat and contemplated for awhile and then said:

"Good for you Jenkins. The fact that he made the offer off his own bat is an eloquent testimony to your persuasiveness. It's a good idea. I'll see to it we get them all there; as an identity parade it may produce more interesting results than the last one—though we can't have Claydon in it."

" How's he getting on, Chief?"

" They're trying some new treatment, but it'll be touch and go. I'm afraid he may not give us any further evidence."

Jenkins sat and cogitated.

" It was his own inquisitiveness did for him. Mind your own business is a safe motto," he said.

CHAPTER SIXTEEN

i

PUNCTUALLY at seven o'clock the same evening Mr. Hardwell arrived at his favourite restaurant, accompanied by Mr. Carringford. The latter had recovered to some extent from the weariness of the previous night and looked more like the quiet detached person whom Macdonald had found interesting to talk to when he first met him. The two men seated themselves at the same table they had occupied on Thursday evening and were served with gin and lime while Mr. Hardwell studied the menu. Shortly afterwards Mr. and Mrs. Ross Lane came in and claimed a table which had been reserved for them a short distance from Mr. Hardwell's. Farther down the restaurant, at a table well removed from the latter, Macdonald and Jenkins also considered the menu. Jenkins looked thoroughly pleased with life: it was not often that duty led him to a good dinner at a good restaurant and he was prepared to do full justice to whatever was set before him.

The restaurant was soon full up, every table occupied by cheerful diners: occasionally someone glanced in from the doors giving on to the lounge to ascertain if a friend had arrived and the waiters bustled around in a manner reminiscent of peace-time festivity. Shortly after half-past seven a dark bespectacled young man wearing a raincoat looked into the restaurant from the lounge and gazed rather anxiously down the rows of tables. Mr. Ross Lane saw him and studied him with amused unconcern. The young man asked a question of a waiter and then withdrew, but ten minutes later he reappeared and walked slowly between the tables to the angle of the L shaped restaurant. He was obviously looking for somebody, and the head waiter went and had a few words with him. As though unconvinced the young man shook his head and continued his inspection of the diners as he walked towards the Paddington Street entrance, and then returned by the way he had come.

146

Macdonald watched with some interest to see if the occupants of the various tables took much notice of the worried looking young man, (his name was Reeves, and he was a member of the C.I.D.) The majority of those dining were too much concerned with their own affairs to take much notice : the habitual ' diners-out ' were concentrating on their food : those who had come with friends—especially the various couples—were concentrating on their conversation.

A few minutes after Reeves had disappeared Bruce Mallaig appeared at the door and stared down the restaurant. He looked nervous, and his hair had more of a tendency to stand on end than usual. After a deliberate scrutiny he withdrew. Certainly Mr. Ross Lane had observed him—the surgeon actually smiled encouragingly at Mallaig : undoubtedly Mr. Hardwell noticed him—he stared long and earnestly at the worried looking young man in the raincoat. Mr. Carringford turned round in his chair and stared also—and then appeared to ask a question of Mr. Hardwell.

Again the head waiter came forward—but Mallaig had withdrawn before that distinguished functionary reached him.

It was now ten minutes short of eight o'clock. Jenkins leaned forward and spoke softly to Macdonald. " Excellent jugged hare, this. I'm enjoying my dinner—but some of our friends are feeling the tension a bit. Mr. Ross Lane has knocked his glass over. Mr. Hardwell has helped himself to pepper three times. Mr. Carringford has just taken another glass of water. Ah, here he comes again . . . good timing. The head waiter's busy, I see. . . ."

Mallaig had re-entered the restaurant, and this time he walked forward for a more thorough scrutiny of the diners. Macdonald watched the pale troubled face of the earnest-looking young man, re-enacting the scene of last Thursday evening. It was now eight o'clock, and Mallaig buttonholed an old waiter and put a question to him. The waiter, preoccupied with the dishes in his hands, shook his head. Bruce then went to the bureau and spoke to the cashier. He was handed a telegram which he opened and read, and then walked out, more quickly than he had come in. It was then five minutes past eight. Five minutes later a waiter went up to Mr. Carringford and told him that he was wanted on the telephone.

ii

At that moment, Reeves, who had been holding ' a watching brief,' left the Paddington Street door of the restaurant and hurried to an alley way just beside the building and unchained a bicycle which leant against the wall and began to ride it through the blackout as though riding a race. A few hundred yards down Paddington Street, left turn into Marylebone High Street, left turn at the Marylebone Road, then up the straight to York Gate and the empty bridge. Three and a half minutes ride—he had timed it before: three minutes on the bridge, and then back the way he had come—the return journey was faster than the outward one. In nine and a half minutes from the time he had left Canuto's, he was back at the door of the restaurant.

Inside the gaily lighted place, Mr. Ross Lane had left his table and moved over to Mr. Harwell's, as the latter sat contemplating by himself.

"Forgive me intruding on your thoughts, sir," said the surgeon pleasantly. "I have an idea we have met before—would it have been at the big sale at Dorrington House? I was trying to get a dower chest which interested me, but you had me beat."

Hardwell studied the other and replied: "I don't remember you, but I remember the chest. 17th century, Spanish workmanship. An interesting piece."

"Have you still got it?"

"I have. Yes. Do you want to bid again?"

"If it's within my means. My wife was anxious to have that chest: curiously enough it's got some armorial bearings on which resemble those of her own family, but with this difference. There was a bar sinister across the shield on the chest."

"A bend sinister," corrected Hardwell. "There's no such thing in heraldry as a bar sinister. It just doesn't make sense. Is your wife Spanish?'"

"No. Irish—but there is Spanish blood in her family—a matter of generations ago."

"Ah—she's of an old family. I should like to meet her. I always try to get at the history of the pieces I buy. Perhaps she could help me to unravel the story of that chest."

Ross Lane produced his card, and Mr. Hardwell sought for his glasses and set them on his nose. Macdonald, unseen, was watching this interview: five minutes had been taken up with the leisurely question and answer of the two men. Ross Lane continued:

"My wife's people had a place near Dublin—a big ancient house—and the contents were sold when she was a child. I believe a lot of antiques went from that house to the sale room in the nineties. It would be curious if the chest was a relic from Kilboyne House. May I make an appointment with you to view the piece, Mr. . . . ?"

" Hardwell, sir."

The dealer had taken out his pocket-book and handed a card to Ross Lane as he studied his diary. Nine minutes, observed Macdonald, and a moment later Mr. Carringford re-entered the restaurant. It was then that Macdonald got up and went to the door, leaving Jenkins to settle the bill and chat to the waiter. The big Inspector had very good ears, and he overheard Mr. Carringford's first remark to Mr. Hardwell when the former returned to his table:

" I can't make out who the devil it was on the phone: some chap who told me I was to go outside the restaurant into Paddington Street and wait for him—said he'd got something that it was essential I should see."

" See, eh? in the blackout? He must be an optimist," rejoined Hardwell. " Are you going? Tell you what, I'll come with you and see fair play . . . In case of any rough stuff, I'll get that gentleman over there to accompany us. He's just moving on . . . and you, sir," turning to Ross Lane who was standing a step or two back from the table: " If you're the sportsman I take you to be, would you care to stand-by and see if a mysterious bloke who's giving visual demonstrations in the blackout is a scoundrel or not?"

" Count me in," said Ross Lane cheerfully. " I'll render first aid to the casualties, but for the love of Mike don't present me with another corpse. People who find corpses in this country have a thin time with the coppers."

Jenkins had come forward and beamed at Ross Lane with his happy smile.

" You will have your little joke, sir. If there's going to be any hocus pocus I shall be glad to lend my support to the law-abiding."

" You're the sort of chap I like," said Hardwell, speaking as though his good dinner had made him feel generally benevolent. " Well, gentlemen—we'll go outside and interview Carringford's mysterious informant, and I'll ask you to come in for a round of drinks afterwards. I'll lead the way just to give you others that feeling of confidence."

iii

When the door shut behind the four men and they stood on the pavement in the blackout not one of them could see anything at all. The darkness was like a pall, it seemed almost tangible. Ross Lane, who was generally good at finding his way in the dark, admitted afterwards that the sudden change from the bright lights and warm air of the restaurant to the black chill of the quiet street nearly made him dizzy. A voice beside him whispered: " Speak up, James. Say you're here."

It was Mr. Hardwell, encouraging his friend to action, for Mr. Hardwell was in that happy state when he had drunk just enough to feel vigorous and confident. Jenkins, as calm and collected as ever, was also unable to see anything yet, but his trained awareness made him conscious that there was more than one person close at hand, invisible in the darkness.

Mr. Hardwell's whisper was answered in unexpected fashion. A deep voice suddenly broke into declamation:

" ' Out, out, brief candle.
    Life's but a walking shadow, a poor player
    That struts and frets his hour upon the stage
    And then is heard no more. . . .' "

Jenkins admitted later that the sound of that amazing voice in the blackout gave him one of the most dramatic moments of a not unexciting career: instinctively he looked in the direction of the voice, and he knew that the men beside him were straining their eyes in the darkness, staring, nonplussed as that vibrant voice tore at their very nerves. Then, as though in climax, a match spluttered and shone in the darkness. Amazingly bright, it illumined a dark face bent over cupped hands—a heavily jowled, dark chinned face. A voice stuttered into breathless speech—Bruce Mallaig's voice:

" There he is—there he is, I say," and Mr. Carringford's voice rose almost to a scream:

" It's the murderer—the murderer at the bridge . . . catch him!"

" And how do you know that, you dirty blighter?" Corporal Nightingale had forgotten all his previous instructions and had broken into furious speech. " Take that, you bastard!" he exclaimed, switching on a torch and lunging towards Carringford.

" Stop it, George!" roared Mr. Rameses, " this isn't your show,"—and the illusionist with the Chaliapin voice adroitly tripped up his aggressive offspring.

Mr. Carringford gave a scream that echoed shrilly down the street, for the sight of Mr. Rameses' masked face seen in the torchlight was enough to shake any nerves. As George tripped over his father's foot, Mr. Carringford broke into a run. Head down he bolted down Paddington Street as though furies were after him.

"Stop him, Reeves—he'll be under that lorry. . . ."

It was Macdonald's shout, but it came too late. Carringford, blind with terror, flung himself across the road and literally hit the front of the lorry before the astonished driver could pull up. There was a scream of brakes and another scream as well as the would-be fugitive went down like a ninepin before the weight of a three-ton lorry which could not stop in its own length.

Mr. Ross Lane's voice spoke from the darkness: "This is another of the occasions when nothing I can do will be of any use . . . but no one can say this was my fault this time."

iv

Five minutes later an oddly assorted party returned to the restaurant for drinks. Mr. Rameses, dangling 'Ananias' by his locks, chose plain soda water. The Commando asked for a Scotch—and got it. Mr. Hardwell joined George in a much-needed reviver. Bruce Mallaig accepted a gin and lime, looking as though he needed it. Jenkins and Macdonald were elsewhere on official duty connected with recent events. Mrs. Ross Lane was still drinking coffee.

"What happened?" she asked.

Hardwell swallowed his drink before replying.

"Carringford—the chap who dined with me—chucked himself under a lorry . . . A nasty business. I still can't believe it. . . . He must have done it, though why he did it, God alone knows—and he was always the world's worst funk."

"That's why," said Ross Lane cryptically, pouring himself the remains of a bottle of Lager. "It's because he was a funk and Timothy O'Farrel knew all about him."

"Who was Timothy O'Farrel, anyway?" demanded Mallaig.

Ross Lane replied tersely: "Timothy O'Farrel was an undergraduate at Dublin University in 1918. So was Carringford. So was my wife—she recognised Carringford this evening. Think it out."

His drink had done Bruce Mallaig good. His wits were working again.

"But that chap Carringford—I had a good look at him this evening—he was about sixty, wasn't he? How could he have

151

been an undergraduate in 1918? He'd have been . . . well about thirty-five then, wouldn't he?"

"Carringford was the same age as Timothy O'Farrel—forty-four last year," said Mrs. Ross Lane, and her husband added:

"That is, thirty-nine when war broke out. And he was a funk. And Timothy O'Farrel knew all about it."

"But *who* was Timothy O'Farrel?" demanded Mallaig helplessly, and Ross Lane replied:

"He was your Irishman, John Ward. . . . You think it out. I've no doubt Macdonald will enlighten you if you can't see daylight."

CHAPTER SEVENTEEN

BRUCE MALLAIG was still "thinking it out" when he arrived at Mr. Hardwell's house, invited by the owner to come to hear Macdonald's elucidation of the "Bridge Mystery"—as the journalists termed it. The room in which the strangely assorted company met had undergone a change since Macdonald last saw it: the Chippendale pieces had gone, and were replaced by Jacobean oak: even the curtains and pictures were different, and Macdonald glancing round, said:

"So your deal went through safely?"

Mr. Hardwell nodded.

"Yes. The stuff's all out of harm's way now: a very satisfactory business."

When Mallaig entered, with his habitually diffident and rather worried look, he found there was quite a party. Mr. and Mrs. Rameses were there, and their son, George. Miss Rosie Willing sat in a corner. Mr. Ross Lane was also present, his wife beside him, and Inspector Jenkins beamed at Mallaig in his usual benevolent way.

"Well, here we are, Chief Inspector," said Mr. Hardwell, "all waiting to hear how you spotted it. I still can't believe that Carringford had the nerve to do it—he was always such a frightened fellow."

"There is an expression ' died of fright,' " said Macdonald. "It is generally prefixed by ' nearly.' In this case two men might have been said to have met their deaths because one was a coward. I think it will be simpler if I give you a straightforward statement of fact, and then tell you how we sorted out the bits and pieces. James Carringford was born in the West Indies in 1899. The place of his birth is only of interest for this fact: men born and brought up in the tropics, notably in the West Indies, do age in appearance more quickly than men born in temperate climates. Carringford's white hair and lined face gave an illusory impression of age. When he was of university age, Carringford was sent to Dublin University. Here he knew Timothy O'Farrel and Mrs. Ross Lane—who was then Josephine Falton, a medical student. The only other actual fact I need put forward now is that Carringford was a coward, and that he had an utter terror of military service and the dangers and horrors of war. When all men and women were called upon to register for purposes of National Registration Identity Cards, Carringford thought things out: he knew that conscription would draw him into the military machine—unless he were medically unfit or over age. He was not unfit—his heart was perfectly sound and he was a very healthy man— so he thought out the notion of adding fifteen years on to his age. It was very improbable that this fraud would be discovered, and he probably had a cousin's birth registration to produce if it were demanded—but it never was demanded. He registered in 1939 as a man of fifty-five years of age, and his white hair helped him to look the part."

It was here that Rosie Willing put a word in: "I'd say he was about the only person in England who pretended to be older than he really was—barring the boys of 16 who said they were 19. Most of the women wanted to be registered as younger than they really were. That business about putting your age on your ration card demand made some of my friends go up in smoke!"

Ross Lane said: "Carringford was far-sighted. Very few men thought of avoiding a call-up some years in advance. However—let's hear the story; I naturally take an intense interest in it, because I must have looked so fishy myself."

Macdonald went on: "You all know what happened at the bridge. A detective has to take very special note of those who report a crime. In this case, although one of my colleagues was sceptical about Mallaig's and Claydon's statements, I was disposed to believe them because they tallied: it struck me that each man had told the exact truth about what he had experienced, and in their different ways they were good witnesses. From their evidence it occurred to me that the assault on John Ward might have been made by a man mounted on a bicycle —experiments bore out the possibility of this—so after I had first examined the ground, I set out with these ideas in my head: a dark complexioned gentleman who could ride a bicycle and wield a hammer—and this same gentleman might be known in his trade or profession as ' doctor.' "

Mr. Rameses gave a good resounding snort: " I was known as ' doctor ' when I toured in South America. The management liked the title—said it was toney."

" Yes," observed Macdonald. " I must admit that a doctorate of that variety seemed indicated to me. Although there are a lot of jokes about doctors killing their patients, it's unusual to find English practitioners bumping off their foes with coal-hammers. However—I kept an open mind on the subject of doctors. Now to get on to Belfort Grove. When I first examined John Ward's room I was convinced that it had been rifled. There was no scrap of paper of any kind save a few ancient novels. If you think it out, hardly anybody destroys every single scrap of paper, old envelopes, old bills, and all the junk which accumulates so quickly. The very negativeness of John Ward's room made me suspicious: I believed that someone had been there between the time he left at 7.0 o'clock in the evening, and the time I arrived just after 11.0 o'clock, and had ransacked his room. I had no actual proof of this, but I was so certain of it that I added the qualification to my other requirements—the gentleman with the blue chin who rode a bike—in the park after dark—had either removed every paper exhibit from John Ward's room—or had got a friend to do so."

" I just can't think why you didn't arrest my Birdie on the spot," twittered Mrs. Rameses, and her husband replied:

" If he hadn't more horse sense than most men I should be languishing in jug. I know that."

" I wouldn't put it as strongly as that myself," replied Macdonald, his face lightening into a grin which made him an exceedingly likeable person. " We don't arrest on suspicion or intuition, you know."

Macdonald paused a moment and added, " The point about the searching of O'Farrel's room was more important than it might appear at first sight. It had been done before I got to Belfort Grove shortly after eleven o'clock, but I think it highly improbable that it was done earlier in the evening before O'Farrel was killed. It seemed to me that the murderer must have waited on circumstances to some extent; that is to say, had Dr. Falton or her representative turned up before O'Farrel's arrival the murder could not have been carried out. That being so, the search of O'Farrel's room would not have been made when there was a chance that he might have returned and discovered it. I argued that the murderer must have had time to search the room some time between half-past eight and eleven. I found later that Carringford left Canuto's at half-past nine. With a bicycle he could have got back to Belfort Grove by nine forty-five. It seems probable to me that Carringford was actually in the house when our sergeant first called to make inquiries about John Ward, and that he was searching the room when the sergeant knocked but failed to gain admission.''

Mallaig shivered: '' It's a pretty grim thought to picture Carringford searching that room, and hearing the knock and saying to himself, ' That's the police . . . and they're looking for me.' ''

Mr. Rameses replied: '' If you're going to murder people, you've got to put all grim thoughts out of your head, because what you've done is grimmer than anything else the world can show.''

Macdonald went on, '' Be that as it may, it was clear that Carringford could have searched O'Farrel's room, removed all his papers and gone out again himself before I arrived. However—to get the story in the right order. I soon found that the name John Ward was an assumed name, and that John Ward's Identity Card had been issued to a man very unlike our friend at Belfort Grove. I also found that an identity disc labelled Timothy O'Farrel had been found in the bombed shelter where the real John Ward once took cover. I then continued my researches at Belfort Grove and met Mr. Carringford. He made a good impression: he talked easily and with confidence. I had no reason to suspect him, and the only thing about him which puzzled me was his age. He was white-haired and his face was lined, but he had none of the aspects of age. I did register vaguely ' This man is much younger than he appears to be at first sight.' I think you all know the story of the bicycle in the basement. At the same time that I found this machine, I had a look at Mr. Claude d'Alvarley's trunk—and realised at once that it had been opened and examined recently. It seemed probable that the same practitioner who had rifled John Ward's room had also been at some trouble to examine d'Alvarley's belongings. It was on this occasion that Mrs. Maloney underlined my own train of thoughts by saying ' Some's older than they looks and some's younger.' ''

'' Do you think she guessed?'' asked Rosie Willing.

'' I expect you all did a certain amount of guess-work, Miss Willing,'' replied Macdonald, smiling back at her. '' Mrs. Maloney is a very shrewd old lady. She had her doubts about Mr. Carringford, but she was much too shrewd to put her suspicions into words. Now I had got to the point of finding the bicycle. Carringford himself provided the next diversion. Because he was of a cowardly disposition, he had not the nerve to sit tight and wait for the evidence to be followed up: he wanted to distract attention from the occupants of Belfort Grove and to focus it elsewhere, so, under guise of a circumstantial account of a meeting at Paddington Station, he gave me a few facts which led me direct to the ' Doctor Joe ' mentioned by Claydon in his account of the telephone conversation. Now I'm not denying that the identity of the doctor, coupled to Mr. Ross Lane's presence in Regents Park at the time of the murder, did seem a straightforward explanation of the murder. Here was motive and opportunity—and the means were very simple. Nevertheless, another question arose—how had Carringford learned these facts? His story about his chance acquaintance at Paddington did not ring true. I was convinced he had come by the facts in some other way. In short, he knew a lot more about John Ward and Timothy O'Farrel than he had admitted. Then came our identity parade. Mallaig, who had seen the murderer, could not identify any of those in the parade with any certainty; curiously enough it was left for Stanley Claydon to provide an odd piece of evidence in saying that he had once heard Carringford lecture on pacificism. Claydon, as was proved by his original action in going to the bridge, is an inquisitive fellow: he couldn't mind his own business. He took the trouble to follow Carringford and to get into conversation with him. Carringford was panic-stricken: he didn't want any inquiries which might lead to the discovery of his real age—and here was Claydon saying, ' You looked quite a young chap last time I saw you.' "

Mallaig cut in here: " Is Claydon still alive?"

" He's not only alive, he's going to recover completely. The surgeons have done a marvellous job with his damaged back: he's in plaster, stiff as a board, but very talkative, so we have his evidence to help towards the total. He says that he went and talked to Carringford and reminded him about that lecture. Carringford let him talk, and asked him what he was doing and if he'd got a job. Carringford then told him to call at Belfort Grove at 10.0 o'clock that evening, and to come straight up to the top floor flat. If he met anyone in the entrance-hall, or on the stairs, he was to say that he had come to see Mr. Rameses. Exactly what Carringford's idea was we shall never know: he may have been going to stage another red-herring involving Mr. Rameses."

" But that was pretty futile," put in Mallaig. " Claydon

would have said that it was Carringford who told him to come."

Mr. Rameses gave another of his resounding snorts:

" And who would have believed him?" he asked. " Carringford would have denied all knowledge of him, and Claydon was semi-suspect, anyway. It was another baby for me to hold —me an Ananias."

Macdonald chuckled. " Incidentally, which Ananias was the prototype—Sap'hira's husband or the other chap?"

" The other chap—Shadrach," replied Mr. Rameses. " Never mind why—just get on with the story."

" This part of the story might well have been ' The Annals of Ananias '," rejoined Macdonald. " During the course of the evening I had had a visit from a gentleman named Veroten, an artist in a variety programme, who, I surmised, resented the fact that the Rameses' turn was more highly considered than his own performance. Mr. Veroten attested with considerable vehemence that Mr. Rameses' performance on the Thursday night was done by an understudy, the understudy being Mr. Rameses' son. Mr. Veroten told me about the masks. I admit that the latter topic interested me considerably, though I was not favourably impressed with Mr. Veroten himself."

" ' A certain lewd fellow of the baser sort,' " quoted Mr. Rameses. " George is going to see him later."

" George has my sympathy, tho' I hope that no action for assault will arise," said Macdonald. " I should hate to be sent to arrest George. My own next activity was to call upon Mr. Rameses—and thereafter, for that evening at any rate, the band played. My arrival at Belfort Grove sychronised with the sirens: on the doorstep was Mrs. Maloney, and almost immediately somebody fled from the house with an abruptness denoting great haste or great fear—or both. I was introduced to the mask named Ananias—and for a moment or two, I admit, the race looked like anybody's. Things could be made to fit in a variety of patterns."

" I've been called a lot of things in my time, but not a pattern," said Mr. Rameses. " I fitted the bill all right. I knew it. He knew it " —pointing to Macdonald.

" I did—but I didn't believe it for long, Samson," responded Macdonald. " You and I did a good job of work together over that fire. It wasn't our fault if the whole bag of tricks collapsed afterwards. While I was fire-fighting with you I still had time to think. If evidence pointed to you as a murderer, then it seemed to me there was something phoney about the evidence. It was plain enough that the evidence against you could all have been planted. However—to get back to Carringford. What his intentions were with regard to Claydon, I don't know. Personally I think he had lost his nerve completely. Fear had dictated his actions up to this point, and fear is a potent urge. But then the sirens sounded. Carringford was terrified of bombs: he simply had not the physical courage to stay at the top of that house any longer. He locked Claydon into John Ward's room and then turned and ran for shelter. When I saw him in the shelter later in the evening, stark fear was written all over him. It was then that I had an idea: here was a man, pretending to be older than I thought he could be, frightened to the uttermost over the prospect of being bombed. What else could that man be frightened of? If he had given a fraudulent statement about his age, and Timothy O'Farrel could prove it, then O'Farrel could have been a living menace to Carringford. With that notion, a number of points fell into line. When Mr. Hardwell suggested to Jenkins that he would dine at Canuto's again and take Carringford with him, I decided upon various tests. Mr. Mallaig—about whom I had never any real doubt, agreed to re-play his original part at the restaurant. Reeves was brought in to complicate things a bit. Mrs. Ross Lane came with her husband to identify a man she had seen over twenty-five years ago as an undergraduate. The telephone call was made to Carringford in order to test Mr. Hardwell's accuracy about assessing time intervals. He had said that Carringford was away from the table for ' a few minutes ' on the Thursday evening."

" Yes," put in Mr. Hardwell. " You taught me a lesson there. When our friend Inspector Jenkins asked me on this second occasion how long I thought Carringford had been away at the 'phone, I said ' three or four minutes.' I never thought it was as much as ten."

" Ten minutes was adequate for what Carringford had to do: the bicycle ensured speed," said Macdonald. " It was an exceedingly clever plan, but the curious part of it was that it was a very risky one, and improvised at very short notice. It was only that morning that O'Farrel had made the appointment at the bridge. It could not have been until lunch time, at the Scarlet Petticoat, where O'Farrel left another man to pay the bill, that O'Farrel could have joined Carringford and told him about his appointment with Dr. Josephine Falton— whom Carringford had known at Dublin. Carringford's preparations were few and simple. He had to get the keys which Mrs. Maloney kept in the basement, and borrow the bicycle and the mask from Mr. Rameses' lock-up. He rode the bicycle from Belfort Grove to Canuto's and left it in the alleyway in Paddington Street."

Rameses interrupted here: "You say his plan for murdering Ward was improvised. The immediate circumstances might have been, but he must have thought out the plan of borrowing the bike and the mask some time back. I know he came to see our show one night: he'd have seen the masks then—and when he went to look for them in the lock-up, he'd have seen the bike. He must have pondered quite a bit over the possibilities of those two properties—plus the blackout."

"Yes. I think you're almost certainly right over that," agreed Macdonald. "He probably waited for an opportunity to use his properties, and when O'Farrel was rash enough to tell him about his meeting with Dr. Josephine Falton, Carringford saw his chance—and acted on it."

It was George's turn to interrupt: "But why in blazes was Ward fool enough to tell the other bloke? That's what beats me."

"But Tim always *was* a fool," put in Mrs. Ross Lane. "It was part of his make-up. When he thought he'd been rather smart, he always boasted about it. He just couldn't keep quiet—that was one of the reasons he was so dangerous. I can just see him boasting to Carringford about the coup he was going to bring off, and trying to borrow a final fiver on the strength of it." She turned to Macdonald: "Did you ever find out what Tim was doing during the past five years?"

"Yes. I've just heard. He was in prison, in Eire, under another name: he had come up against some Irish desperadoes who had put a price upon his head. When he came out of prison he managed to give everybody the slip—and he reappeared eventually under the name of John Ward. He came across Claude d'Alvarley, and learned something which the latter was anxious to keep secret—about a woman, I gather—so to keep him quiet d'Alvarley lent Ward his room, and at Belfort Grove he met Carringford and remembered him."

"Do you mean you've got in touch with d'Alvarley, too?" asked Mallaig, almost fearfully.

Macdonald laughed. "Yes. He was at his base, fortunately, and his C.O. got a statement from him and wirelessed it to us."

"Good work," growled Mr. Rameses. "You're thorough, I'll say that for you."

The latter sentence set Macdonald laughing, for the voice was the voice of Mrs. Maloney—a perfect piece of mimicry.

Mallaig went on: "You frighten me rather, Inspector. You

seem capable of finding out anything. One last question: how did you *know* that Ward met Carringford at the Scarlet Petticoat?"

" I knew because a very efficient laddie named Reeves almost camped out there, armed with a series of photographs which included every contact in the case, including Ward's, Carringford's—and your own as well if it interests you. Here they are, taken at odd moments when you least expected it."

" Well I'm dashed," said Mallaig, and suddenly Miss Willing put in:

" We ought to have asked Mrs. Maloney—she'd have been so thrilled."

Mr. Hardwell chuckled: " If you call here to-morrow, you'll see her. She's taken me on—' to oblige,' as the saying is. She says frankly I'm a second-best. It was the Chief Inspector she'd set her heart on. To clean his boots would give Mrs. Maloney the keenest pleasure."

Macdonald turned to Mallaig, deliberately changing the subject: " When is that delayed dinner party coming off? Has Corporal Pat recovered from 'flu yet?"

Mallaig blushed to the roots of his red hair. " Oh—how decent of you to ask. Yes, she's better and she's coming up next week—she's got a whole fortnight's leave."

" I'm so glad—and the best of good luck to you both," replied Macdonald.

Mr. Rameses got up and stretched his massive self.

" Well—that's the curtain, and a very good one," he said. " I've only one regret over this case. It's finished, and this chap,"—(patting Macdonald on the shoulder) " won't come and talk to me any more."

" Don't you believe it, Samson. You're a fellow I'm not going to lose sight of," rejoined the Chief Inspector. " We work well together—and we'll do some more jobs yet."

" Suits me," rejoined Mr. Rameses contentedly.

THE END